IF SOME PEOPLE DIDN'T KNOW RIGHT FROM WRONG, JODY WOULD SHOW THEM SHE KNEW THE MEANING OF LOVE.

GURNEY DOWD
Who was openly drawn to Jody for the same quiet loveliness he had married her mother for . . .

VERNA DOWD
Who tried not to see the dangerous feelings stirring between Jody and her step-father . . .

MARV DOWD
Jody's big bully of a step-brother, whose shameless hankering for Jody forced her to grow up fast . . .

TAY BRANNON
The decent young loner who respected Jody enough to let her do what she must to save the promise of their love.

THE GROWING SEASON

JAN COX SPEAS

AVON
PUBLISHERS OF BARD, CAMELOT AND DISCUS BOOKS

AVON BOOKS
A division of
The Hearst Corporation
959 Eighth Avenue
New York, New York 10019

Copyright © 1963 by Jan Cox Speas
Published by arrangement with
William Morrow & Company.
Library of Congress Catalog Card Number: 63-16093
ISBN: 0-380-44131-4

First Avon Printing, April, 1979

AVON TRADEMARK REG. U.S. PAT. OFF. AND IN
OTHER COUNTRIES, MARCA REGISTRADA, HECHO EN
U.S.A.

Printed in the U.S.A.

For Cindy and Greg

{1}

THE girl walked steadily up the hill, hands in her pockets, head slightly bent. From the darkness beneath the trees, where her dress was only a faint blurred flicker of movement, she emerged into the yellow circles of street light at each corner, then disappeared again in the thick shadows of the next block.

As she followed the rough dirt sidewalk, separated from the street by a wide drainage ditch, she stepped carefully to avoid the potholes and small gullies left by the eroding rains of early summer. Once, in the middle of a block where the hill sloped sharply up to its final ridge, the sidewalk had been eaten away until only the ditch remained, and the girl crossed a plank bridge at a driveway and walked along the edge of the graveled road.

The August night, hot and still, rested heavily on the small frame houses that lined the road. Most of them were dark, seemingly deserted, but as the girl walked up the hill she could hear the squeaking gliders, the rattle of chain as a swing was pushed back and forth, the voices withdrawing into a curious silence that watched the moment of her passing. For that brief interval of time the silence seemed absolute. Then, behind her, the porches were once more alive with people and the darkness brimmed with all the familiar noises of a Saturday night on the Hill.

A television set crackled with gunfire and galloping horses. Down on the highway a siren rose and ebbed,

7

its whine softened by distance. Nearer, a car backed out of a driveway, spinning its wheels on the gravel, and passed the girl with a blare of horn. Several small boys jumped the ditch, eddied around her, then ran on down the street, their shrill voices trailing behind them.

The girl crossed the road, angling toward the next corner. But before she reached it her steps slowed perceptibly and she lifted her head, listening. Then she stopped, turning to stare down the length of the road.

The siren was louder now, more insistent, mingled with the excited cries of the children who had been playing in the road. From the bottom of the hill headlights swept upward, shattering the night, moving so rapidly that the girl barely had time to retreat to the dirt shoulder of the road before the police car passed her in a squall of light and noise.

Her face, caught briefly in the glare, was drained of color, childishly pale and thin under her short dark hair. Then the headlights raced past and the flickering red light touched her for an instant, darkening the wide startled eyes, warming the full mouth and delicate curve of cheek. Then it was also gone and she was left in darkness again, watching the car as it turned the corner, flinching slightly as the siren wailed to another crescendo.

The road was suddenly full of children, noisy with exhilaration as they scampered up the hill behind the police car. One of them, seeing the girl, slid to a stop on the gravel.

"Hey, Jody, it turned into your street! You think it's gonna stop at your house? Billie Mae'll have fits, she's so scared a' cops."

Jody looked down at the little girl, skipping sideways in jerky hops and jumps. "Billy Mae's in bed asleep, Linda," she said, holding out her hand. "Why aren't you?"

Linda accepted the hand, but only for a moment. "I'm a year older'n her. Besides, nobody told me to go

8

to bed. Ma's down to the Greek's, drinking beer." She turned the corner, pulling away from Jody to run ahead a few feet. "Hurry, Jody, it's stopped!"

In the next block the police car had pulled off to the side of the road. Its siren was finally silenced, but the red flasher still turned and the headlights stared across a dirt yard at a small square house cowering behind a row of straggling snowball bushes. All along the road people had left their porches to stand in little groups on the sidewalk or under the trees, talking in low voices, watching the police car and the lights and the marked house.

Linda's thin little legs jiggled up and down in an agony of curiosity. "It's not your house, Jody, it's the Johnsons'. Reckon that old man's been beating on his wife? My ma says he's meaner'n sin, and I believe it. He run me and Billie Mae outa his yard just yesterday."

"What were you kids doing in his yard?"

Linda giggled. "We like to listen to him. He cusses something awful, Jody, you ought to hear him."

"And you ought to be home, this time of night," Jody said. "Why don't you run along, honey, and surprise your mother by being in bed asleep when she gets home?"

"And miss all the fun?" Linda asked incredulously. "I'm gonna see what's happening. Tell Billie Mae I'll be up and tell her all about it in the morning." She started to run, then turned and jogged backwards. "Anyway, it wouldn't do no good to go to bed," she said with a malicious amusement. "Ma'll bring some guy home with her and I'd just have to get up again."

She laughed and darted across the road, squirming her way through the barrier of people standing around the police car. The radio inside the car grated with static and a voice that occasionally droned out unintelligible words; from the Johnson house the voices were clear and plainly audible, one rising above the others with a steady flow of curses.

9

"They won't have an easy time taking Ed Johnson," a man said from the darkness of a lawn just beyond the ditch, and someone beside him laughed quietly. "He'll tear up the house first."

Jody began to walk again, hurriedly, keeping to the shadowed edge of the road opposite the police car.

"Wait up, Jody, you going to a fire?"

Her whole face stilled, tense and startled. She kept on walking for a few steps, then stopped with obvious reluctance and turned.

The breath she had been holding escaped with a small sighing sound.

"Bob McGee," she said, and stopped. She shook her head, smiling faintly. "You ought not to creep up on people like that."

"No such thing. I've been following you all the way from the drugstore, right out in the open."

He was slight and thin, with a dark narrow face and dark eyes, and he came toward her with a quick easy grace, moving lightly on his feet like a dancer. In the red glow from the revolving light his smile had the same quality, easy and adroit, restless, playing across his face in the bright pattern of light striking water.

"For a minute," Jody said, "I thought you were Marv."

"Thanks," he said, drawling the word. "I don't think."

Only for a minute," she said quickly. Her voice trailed away and she was silent, her eyes going back to the growing crowd around the police car. Then she asked casually, "Have you seen him around anywhere tonight?"

"Yeah, down at the Greek's. An hour ago, maybe more." His smile flickered, then was gone. "You got any special reason for wanting to know? Besides making sure he's not creeping up on you from behind?"

After a pause she said, "I just wondered," and the boy looked down at her thoughtfully and then away, putting his hands in his pockets, rocking back on his heels.

"What's going on, anyway? Ed Johnson hanging one on?"

Across the road the screen door slammed back against the house siding and a policeman came out and stalked down the steps. He ignored the people in the yard and pushed through those clustered around the police car. Someone asked him a question and he answered curtly, opening the door to sit at an angle on the seat as he picked up the radio mike.

"Old Ed must be giving 'em a hard time," Bob said softly. "Nothing like a jug of corn to make a man feel big." He laughed under his breath. "If it don't kill him first. Ed gets it from some joker who's been caught so many times he makes it up in a car radiator. That ought to give it a real bite, you know?"

Jody smiled. "I hope he's finished all he's got on hand, then, or they're liable to put him on the roads again."

"He don't care. It's like taking the cure, he says, only the County pays for it." He waited for her smile again, and his own touched his thin mobile mouth. "No point in sticking around to watch the same old show. Come on, honey, walk back down to the Greek's with me. Just to show you what a big man I am, stone sober, I'll buy you a large beer."

"I'm sorry, Bob, I've got to hurry. I've been gone too long already." She turned away, her smile already gone. "See you around."

"Hey, wait." He took a long stride and caught up with her. "What's there to do when you get home?"

"Mom works till eleven," she said, "and somebody has to stay with the kids. I only ran out a minute to get something at the drugstore, and I should've been back ages ago."

"Where's Gurney?"

"Home, I hope. He said he'd stay till I got back."

"Couldn't he watch the kids for a few minutes longer?"

"Men don't know anything about kids," Jody said, her voice soft and hurried, slurring the words together. "Besides, he'll have to leave soon to pick up Mom."

"I'll walk you home then. Need another baby-sitter? We could hold hands and watch television, or something wild like that."

Jody came to an abrupt halt. "Not tonight," she said quickly. "Honest, Bob, I'm sorry."

"Okay," he said easily, "I'll just walk you to the door."

"I'm in a rush, Bob. Some other night, please?"

He looked down at her silently. The night was dark beneath the tall oaks that leaned together above the road, but the street light from the next corner filtered through the thick leaves and fell across her face in pale narrow filaments.

"Yeah, some other night," he said finally. "Only there won't be another one, there never is."

She made a little movement with her hand, but she didn't speak.

"It's Gurney who sees to that, right? And maybe Marv, too, he's just that kind of bastard." He said it lightly, without emphasis. "They got something on you, kid, you got to let 'em get away with being the way they are?"

She shook her head, looking away from him.

"Listen, kid, I've known Marv Dowd since he was a nogood bum and we used to skip school together. There's not much you could tell me about him I don't already know, and a hell of a lot besides, and I don't figure he's changed much just because his old man married your mother. They may have moved in with you, but that don't give Marv any rights, or Gurney, either."

After a long pause she said, "Gurney's got all the

rights he wants. Mom's married to him and it's up to me to get along with him, you ought to know that."

"Does that mean you have to play along with Marv, too?" Some of the easy quickness fell away from his voice. "Must be a happy little bunch over to your house. Everybody loves everybody else, it's Christmas every day of the year."

He looked down at her face and stopped abruptly. Putting his hands in his pockets again, he hunched his shoulders, then relaxed them. Behind them the headlights swung across the road and slid away into darkness as the police car turned the corner and went back down the Hill.

"You ought to take off, you know it?" Bob said carelessly. "There's no good reason you have to stick around in a lousy setup like that."

She raised her eyes swiftly, giving him a brief intent scrutiny. The street light glimmered in her eyes, then she moved slightly and they were dark and secretive again, shuttered by the heavy lids and curving fan of lashes.

"Maybe that's what I'll do, one of these days."

"Sure," he said, and laughed. "Let me know when, will you, so I can send Marv a nice wreath and a sympathy card."

"Is that all you'd do?" A small smile, held in and guarded, lifted her mouth. "What if I asked you to lend me some money, or take me to Charlotte, or maybe help find me a job some place?"

He was silent, staring down at her. Then he asked slowly, "You serious?"

"Maybe."

"Been thinking about it long?"

"You brought it up," Jody said softly. "It was your idea." She saw his quick frown and her smile deepened. "What's the matter, you scared of Marv and Gurney?"

13

"The hell I am," he said shortly. "Gurney, maybe, I don't know, but you'll never see the day I'd worry about Marv Dowd."

"He carries a knife," she said, almost absently.

The soberness left him. "Well, sure," he said with a bright narrow grin. "He's a big tough, that Marv." He shook his head, hunched his shoulders, grinned down at her. "Honey, any time you're ready to run, just give me the word. Day or night, but day'd be better unless you don't mind sharing a bed with two or three Mc-Gees. We're a little crowded since Ma had her last two. And make it a Saturday or we've had it, I'm broke every day but payday."

Jody laughed. "Crazy," she said, her voice warm with the laughter, her whole face changing with it, coming out of itself, suddenly very young and open. "Thanks, I'll be sure and make it high noon on a Saturday." She added, "Be seeing you," and turned away.

But his voice followed her. "Just let me know, honey, and don't worry about Marv. My switchblade's sharper than his, any day."

She didn't look back. Almost running, she crossed the ditch again at a driveway and brushed through a stunted evergreen hedge bordering the sidewalk. Cutting through a dark yard, she circled a car parked in a driveway and went into the next yard. There she was forced to a walk to avoid a tire swing hanging from an oak tree that stood in the center of the yard, its roots stretching out greedily to hump across the sidewalk and dangle, naked and groping, from the eroded funnels of the ditch.

The light from the house streamed across the porch and the hard packed dirt beneath the tree. Jody, hesitating on the edge of the light, glanced toward the open door. Then, taking a deep breath, she walked steadily across the square of light and turned the corner of the porch into darkness again.

"Jody, come here."

She stopped short, still in the dark shadows of the house, and looked over her shoulder indecisively.

"I see you, it ain't no use to hide. Come sit with me a spell, it won't hurt you. One of the kids needs you, Gurney's only got to holler and you'll hear."

Jody sighed. Crossing the driveway, she went through the opening in the tall hedge that straggled around the Hackett place. The big rambling old house was dark except for a light in the front hall, but she moved across the lawn with the certainty of long familiarity, knowing that Mrs. Hackett's chair would be in its usual place on the porch, drawn up to the very edge of the steps.

"What's going on down the road? Addie's down to the church, trust her to be gone when anybody needs her." Mrs. Hackett's voice was plaintive and put-upon. "I saw you sneaking out, hour or so ago, and knew you'd be back sooner or later. Didn't know if I could stand it, though, waiting for you."

Jody sat down on the top step. "I didn't sneak out," she said mildly. "I had to get some shampoo at the drugstore."

"Well, you were sure as sin sneaking back. Took you long enough to walk a few blocks, didn't it?"

"I stayed around to see all the excitement," Jody said gravely, "knowing you'd be waiting to ask me a million questions."

"Smart aleck," Mrs. Hackett said. She leaned forward eagerly in her chair and the rockers tipped dangerously close to the steps. "I heard the siren, it's enough to raise the skin on your neck, ain't it? Down a couple of blocks, I could tell that, but who was it? If Verna'd have that worthless oak tree cut down outa your yard, people could look up and down and see what was going on in the world."

Jody lifted her face innocently. "Nothing very exciting going on, really. Anyway, Addie says you've got

15

a heart condition and ought not to get worked up about things."

"Jody," Mrs. Hackett said. "Jody, I'm warning you." She drew a sharp breath and leaned back. "Let me see, now. Could've been Nancy Sykes, I hear she's running with some fellow from town. Vernon's a fool if he don't do something about it, and her with four kids and maybe another one on the way that won't be his. Or Ruthie Maness, the Lord knows she's been asking for trouble so long she won't even know it when it comes."

"I saw her little girl down the road. Something ought to be done about that, too, but I don't know what it'd be."

"Nothing to do," Mrs. Hackett said definitely. "Ruthie raises that child the best way she knows. Keeps clean clothes on her, anybody can see that, and feeds her well enough. A lotta kids right on this road live worse'n that, and nobody but the Welfare'd complain. It's Ruthie worries me. She's never been lucky with her men and she ain't gonna be, she keeps on the way she's going." She paused, rocking back and forth carefully before adding, "Don't you try me too far, Jody, not as hot as it is."

Jody laughed. "It was only Ed Johnson. The neighbors complained, I reckon, or maybe his wife got up enough nerve to call the police."

"Is that all?" Mrs. Hackett said, disappointed. "Well, no wonder you didn't tell me straight out. I shoulda known. The old fool, they'll put him away for good one day and we'll be shed of him."

Jody lifted her skirt and let it fall, creating a gentle rush of air. "It's so hot," she said absently. "Hot enough to make anybody do things they ought not."

Mrs. Hackett sighed. "Ain't it so. The thermometer on my back porch went over a hundred today for the fourth day running." She moved restlessly in her chair. "Not that I got a flea's chance of doing anything I

16

oughtn't to. I'd have to rise right up and click my heels together, and there ain't much chance a' that."

Jody sat with her chin in her hands, looking out across the yard. Close to the steps a row of forsythia bushes drooped long languid branches toward the ground, and immediately beyond them an overgrown magnolia tree bunched its unwieldy height up above the porch roof, its enormous stiff blossoms wrapped in a pungent sweet scent too heavy to drift away in the still air. But it did not screen the yard completely, and the trees across the road were spindly and thin, neither hiding nor softening the bleak square houses that faced the Hackett place.

Beyond them rose the black bulk of the mill with its line of blue windows staring blankly at the Hill. Four blocks of houses stood between the mill and the high ridge, but the ground dropped away so sharply that nothing could be seen of them, even in daylight, but an occasional chimney pushing through the trees. Now, at night, there was nothing but darkness to hold the mill in check, and the long rows of lighted windows advanced so closely that they blotted out the stars, substituting their own cold blue light in the night sky. The mill did not own the Hill now, as it once had; the blocks of identical houses that had been built by the Company now belonged to anyone with the money to buy or rent, and for a dozen years there had been more people living on the Hill who worked in town than in the mill. But the mill continued to dominate the Hill and the hollows below; it still stood, a long pile of red brick and blue windows, to glower down at its domain as if it yet owned every leaking faucet and sagging porch of it.

Jody wiped her moist upper lip with the back of a finger, then lifted the short hair away from her neck and held it there for a moment before letting it fall. "If Addie had her way," she remarked idly, "she'd have another magnolia on this side of the yard to block

17

out the view." She smiled faintly. "You want to see everything, and she'd like to shut it out."

"Addie's a fool," Mrs. Hackett said crossly.

"She can't help it if she's different from you."

Mrs. Hackett snorted. "She's a curse, brought on me by my sins. I had seven kids, every one as bright and sassy as a two-dollar gold piece, and then Addie come along, so skinny and puny nobody figured she'd last through Easter. Now three's dead and four's married and scattered, and all I've got to comfort me in my old age, bless Pat, is Addie."

"You ought to be thankful," Jody said. Her voice trailed off and she fell silent, but after a lengthy pause she seemed to rouse herself again. "She came over before supper and borrowed some cream of tartar. Did you get your lemon pie?"

"I did," Mrs. Hackett said with satisfaction. "Addie can cook, I'll say that for her. Ate close to half of it myself. Go on in and get you a slice, Jody, it's on the kitchen table."

Jody shook her head. "Thanks, but I'd better be getting back." She stood up and went slowly down the steps, one by one. "I've still got some ironing to do before Mom gets home."

"Too hot to iron tonight. You go on to bed and get up early, say five or so. House won't be all heated up, it's right cool that time of day."

Jody put her hand on a forsythia bush, moving it back and forth. She took a step and then stopped again, breaking off a dry leaf to crumple in her hand. She glanced briefly at the house across the driveway, then down at the tiny particles of leaf sticking to her moist palm.

Mrs. Hackett hitched her rocker closer to the steps and looked at Jody's bent head. Finally she said, "Addie and me were talking about it being such a long hot spell. She says decent people stand the heat, and them that ain't start causing trouble."

Jody didn't speak. From the house next door the sudden noise of a television set broke the silence.

"Well, there ain't a word of it so. You said it yourself, people can get to the place they'll do anything, even if it's wrong. Decent people, too, they got to live in their skins like anybody else." Mrs. Hackett stopped, apparently searching for words that did not come readily. "Wait till the weather breaks, Jody, and likely it'll be easier. Gurney's got a lot of faults, but he ain't mean clear through."

"You worry too much," Jody said gently. "It'll be all right."

Mrs. Hackett frowned. Then, with a harsh little burst of words, she said, "Why don't you spend the night with Addie and me? When you was a little thing Verna used to let you stay real often, it made a nice change for everybody. All our upstairs bedrooms get a good breeze, it'd be a sight cooler than that stuffy back room of yours."

Jody smiled. "No breeze tonight, anywhere," she said, "and I wouldn't know how to act, being company." She started across the yard. "Goodnight. Don't you try to go to bed till Addie gets home."

Mrs. Hackett watched her as she went through the gap in the hedge, detoured around Gurney's car parked before the garage, and disappeared behind the house. When she saw the kitchen light go on she leaned forward, turning her head sharply to one side. But although she held that strained position for some time, she could hear nothing above the sound of the television.

She leaned back at last and began to rock again, back and forth with monotonous regularity, the uneasy squeaking of the cane seat keeping time with the thump of her feet on the floor, the rockers creeping across the porch until they bumped the railing and had to be jerked away. Then, after a tiny pause of silence, the squeak and the thump began again.

2

IN the Dowd kitchen, Jody had placed the ironing board by the open back door. Her head was bent in absorbed concentration, her lower lip caught between her teeth, and the steam from the dampened clothes eddied upward and formed small beads of perspiration around her mouth and along the edge of her hair. Finishing a heavy white coverall with the name G. Dowd sewn in red across the pocket, she folded it skillfully and added it to the pile of clean coveralls on the table. Then she took a yellow dress from the plastic basket at her feet and slipped it over the end of the board.

She frowned slightly whenever a movement of her arm cast a shadow across the board. The light was behind her, a single bulb hanging by a long cord from the ceiling, its inadequate radius of light further obscured by a cracked yellow shade. But it shone brightly on the red-flowered plastic tablecloth and tactfully avoided the faded linoleum on the floor, the maze of stained pipes under the sink, the soiled wallpaper with its dismal clusters of paper fruit, the uneven cracks along the baseboard from which, despite Jody's vigilance with soap and hot water, the shiny brown roaches scampered in companionable hordes during the silent hours of the night.

"They're all the same," Addie said contemptuously of the old Company houses. "Full of bugs and dirt and common people." She liked to point out to Jody that everyone on the Hill, with the exception of the Hacketts, ate, slept, bathed and breathed in precisely the same pattern as his neighbors on either side. Even the beds, crowding the tiny bedrooms, pushed their heads against the same walls in each house, for the Company had designated only one wall wide enough to hold a bed. "Just like the mill," said Addie. "Everything cut from the same cheap bolt of material."

The Dowd house might be full of people, but Jody knew better than anyone else that it wasn't dirty. "And we aren't common," she said loyally. "People aren't the same, Addie. Even on the Hill, there's a difference."

Jody couldn't deny that the Company houses were built alike, from the peeling paint outside to the colonies of roach families inside, but somehow she felt Addie was wrong to think that the pattern mattered so much. No house on the Hill, after all, needed a number for identification; each tenant left a mark on everything he touched that was as personal as his name. The McGee yard, for instance, had been worn down to hard dirt by the horde of youthful McGees, and was scattered with rusty playcars and scooters, old tires, broken toys, bits of derelict cars scrounged from the filling station down on the highway, and garbage dragged there by the McGee cats and dogs and the youngest McGee baby. But Gladys Odell, the McGee's neighbor to the south, pruned her yard with the fanatical care of the dedicated gardener; the Odell hedge was always trimmed, the lawn thick and green, the flowers brilliant. "Fool woman," Mrs. Hackett said frequently, "spends all her waking hours trying to keep the McGee kids outa her yard, and what's she got to show for it? The stingiest husband in the county and a wart on the side of her nose."

But Jody suspected that Addie thought nothing in the world would be quite so satisfying as the possession of a quiet green yard protected by a hedge too thick for children to penetrate and too tall for the rest of the world to see over. "You can't have a garden with children around," she once said wistfully to Jody. "We used to have such lovely flowers, and look at our yard now. Look what happened to your tulips."

"I hope she learned a lesson," Mrs. Hackett said crossly. "It ain't good to set too much store in things. Or people, if it comes to that."

Jody had smiled without answering, not wanting to admit that the lesson had been such a hard one. Whenever she remembered the tulips she knew again the bitter disappointment of that March day when she discovered that Billie Mae had not only dug up all of the two dozen bulbs planted so tenderly in the fall, but had devoured several of them in the mistaken belief that they were a sort of expensive onion. The two of them had sat on the steps in the pale sunlight and wept together, Jody from the depths of some wordless desolation and Billie Mae from the terrible remorse of admitting she had purposely hurt Jody.

In the hot kitchen, ironing a yellow dress for Billie Mae, Jody thought of the lost tulips with their upturned yellow petals, cool and fragile yet glowing with a warm liquid gold. She had dreamed about them all through the winter, imagining the thin green spires thrusting up through the soil, seeking the sun and sky and rain. "You won't get a single bloom," Addie predicted sadly. "I could have told you bulbs need good rich garden dirt to grow in, with a bit of mulch to protect them. That hard red clay never grew anything but weeds." But Jody had waited, with a secret anticipation she thought she had outgrown; for a long while the tulips had seemed the most important thing in the world.

But she had been greedy, she had wanted too much. "I'll buy you some more flowers," Billie Mae said tearfully. "I'll give you all the money in my dime bank."

"Never mind," Jody said.

"But I've known all this time," Billy Mae said. "For ages and ages, and there wasn't anybody to tell."

"Never mind," Jody said again. "It won't be so bad now that you've told me."

Billie Mae looked uncertain and forlorn. "I wish I hadn't eaten them," she said fiercely. "They tasted awful."

Gurney, of course, had found out about it. He had thought the whole thing very funny; for a week he could not look at Billie Mae without laughing. Then he came into the kitchen one night while Jody was doing the dishes and threw a five dollar bill on the table. "Don't say I never gave you nothing," he said. "Go buy yourself some flowers and stop moping around like you had a bellyache." The bill lay on the table for almost an hour. Then Marv came through the kitchen on his way out. He looked at the bill, then at Jody, and slipped the money into his pocket. "You don't need it, honey," he said, grinning a little, "and I've got a big date tonight. I'll pay you back some day when I'm loaded."

He did not pay her back, however, and Gurney never mentioned the flowers again. The tulips were forgotten, except by Jody and Addie. By the end of August the only flowers on the Hill were zinnias that wilted in the hot sun and red dust and gave off an acrid musty odor in the heat.

Finishing Billie Mae's yellow dress, Jody put it on a hanger and hung it on the back of the door. Then she stood erect, stretching her cramped fingers, moving her shoulders gently to loosen the damp dress clinging to her back.

Behind the house, where the Hill sloped off to the highway, she could see the garish neon sign over the truckers' all-night cafe. To its left was the white brilliance of the filling station where Bob McGee worked, then the circular sign, shaped like a hamburger, that marked the first of several drive-ins. The Greek's was

there, and Jody thought fleetingly of Ruthie Maness
and wondered if she ever worried about her little girl
wandering around the Hill alone, night after night.
Probably not. Ruthie knew the neighbors looked after
Linda as much as they could, and kids on the Hill
usually learned to take care of themselves. Ruthie loved
Linda, in her way, but she also loved liquor and men
and music, and no matter what time of day you walked
into the Greek's you could find her there, a beer on
the table before her, her pretty dark eyes lost and
dreaming with the music from the juke-box.

Sometimes, if the night was still, Jody could hear
the music, faint and far-away, drifting like smoke up
the Hill, but tonight the penetrating voice of a television comedian, punctuated by explosive bursts of ap-
plause and Gurney's laughter, filled the small kitchen.

Hearing a small noise, Jody glanced toward the
closed bedroom door to her right. She waited, watching the door as it creaked open.

Billie Mae stood there, her tiny face twisted comi-
cally against the kitchen light. "Jody," she said plaintively, "I can't go to sleep."

Jody moved swiftly across the room. She lifted Billie
Mae in her arms and slipped into the bedroom, closing
the door behind her. "Don't wake the baby," she whispered. She deposited Billie Mae on the double bed
under the window and smoothed the hair back from the
hot little face. "You've been asleep for hours, honey.
Be quiet now, and close your eyes."

"I don't wanna go to sleep. I'm gonna watch television."

"Hush, Billie, you'll wake Neal."

But Neal was already awake. He whimpered in the
darkness and staggered clumsily to his feet. As he
bumped against the headboard of the crib the whimper
became an outraged cry.

"I wanna see Daddy," Billie Mae protested. "I
wanna watch television with Daddy."

"It's late," Jody said firmly. "If you go in the living room your Daddy'll give you a spanking."

After a moment of indecision Billie Mae said, "But I'm hot, Jody. Get me a glass of water."

The baby continued to cry, with a sleepy insistence, and Jody finally took him from the crib and held him on her shoulder.

"I'll get you some water in a minute," she said. "Don't cry, Neal, Jody's here." She felt the baby's arms go around her neck and a tearful cheek rubbed against hers; in the hot close air of the bedroom his pajamas were damply wet, sticking to her bare arms and smelling of baby oil and sour milk. She held him gently and walked back and forth in the narrow space between the bed and crib, patting his back with her hand and whispering small comforting words until she felt him slipping back into sleep.

There was no protest as she lowered him carefully into the crib, and from the bed under the window Billie Mae breathed in even little grunts of sleep. Jody tiptoed to the door, taking the familiar long step at the foot of the bed to avoid the squeaking board there.

As she opened the door, the screen door leading to the back porch opened and slammed shut. The ironing board scraped harshly along the floor as it was pushed aside and Marv's voice, pitched against the noise of the television, scraped with the same harshness against Jody's nerves.

"This is it," he said to someone behind him. "Not much, but it's home. Make yourself comfortable."

Neal, twice shocked from sleep, wailed miserably from the crib and Jody ran to pick him up again. For a moment she stood holding him, resting her face against his topknot of hair, one hand pressed tightly against her mouth.

In the kitchen Marv said loudly, "Have a seat. I'll hit the old man for the car."

Jody lifted her head wearily and went to close the door, keeping in the shadows until Marv had disappeared into the dining room. Marv's friend stood directly opposite her, his shoulder propped against the refrigerator. His head was slightly bent, his eyes narrowed as he watched the slow spiral of smoke from the cigarette in his hand, and Jody studied him briefly, her whole body feeling cold and rigid with distaste.

He looked up suddenly, catching her unawares, and for a long silent moment they stared at each other over Neal's head.

"Hello," he said at last, his voice quiet. "Hope we didn't wake the kid."

Jody said nothing. From the living room the sound of the television mingled with a shouted conversation between Marv and Gurney; out on the street a car door slammed, someone hit a piercing tattoo on the horn, several people laughed.

"Saturday night," he said, somewhat ruefully. After a pause he added, "I'm Tay Brannon. Marv told me to wait here."

Jody stood there, motionless and silent, and he said nothing more but looked back at her steadily.

She had never seen him before, but he looked, Jody thought, like all the other young men on the Hill. His brown hair was streaked unevenly by the sun and clipped short, unlike Marv's long waves that swept into a cultivated point in the back; but he was not much older than Marv and he wore the same uniform, cotton shirt and faded blue jeans, the shirt unbuttoned at the collar and the jeans fitting his legs snugly, seemingly supported by nothing but his hipbones. Over one arm, despite the hot night, he carried a battered leather jacket.

Neal stirred and pushed his moist face deeper into Jody's neck, and she stepped back and closed the door.

Slowly and deliberately, she lowered the baby into the crib. After one muttered protest he put his thumb in his mouth, curled into a fat round ball, and was instantly asleep. Jody turned away, hugging her arms against her. She paused by the door and took a deep breath, closing her eyes. Then she pushed her hair back from her face, lifted her chin, and went back into the lighted kitchen.

Gurney and Marv were there. Marv leaned indolently against the kitchen table, absorbed in a study of his fingernails; Gurney stood in the dining room door, almost filling it, one big hand on either side of the door jamb above his head.

"I got to pick up Verna, I tell you," he said impatiently. "You take the car, I won't see it till morning."

"I'll get Verna. Time for her right now, ain't it?"

"Don't give me that. You say you will, then she never lays an eye on you."

"Saturday night, Pa," Marv said. "You getting so old you forgot what it's like?"

"I know what it's like. I know enough to keep you outa my car on Saturday nights."

Jody went quietly to the ironing board and took a shirt from the basket of dampened clothes. The boy called Tay Brannon had not moved. Still leaning against the refrigerator, hands in his pockets now, he was watching Gurney and Marv, his eyes remote and disinterested. Jody, glancing at him briefly from beneath her lashes, noticed that his shirt was very clean and white, as spotless as the one of Gurney's stretched across the board. Where he had rolled the sleeves to the elbows his forearms looked brown and hard; on one wrist was a startlingly white mark in the shape of a watch, now missing, that he must have worn for a long time in the sun.

Marv said, "Aw, give me a break, will ya? I got to go over to Ashton."

"You ain't got to do nothing but die," Gurney retorted.

"Pretty funny. Look, I got an important date. You want me to walk twenty miles?"

"Might slow you down to size. You want to splatter yourself all over the highway, that's your business, but not in my car."

Marv flung up his head; the long waves moved uneasily, settled again. "You ever caught me putting a single scratch on that precious Ford of yours?"

"I paid enough tickets for speeding, that's all I know."

Marv shrugged. "Some dumb cop earning his pay. They got to raise money some way."

"Not my money. That dumb cop catches you once more, and maybe drinking, and you've had it."

"Now, Pa," Marv said insolently, "you'd come down and bail me out, wouldn't ya?"

Gurney's black brows met in a scowl. "You get picked up, car or not, and you'll have a long wait before I bail you out." The thought seemed to restore him to a fleeting good humor. "Might do you good, a coupla months on the roads. You'd get them pretty waves cut off, first thing, and then maybe learn what it's like to put in a hard day's work. Make a man outa you, might be."

Marv's grin faded. "Lay off, Pa."

Jody did not raise her head, but she knew how Marv would look, pale and stiff, his dark eyes glittering with a barely suppressed anger that came close to hatred, his restless hands looking as if they itched for the switchblade knife in his pocket.

"Go on, beat it," Gurney said. "You can't have the car."

After a moment Marv said, with a forced nonchalance, "Then how about a ride to town? Like you to meet a friend of mine, Tay Brannon. He's only been in town a day or two."

From the corner of her eye Jody saw Tay Brannon straighten, shake hands with Gurney. When Marv

28

turned he had masked his anger behind a thin smile, as if Gurney's words, in themselves, were not so galling as having them spoken before this stranger.

"New in town, huh?" Gurney said. "Where you from?"

"Kansas," Tay Brannon said, and then added, "The last stop."

"Looking for a job?"

"I'm just passing through."

"Better settle down to a steady job and quit bumming around," Gurney said. "Nothing sorrier than a man who won't work." With his insolent grin, the resemblance between Gurney and Marv was suddenly stronger. "I always figure a man's got only two reasons for keeping on the move. He's scared of cops or scared of work, and I got no use for him either way."

Watching Tay Brannon, Jody thought she had never before seen such stillness in a face. Gurney might have been prodding a cake of ice; there was no reaction at all, not even the barest flicker of anger or resentment.

"Thanks for the word," he said. "It's nice to meet a guy who's got it all figured out."

There was nothing hostile in his voice, only the stillness, the unnatural restraint. But something about it stopped Gurney; he pushed his head forward belligerently, but he didn't speak at once.

Tay Brannon met his stare calmly, and it was Gurney who looked away first, a dark flush staining his face. His eyes fell on Jody, standing by the ironing board with her iron forgotten in her hand.

"What you gawking about? Ain't you never seen a man before?"

Caught off guard, Jody stared at Gurney helplessly.

"You lost your voice?" Gurney asked with a heavy sarcasm. "Somebody speaks to you, they deserve a decent answer."

Marv snickered a little. By the refrigerator Tay Brannon straightened slowly, putting his leather jacket over his shoulder.

"I've got to be going," he said.

Jody resumed her ironing, lowering her head over the board so that her face was hidden. The waves of humiliation came and went, burning through her until she felt scorched and weak with the heat, burning even in her eyes so that the white shirt on the board blurred and glared like hot sunlight.

"God knows why you got to be ironing this time of night," Gurney said roughly. "What you been doing all day? Setting on old lady Hackett's steps, I'll bet, doing nothing. Or maybe you ain't been home at all today." He stared at her, all his anger directed toward her now. "You went chasing out tonight, too, dammit, you got some guy you're sneaking out to see?"

Tay Brannon had reached the screen door. "Coming, Marv?"

Gurney looked up. "I'll give you a ride. I'm going into town, anyway, to get the wife." He walked across the kitchen, paying no more attention to Jody. When he passed Marv he asked brusquely, "You need some cash?" Without waiting for an answer he took a worn wallet from his back pocket and pulled three five dollar bills from it, tossing them on the table. "Have yourself a time, boy, but watch out for them dumb cops."

He brushed past Tay Brannon and went down the back steps. Marv picked up the bills and stuffed them in his pocket; his eyes moved over Jody, then fell away.

"Look, Tay," he said carelessly, "I think I'll grab a bath and change clothes. You go on in with Pa and I'll meet you in front of the bank, say, in an hour. Maybe I can whistle up a car from somewhere."

Tay Brannon hesitated. He stood with one hand on the screen door, looking at Marv. Finally, he shrugged and said coolly, "See you later, then."

Jody listened as his feet sounded on the steps; for a moment of desperation she wondered what he'd say if she called him back. But she turned to her ironing, and after a moment she heard Gurney's car go down the driveway. His departure left a void of uneasy silence, despite the sound of the television; the sweltering night lay like an oppressive weight over the house, its air so heavy with heat that the very act of breathing became slow and labored.

Behind her Marv sat on the edge of the table. "Don't let Pa get you down. He's been on a tear all day. Somebody musta slapped him down at the garage."

Jody didn't raise her head. "He doesn't bother me."

"I know better. I got to put up with it too, you know. He must have it in for both of us."

Jody said nothing.

"I wish I could do something about it, kid. It sure gripes me, seeing him jump on you like that."

After another moment of silence Marv slipped from the table; Jody could hear the soft thud as his rubber-soled suede shoes hit the floor. Her hand clutched the handle of the iron with such rigidity that the knuckles ached, and she loosened her fingers carefully, one by one.

"Hey," he said, close behind her, "somebody told me they saw you down the road tonight with Bob McGee. How come you'll take up with a goon like that and not let me get inside speaking distance?" The words dropped, grew sly and low. "Come on, honey, be nice to me. I'm as good as your brother, ain't I?"

"I was on my way back from the drugstore," Jody said steadily. "I haven't taken up with anybody."

"Time you started, then," Marv said. He put his hand on her wrist. "Can't hold out forever."

Jody spun around, took a long step backwards. "Don't touch me, Marv. I'm warning you."

He grinned. "Who's gonna stop me?"

Jody retreated before him, moving backwards step

31

by step toward the dining room door. "Leave me alone," she said, furious that her voice sounded high and strained, not like her voice at all.

He advanced, deliberately matching her steps, still grinning. "Sure," he said, "when I'm good and ready." Jody reached the dining room door and turned to run toward the living room, but Marv's thin hand grabbed her arm and held it tenaciously. "You been putting me off for a long time," he said, pulling her toward him. "You had your fun, now I'm gonna have mine."

She didn't make a sound, even when he twisted her arm behind her with a crude jerk that sent tiny streamers of pain through her body. He pushed her against the wall and she forced herself to stand quietly, not moving, biting her lip to keep from crying out.

"I didn't figure you'd fight," Marv said under his breath. "I shoulda got rough a long time ago. Bet you been pretty impatient, me pussy-footing around, being so nice and polite." He put his hand on her averted face and forced it up, bending his head. Then, for a long time, there was no sound but the slow beat of music from the television.

Marv lifted his head abruptly and moved her slowly along the wall toward the open bedroom door to his left. When she stiffened and pulled back he twisted her arm behind her a little higher, grinning slightly when he heard her quick, involuntary sigh.

Then the back screen door slammed. From the kitchen Mrs. Hackett called querulously, "Where are you, Jody? The Lord knows you oughta be hot enough without leaving an iron setting around to fire up the house."

Marv cursed violently and threw Jody away from him, then turned toward the kitchen. Jody heard another curse as his leg hit a chair, then the clatter as he kicked it out of his way. He did not speak to Mrs. Hackett. The back door slammed with a staggering crash, and Jody heard the slap of his shoes on the steps.

She walked into the kitchen, rubbing her arm where Marv's fingerprints still burned painfully crimson against the white skin.

"Marv's sure in a pucker," Mrs. Hackett said mildly.

Jody stared at her, frowning slightly. "Did you come over all by yourself?" she asked blankly. "You'd better sit down."

"Reckon I can walk across the yard without falling on my face." But the old woman sat down heavily at the table, hanging her cane on the back of the chair. "Addie's home, but I was in too big a hurry to call her."

Jody sat down opposite her. "How did you know?" she said, almost inaudibly.

"Can't nobody live next door to the Dowds," Mrs. Hackett said with asperity, "without knowing a few things. If you mean Marv, I seen him come in with that strange man, but I didn't see him go out again."

"You shouldn't have come. Not without Addie, anyway. You might have fallen."

"I might've got clonked on the head, too, the way Marv was feeling, but I didn't." Mrs. Hackett folded her hands together on the table, absently smoothing at the wrinkles along her fingers. "I don't like to push my nose in where it don't belong, Jody, but you hadn't ought to stay here alone with Marv."

"I didn't want to," Jody said with despair. "There wasn't anything I could do about it. I didn't know he'd stay behind when Gurney left."

She met Mrs. Hackett's eyes. Without warning her face began to burn again and she hid it with her hands, pressing her stomach into the edge of the table until it hurt, and still she could feel the blood flaming in her face, dry and burning against the palms of her hands.

"What am I going to do?" she asked, and with the words there was something else to fight, the fluttering inside her that was the beginning of panic. "I don't know which way to turn, any more. I don't know what to do."

"There ain't but one thing left for you to do," Mrs. Hackett said, "and that's tell Verna."

"It won't help, talking about it."

"Verna was your mother before she married Gurney Dowd, and it's up to her to put a stop to any such foolishness as this."

"Mom can't do anything," Jody said dully. "Gurney won't let anybody say a word against Marv, and if they get to fighting about it, Mom's liable to get hurt. You know what Gurney's like when he gets mad."

"I know what you and Verna's like when he gets over being mad. Verna carried a black eye all last week, and that bruise still shows on your shoulder."

Jody hastily put her arm behind her. But the bruise still showed, faintly purple and yellow, against her upper arm.

"I can't change him," she said. "I can't make him stop hating me. And I can't keep out of Marv's way, living in the same house with him."

She stood up abruptly and went to the ironing board. Finishing the white shirt still on the board, she folded it and added it to the things on the table. She closed the board and leaned it against the wall behind the back door, then put the hot iron on the stove to cool. Taking the pile of clothes from the table, she took them into the front bedroom. On her way back she turned off the television, and the silence seemed to lift a burden from the night.

When she came into the kitchen she didn't sit down. She rested her hands on the back of her chair, looking down at Mrs. Hackett.

"I thought I might leave," she said, very quietly. "Without saying anything. Just leave, and never come back."

Mrs. Hackett did not look surprised. "I don't know

where you'd go, Jody. You ain't got money enough to get far and you don't know anybody that'd take you in till you found a job and got straightened out. Gurney'd go after you, anyway, maybe call the police to help him find you. And where'd you be then, Gurney bringing you home by the scruff of your neck?"

"He might not want me back."

"The world might not go around tomorrow, either, but I don't reckon I'd put too much store in seeing it."

"But you'd think he'd be glad to see me go," Jody said, her voice sliding up, breaking slightly.

With great care, Mrs. Hackett traced the outline of a red flower on the tablecloth. Then she said calmly, "And who'd cook and clean house, and wash his dirty work clothes, and tend Billie Mae and the baby? Who'd wait on him hand and foot, and shiver and shake every time he comes in the door?"

"Mom could stop working," Jody said doggedly.

"Verna's paying for this house and she won't quit till she gets it done. I been meaning to ask you, Jody, did Verna ever make the deed over to Gurney?"

"No, they fight about that, too."

"I didn't give her credit for that much sense."

After a long silence, Jody said, "I've got ten dollars."

"Wouldn't take you far enough," Mrs. Hackett said gently. "Ain't no end to running, Jody, once you get started."

They looked at each other. For once Mrs. Hackett seemed to be weary of talking; she looked tired and worn, her mouth drooping at the corners, a muscle twitching every now and then in one cheek. They sat without speaking for a long time, and the night was also quiet; from the highway below the distant sounds of music and cars and Saturday night laughter were muffled and remote.

"Jody," Mrs. Hackett said finally, "Does Gurney ever bother you?"

"No," Jody said. Then, "At least, not the way you mean."

"Well, thank the good Lord for that."

Some quality in her voice, a fleeting inflection that was not a familiar one, caught Jody's attention. She raised her eyes quickly, but Mrs. Hackett was looking down at the table again.

"It's hard on Verna," she said, "standing between you and Gurney all the time. But you ought to tell her, just the same." She reached over and patted Jody's hand. "I'll stay till she gets home. Gurney Dowd tries to cross me, I'll take my cane to him."

{3}

IN her upstairs bedroom, facing away from the mill, Addie went about her preparations for bed with a slow deliberation.

The clean counterpane was folded neatly to the foot of the heavy mahogany bed and the long bolster laid across it; the sheet was turned back, her muslin gown waited on the pillow, and on the table beside the bed she had placed her Bible, the alarm clock and a glass of water. The old-fashioned lamp was too dim for reading, but a swarm of night insects were already fluttering against the window screen behind the table; it would never do to put a brighter bulb in it, and she didn't need to read the Bible when she was comforted just to know it was there on the table, within the reach of her hand.

The muscles in the small of her back ached dully and she stood in the center of the room and rubbed them with both hands. She kept her eyes resolutely away from the bed; she couldn't undress until her mother was safely in bed, and there was no way of telling how long she intended to sit on the porch. All night, if she took the notion. She had been out of sorts since breakfast, and now she was still down there rocking back and forth, staring into space, not willing to let the day go and be done with it.

Maybe it was only the heat going on so long, or maybe her old bones pained her more than usual. But other people suffered from the heat, Addie thought tiredly, and other people's bones ached now and then.

Ashamed of her resentment, she went into the hall. At the top of the stairs she hesitated, as she always did, with her hand on the newel post, listening with the contentment of old habit to the quiet emptiness of the upstairs hall and bedrooms.

She kept them aired and dusted as if company was expected at any moment, but it was pleasant to know that no one would be likely to disturb their neat serenity. At least once every day she climbed the stairs and went to one bedroom after another, standing in each doorway for a moment or two. That was enough, usually, and she could go downstairs again and finish the day with a sort of peace inside her that would last, with luck, until she went up to bed. She had sewn each of the ruffled bedspreads and matching curtains, all alike except for their colors, lavender, pink, blue and pale green; every ruffle had been gathered by hand and finished with careful stitches. The lamps, with flowered china bases, were bought with Green Stamps saved over several years; the flower pictures on the wall were prints cut from magazines and framed behind shining glass. Except for the dark furniture that had always belonged to the house, everything pretty and ruffled had been added by Addie herself. Now that Mrs. Hackett could no longer climb the stairs no one ever set foot in them but Addie, and if she could hold her own against her mother, no one else ever would.

Verna Dowd, who frequently suggested that Addie might do well to take roomers, had an eager ally in Mrs. Hackett. "Empty old barn," she said. "Addie's working herself into an early grave, trying to keep it clean. Might as well make some money out of it."

"Three bedrooms you could rent," Verna pointed out. "Even with only one to a room at, say, five dollars a week, that's about sixty a month. And you'd want men, of course."

Mrs. Hackett received this with a delighted cackle. "Sure, we'd want men."

"I won't have it, Mama," Addie would say firmly. "You needn't make any plans."

"But you rent to girls," Verna said, "they'll use all the hot water and want the front room for dates and ask to cook in your kitchen. Men are no trouble at all, they keep to themselves."

"It doesn't matter which," Addie said, "I'm not renting any of my bedrooms."

So far she had held out against the two of them, and she suspected, once her fear and panic had died away, that her mother didn't want to take in roomers as much as she enjoyed being contrary. It had been the same way when she insisted on painting the house gray, saying, "It's easier to keep up. Looks don't count for everything, Addie, and white paint once a year costs money."

It had taken Addie a long time to get used to the change a coat of gray paint made in the house. White and green under its oaks, it had looked like a sturdy, prosperous farm house, its respectability holding back the encroaching Company houses. Just a little better than the company it kept, it seemed to say to the world passing by; and if the passing world was almost exclusively of that company, no matter. Addie knew they were the very ones the house wished to impress.

But Mrs. Hackett said, "Needn't look down your nose at anybody. Your Pa worked for the Company till he died, a mill hand and proud of it, so long as he could bring home a pay check regular once a week. That mill put clothes on your back and food in your belly for a long time, Addie Steed, and don't you forget it."

"If Pa had worked some place decent," Addie said, "he could have bought more insurance and left you to live in comfort."

Mrs. Hackett always had the last word. "We ain't

starving. I can't see your man did any better by you,
selling ladies' shoes in some crummy store downtown.
He might've wore a white shirt to work and left plenty
of insurance behind, but here you are, right back where
you started."

Addie sighed and went down the stairs. She wasn't
really hungry; still, a piece of that lemon pie would
taste good. Not one of her best, but light and fluffy;
at supper she had considered taking a slice over to
Jody, only there hadn't been any chance once Gurney
got home.

She stopped by the sewing machine, set up in the
corner of the kitchen, and put her hand softly on the
yellow material there. It would be a dress for Jody, if
she ever managed to finish it in such weather, so hot
that her hands stuck moistly to the material and left,
to her dismay, little streaks of perspiration on the crisp
cotton. She'd laid it aside for a day or two, but it'd be
a pretty thing when she was finally done, and like
Jody, there'd be nothing cheap or ready-made about it.
It ought to be Verna doing it, she knew. It was a
mother's place to do for her daughter. But Verna never
had time; it never seemed to give her pleasure, the way
it did Addie, to do little extra things for Jody.

"That don't mean you love her any better'n Verna,"
Mrs. Hackett said cruelly. "Verna's no hand for doing
around the house, and besides, she's got Gurney to
think about."

The very name could arouse a storm of contradic-
tory feelings in Addie. "I don't know why she hasn't
had enough of him by now," she said scornfully. "She
did all right for herself before she married him."

"She had enough to eat, I reckon," said Mrs. Hackett, "but that ain't enough for a woman, Addie."

"It's enough for me."

"Well," said Mrs. Hackett.

Addie's feelings were not hurt. She had been married once, she knew how it was. Not for all the treas-

ures of the earth would she have traded places with
Verna Dowd; never had she ceased to be grateful that
she was neither young nor pretty, that there was nothing about her to draw Gurney's attention.

Sometimes Addie could not remember a time when
the house next door had been empty of Gurney Dowd.
That there had been such a time, quiet, peaceful, and
blessedly uncomplicated, she frequently reminded
Jody; but it seemed unreal and hazy to both of them.
The present was all that mattered, and the present was
dominated, was filled to overflowing, by Gurney and
his loud laughter, his vulgarity, his violent and un-
predictable temper, his vitality that swept through the
house, reaching into every corner, searching and prying
as if he must possess not only Verna and the house
but every action, thought or emotion that breathed the
same air with either.

Addie hated him until her hatred threatened to tear
her apart inside. Whenever she saw him striding down
the sidewalk, big and dark, his head thrust forward and
his arms swinging as though he had only to lift them
to seize the whole world, whenever Jody came over,
worn and exhausted, bruised in spirit and body, whenever voices from the Dowd house rolled harshly across
the yard to the Hackett porch, Addie felt such an
overpowering frenzy of hatred that she could hardly
control herself.

One night Mrs. Hackett caught Addie with her hand
on the phone, ready to call the police. "Don't be a fool,
Addie, that ain't gonna help Verna. He's got a lot of
faults, ain't any man perfect, but he's worth keeping
and Verna knows it. She's got to learn how to handle
him, is all."

Addie had put the phone down, knowing it was useless. She could not understand women like Verna, and
sometimes it was hard to understand her mother.

Mrs. Hackett, to Addie's chagrin, got along with
Gurney Dowd better than anyone else on the Hill.

Their frequent skirmishes, conducted at the top of their voices from the Dowd yard to the Hackett porch, could reduce Addie to embarrassed tears; but neither Gurney nor Mrs. Hackett ever retreated an inch or seemed to think there would be any pleasure in doing so. There was the time, Addie remembered, when Gurney came over and tossed two apples in Mrs. Hackett's lap. Apples—large, juicy, crimson, expensive ones—had always been Mrs. Hackett's favorite indulgence, and these were the first delicious Winesaps of the year. Addie, seeing her mother's childish joy, had almost warmed to Gurney for displaying a Christian charity so unlike him.

It had taken them an entire day and part of the night to find the glass containing Mrs. Hackett's dentures. Finally Billie Mae accidentally discovered it under the magnolia tree, where Gurney had hidden it, but not before Mrs. Hackett had spent a wretched, harrowing day of agony, looking plaintively at the hard crisp apples in her lap and running her tongue along the smooth useless edge of her old gums.

When the teeth were found, pearly white and even, set in a faintly mocking smile, Addie was amazed and bewildered at Mrs. Hackett's reaction. "You laughed the rest of the week," she accused.

"That Gurney," Mrs. Hackett said, and the memory always brought a chuckle. "Nothing I like better'n a good joke." Then, with a small vain smile, "Hope you noticed he liked my red dress you was so set against me buying."

"When a woman gets to be eighty," Addie said, exasperated, "she ought to have enough sense to stop thinking about men noticing her."

"Well, I ain't dead yet, Addie," said Mrs. Hackett. "I ain't eighty, neither."

Close enough, Addie might have said, but there her mother sat, pushing seventy-five, bent and twisted by pain, seldom neat and not always clean despite Addie's vigilance, contrary by choice as well as nature, an old woman living out her useless days in a rocking chair on the porch.

And yet, Addie thought, it was Mrs. Hackett Jody loved best, it was Mrs. Hackett who could make her laugh, it was Mrs. Hackett who always seemed to know the words to reach Jody in the secret place that lay hidden behind the guarded hazel eyes.

Addie put the yellow material aside with gentle fingers and sat down at the table. She cut herself a slice of pie, wondering if her mother might like another piece; it might be just the way to tempt her to come inside and get ready for bed.

She went down the hall and pushed open the screen door. "Mama, come inside and have some pie with me."

It took her a moment to realize that the rocker was empty. Surprised, she stepped out on the porch and called, "Mama?" Then she turned back to the door and called again, her voice echoing down the hall. With a quick stir of alarm she ran down the steps, turning her head to look up and down the road. But nothing moved in the yard or on the road, and all of the houses were dark except the Dowd house next door, lighted from front to back.

She let out her breath in a long sigh and crossed the yard. Relieved to see that Gurney's car was not in the driveway, she went up the back steps and knocked lightly on the kitchen door.

"Mama, I've been looking all over for you."

"Must not have looked very far. I've been right here, talking to Jody."

"You're not supposed to go walking in the dark alone. What if you'd fallen, and nobody knowing where you were?"

"You'd have to spend all night looking," Mrs. Hackett said cheerfully, "and then work your fingers to the bone nursing me back to life. That's what you get,

Addie, spend all your time down to the church, praying to be a good woman, and folks just naturally expect you to be one."

"I don't feel like one now," Addie said, her voice sharper than she'd meant it to be. "It's too late to be visiting people, Mama."

Jody smiled up at her. "You look nice, Addie. Did you have a good crowd at the church supper tonight?"

Addie came to the table, but she didn't sit down. "Not much of one. Nobody felt like eating, I reckon, hot as it is. Where's your cane, Mama, I'll help you down the steps."

"I ain't going now," Mrs. Hackett said. "Verna'll be home in a minute, and I want to talk to her."

Addie was too tired to argue. "I'll go along home, then," she said, feeling the nagging ache in her back again. "Jody'll have to walk you back."

But it was too late. Before she reached the screen door, she heard the car stop in the driveway outside. Turning back quickly, she saw the look that passed between Mrs. Hackett and Jody.

"Please," Jody said, a queer little jerk in her voice. "Please don't say anything about it."

"God knows I hate to cause more trouble for you, Jody," Mrs. Hackett said. "But you got more'n you can handle, looks like, and if you ain't careful it'll get outa hand. Somebody's got to stop it and it might as well be me. I ain't scared to speak up."

Gurney flung open the screen door and came into the kitchen on a shout of laughter. The door thudded against the outside wall and hung there uncertainly until Verna, just behind Gurney, pulled it shut again.

"Well, look who's visiting," she said, dropping a heavy bag of groceries on the table. "Goodness, I shoulda let you carry them groceries, Gurney. Prices the way they are, you wouldn't think five dollars' worth could weigh so much."

She sank into a chair at the table and eased off her

shoes, drawing a long breath of relief that pushed against the seams of her soiled white uniform.

"Gurney, how about putting up the groceries for me?"

"You still got two good hands," he retorted, but he lifted the sack from the table and took out several heavy cans, putting them away in a cabinet above the sink.

"First time you've been over in a long time," Verna said to Mrs. Hackett. "I've been meaning to come over, every morning this week, but there's always something." She smiled at Addie, still standing against the wall by the door. "Hot enough for you? Jody, get up and give Addie a seat."

"I was just going," Addie said.

"Don't let me run you off," Gurney said amiably. "Why don't you sit down and visit?"

Addie regarded him with a growing suspicion as he opened the refrigerator and took out a can of beer touched with white hoar frost that immediately began to drip.

"I can't stay," she said hurriedly.

Gurney grinned. "Aw, come on, Addie, have a beer before you go. Nothing like it for curing what ails you."

Addie's mouth tightened. "I don't drink."

"Maybe that's what ails you," Gurney said. He punctured the can with an opener and drained half of it at a gulp. "You oughta take a case of beer down to prayer meeting some time, Addie, see if it don't jazz things up a little." He laughed, his teeth white and strong in his dark face. "Wash everybody's sins away, I'll bet. You won't even need the preacher to pray over you."

Verna protested, "Gurney, don't talk like that," but she laughed a little. She was a small woman, soft and plump, her short hair frizzled on the ends with too many cheap permanents, graduating from a yellow blonde to natural brown at the roots. Her face was tired now, its fullness emphasized by the sagging flesh and the damp flush of perspiration; but when she looked at Gurney and laughed, some of the weariness left her face. She was almost pretty, Addie admitted reluctantly, with her soft red mouth and soft skin.

"I've lugged so many beers around tonight," she said, "I don't care if I never see another one. Steak, french fries and beer, that's all anybody wanted to eat. Almost made me sick, hot like it is." She looked across the table at Jody. "How're the kids? They give you any trouble today?"

Jody shook her head silently. But Mrs. Hackett cleared her throat and said, "I'm glad you brought it up, Verna. There's been trouble, all right, but not with Billie Mae and the baby."

The silence lasted only a few seconds. Gurney finished his beer and slammed the can on the yellowed porcelain sink. Addie jumped at the sound and looked instinctively at Jody, seeing her clasp her hands tightly together, the knuckles showing white and thin.

Verna frowned at Mrs. Hackett. "What do you mean, trouble?"

"I mean Marv Dowd," Mrs. Hackett said bluntly, "and that's trouble enough for anybody."

Gurney stared at her. "You better go on home," he said abruptly. "And if I was you I'd stay there, keep my nose outa other folks' business."

"You know what I'm fixing to say?" Mrs. Hackett asked calmly.

"No," Gurney said, "and what's more I don't want to know. Addie, you take her on home."

"I ain't going any place till you and Verna hear what I got to say."

"Listen," Gurney said, "you set on that front porch of yours all day, rocking and spying, and maybe you think that gives you the right to run everything on the Hill to suit yourself. That's okay by me, any fool wants to let you tell him how to live, but you ain't telling me nothing."

"Nobody has to spy to know what's going on in this house. You don't want anybody knowing your business, you oughta keep it a little quieter."

Verna's frown deepened, creasing tiny uneasy lines in her round face. But she was still silent, looking from Mrs. Hackett to Gurney and back again.

"I'm warning you," Gurney said softly. "Old woman or not, nobody's gonna meddle in my business."

"I don't scare easy as Verna," Mrs. Hackett said. "Lay a finger on me and I'll have the police out here, serving you with a warrant." She looked at him smugly, a little contemptuously, as if knowing her own threat to be far more powerful than any of his. "It ain't just your business, or Verna's. I'm making it mine."

"Mrs. Hackett," Verna said, "what's wrong? What're you trying to say?"

"I'm saying it's time you opened your eyes and saw what's going on in your own house. Gurney gives Jody a bad time, always has, and there's not much chance of making him be decent if his mind's set against it. But when it comes to letting Marv act the way he does, Verna, it's time somebody saw to it Jody don't have to put up with that kind of thing."

Verna pushed back her chair and stood up. "What's Marv done?"

"Marv ain't done nothing," Gurney said roughly.

"If he ain't," Mrs. Hackett said, "it's because I come along in time to stop him. But that don't mean he didn't try."

Verna's anger was slow and deliberate, like everything else about her, but now her whole face was flushed with it. "Jody," she demanded, "what's Marv done to you?"

Jody put the back of her hand hard against her mouth. Mrs. Hackett said quickly, "No reason you got to have it spelled out, Verna. It oughta be enough for you, just to know the girl can't stay alone in the house for fear that young punk'll attack her."

They all stared at Jody. Addie, her throat rigid and tight, stood with her back pressed against the wall, the georgette of her dress sticking damply to her flesh. None of it could be true, she thought numbly, it was too terrible, too vile even to be put into words where Jody could hear. She was only a child, a thin worn child too young even to know such disgusting things existed in the world. Only a child, Addie repeated helplessly to herself, and the pretty yellow dress wasn't finished yet.

"I don't believe it," Gurney said with biting contempt. "She told you that, it's a dirty lie. Marv never touched her."

He pushed Verna aside and went around the table to Jody, towering above her, his big hands clenched. She didn't move or flinch away. She sat looking up at him, silent, her face pale and frozen.

"Tell 'em you were lying," he said loudly. "Marv ever got that close to you, you musta drove him to it. Maybe that's true enough, you playing up to him when nobody's home, teasing him and leading him on just so's you could run tell some old woman what it's like to have a man hot for you!"

"Shut up, Gurney," Verna said, "I've heard enough of that kind of talk."

Gurney ignored her. His back to her, he went on furiously, "Marv wants a woman, he ain't got to mess around with some runny-nose little sneak who'll spread dirt about him behind his back!"

His eyes were hot and black, narrowed as he looked down at Jody. Abruptly, he put his hands on her shoulders; and Addie, feeling the perspiration break out all over her body, waited without breathing for the explosion of violence that must surely follow.

But he said, the words queer and difficult, forced out with a grating harshness, "He didn't touch you, did he? You were lying about it. Go on, say it was a lie. Tell 'em he never laid a hand on you."

Addie watched his hands move from Jody's shoulders to her thin arms, then back to her shoulders, not gentle but curiously without violence. He had forgotten the rest of them in the kitchen; his eyes were on Jody's face, his hands holding her still, his mouth pulled back against his teeth.

Addie also stared at Jody, and for the first time she noticed the full mouth, soft and forlorn now, and the way the dark lashes swept upward for a brief instant so that the light was caught shining in clear wet hazel. *She's only a child,* she said the words over and over inside, *no more than a child.* But her eyes prickled and for a miserable moment she felt a rising nausea in her throat.

"It's not a lie," Jody said, low, unsteadily.

Gurney took his hands away. "Dammit, don't say that," he said rapidly. "Don't say it, Jody!"

"Leave her alone," Verna said behind him, and caught at his arm. He shook it off, throwing her away from him. Then, as if goaded beyond endurance, he struck Jody with the flat of his hand, a backhanded blow that caught her on the side of the head and threw her off balance. The chair tottered and she grabbed the edge of the table to keep from falling.

Into the stunned silence he shouted, "I warned you not to tell me no lies!"

Mrs. Hackett's attention was on Jody, and Verna, behind Gurney, could see nothing. But Addie, watching Gurney with disbelieving horror, saw the way he stared down at Jody, his face white and drained of blood.

Verna came around Gurney and pushed Jody back, out of the way. "Keep your hands off Jody," she said hotly.

Gurney drew a deep shuddering breath. "Get outa my way," he said. "I ain't finished."

Verna held her ground. "I mean it. You touch Jody once more and so help me God I'll call the cops."

"You ain't calling nobody." Gurney rubbed his mouth with the back of his hand. The queer look had gone from his face; his anger was back, directed now at Verna. "Get outa my way or I'll knock you out of it."

Verna didn't move. "You'd better not try it," she said, her breathing shallow and quick but the words holding steady. "I'm getting pretty tired of hearing what you're gonna do. I'm tired of being knocked around, going to work black-and-blue. It's gonna stop, Gurney. It's gonna stop right now."

"It's gonna stop," Gurney mimicked harshly. "Who's gonna stop it? Call the cops, see how much good it'll do you. No law in the books says a man can't run his family the way he wants to."

"I don't know much about the law, but I know one thing for sure. You leave Jody alone, and you keep Marv away from her, or I won't guarantee what'll happen."

"Listen to who's giving orders. I'll do what I please and so'll Marv."

Verna's anger was weary now, robbed of urgency.

"Not in my house, Gurney," she said.

The kitchen was instantly still. Gurney stared at Verna as if he could not believe the words had actually been spoken; Jody stood beyond the circle of light, eyes wide and dazed, her face a pale oval in the shadows; Mrs. Hackett looked from Verna to Gurney with a grim curiosity.

Gurney recovered his voice. "That's the way you feel about it, we'll get out, Marv and me. The day won't ever come I'd let a bunch of women tell me what I can and can't do. Keep your house and welcome to it, Marv and me'll get along fine!"

"It's up to you," Verna said. "I've said all I'm gonna say."

Gurney cursed her, a long ugly spate of words striking her face as violently as blows. "First thing in the morning, I'm leaving. You wanted to get rid of me, you done a damn good job of it!"

He flung himself into the dining room. In a moment the door of the front bedroom slammed shut.

Verna sat down at the table and put her face in her hands. From the bedroom behind her Neal began to cry sleepily. Jody had not moved since Verna pushed her from the table. Now, with a small noise like an uneven catch of breath, she turned and opened the bedroom door, slipped inside and closed the door behind her.

"Well," Mrs. Hackett said slowly, "looks like I've gone and done it."

"You had to say something," Verna said heavily. "Anything happened to Jody, I'd always blame myself."

Addie, taking a step forward, looked down at Verna's bowed head, at the dark roots and yellow bleached curls falling damply on her neck in the cheap net that held them. The plump shoulders were shaking under the white uniform. Without seeing them, Addie knew exactly how the wet tears would look streaking the round pink face, how the soft mouth would quiver, like Jody's, with some lonely wordless despair. But Addie could say nothing to comfort her.

Mrs. Hackett stood up. "You better go make some kind of peace with Gurney," she said softly. "It ain't easy, living with him, but it won't be any easier without him."

Verna took a damp handkerchief that had been tucked in her belt and wiped her face with it, but she kept on crying, making no sound, the handkerchief growing sodden and lumpy in her hands.

"I don't reckon he intends to leave, he's just talking," Mrs. Hackett said. "But a man's got his pride. You go talk to him."

"I've got a little pride left, myself," Verna said, low.

"It don't matter so much to a woman," Mrs. Hackett said. "You stood up to him, Verna, and that's what counts." After a pause she added thoughtfully, "Just keep after him about Marv, every chance you get. Best time's at night, when he's all softened up with his mind on something else. No need to keep fighting about it, just let him know you ain't forgot."

Addie stared at her mother incredulously. She started to speak, then clamped her lips together.

"You speak to Jody, too," Mrs. Hackett said. "She'll be needing somebody to comfort her."

"Come on, Mama," Addie said tiredly, "let's go home."

Mrs. Hackett went with her without argument, shrugging off her hand. "I ain't blind, you don't have to lead me."

She took the steps slowly, feeling her way with the cane. Neither of them spoke as they rounded the house and crossed the driveway.

Then, as they reached the porch, Mrs. Hackett asked, "Addie, you got any money to spare?"

"No," Addie said shortly. "You know I went to the A&P this afternoon. I've got two dollars to last us till the check comes Monday."

"Two dollars won't help," Mrs. Hackett said absently. She accepted Addie's help up the steps and sank into her rocker with a long sigh.

"You had five dollars," Addie said, "when I left for church. I asked you for some change, and you only had the one bill."

Mrs. Hackett said quickly, "You go on up to bed, Addie. I'll just set here a while, enjoy the night air."

"Mama, what did you do with the five dollars?"

"I don't have to account for every cent. Not to you, anyway. It's my money, all of it, ain't it?"

"That McGee boy was here, wasn't he? Mama, did you give him money again?"

"Bob McGee's got a good job, he don't need money."

"The other one, then," Addie said.

"Well, no crime if I did."

"We could starve, for all you care," Addie said despairingly. "No matter how little we've got, you'll give it away to anybody who comes down the road asking for it."

"Not just anybody," Mrs. Hackett said.

"You know what he'll do with it. Spend it on beer or some girl, and that's the last of it. You'll never get it back."

"Worse things to do with money," Mrs. Hackett said, "and I never asked for it back. Only thing, I didn't think Jody might need it."

Addie turned sharply. "What does Jody need money for?"

After an interval of silence Mrs. Hackett said, her voice very tired, "I hope she don't need it for anything, Addie. I hope to God she don't."

"Why'd you have to go and meddle in that business?" Addie asked, the prickling back in her throat and eyes. "You see what happened, you only made it worse for Jody."

"I know it was bad," Mrs. Hackett said, "but it had to come. Go on to bed now, and don't keep asking questions. I'm tired of talking. I'm tired of people, even myself."

Addie sat down on the steps, leaning her head on the porch railing. She didn't try to speak again. Closing her eyes, she felt the tears tracing down her cheeks, and she pressed her hand against her side as if that might ease the hurting inside.

She forced herself to think of the pretty bedrooms upstairs, unsoiled, undisturbed, where no man's footsteps or voice would ever again break the silence or wrinkle the ruffled bedspreads. But the tears still came, slow and relentless, falling in wet circles on the limp collar of her best georgette dress.

{4}

LYING on the bed beside Billie Mae, Jody looked
across the small humped body under the sheet to
the window and the darkness that pushed up to it and
then through it, growing darker inside the room as if it
had been searching for walls and a ceiling to shelter it.

She lay on her side, forgetting to move for so long a
time that the arm under her head ached and prickled
and then cramped sharply. Rubbing it absently, she
prodded the pillow into a ball against the iron bars of
the bedstead and went on watching the night and waiting.

Sometimes, at this hour of the night, the air left
over from the day began to stir outside in the yard,
not really a breeze, not enough to rustle the window
shade, but there suddenly, before you knew it, a cool
feel against your face that came and went without
sound or movement. But the air wasn't restless tonight, or if it was it stayed outside, not strong enough
to follow the dark in through the window, maybe not
wanting to, knowing it belonged out under the trees
and along the ridge of the Hill where nothing saw or
felt it except the things meant to be outside in the
night.

A faint trembling broke out along Jody's bare arms.
Once more she thought her way in the darkness across
the yard, down the hill that sloped to a gullied ravine
and a straggle of pine trees, past the filling station and
over the highway to the narrow asphalt road going off

at an angle toward the woods. It ran for five miles, more or less, between fields and pines and tobacco barns and a few small white houses, up hills and down them, flat and straight beside an old swamp, pushing through a red clay hill covered with growing vines to the other highway that headed south away from town. It was a familiar road for a mile or two, at least as far as the dirt track that went off through the pine woods past a row of shacks belonging to colored people and finally trailed away into two dusty ruts. She and Billie Mae had gone hunting for blackberries one day, following the ruts until they disappeared and then cutting across fields to the river, where they found blackberry tangles and swamp flowers and slow muddy water running between old trees.

Then, one Saturday morning four or five years ago, Jody and Bob McGee and one of the girls down the block had walked the whole five miles. At the junction with the other highway they had stopped at a filling station and drunk cold bottles of orange pop, sitting beside the gas pumps in the winter sun and watching a Greyhound bus pick up two passengers. The sign above the wide windshield had said Miami, and Jody still remembered the faces looking blankly down out of the windows, not smiling or frowning, staring without interest across the chasm that separated the three drinking orange pop in the sun from those sitting in the big bus going south to Miami.

"They got a nerve," Bob had said, laughing straight into their faces, his eyes narrow and squinted against the glare, an old baseball cap on the back of his head, looking like a tramp with his coat collar turned up so that the fresh underside showed new and brown beside the faded shoulders. "Going all the way to Salisbury, some of 'em, and the rest'll be getting off at every cow path down the road. World travelers, you know?"

They had laughed up at the bus as it wheeled clumsily back to the highway with its Miami sign and its rows of blank white faces. Then they were finished with the orange pop and had to walk the five miles back home. They'd tried to hitch a ride, but there wasn't much traffic on the blacktop road and the few cars that passed them speeded up when they got close enough to see Bob, sticking out his thumb and dancing a crazy jig in the dust beside the pavement. Some farmer with an open truck finally picked them up but it was only a hundred yards or so to the highway running below the Hill and they had to yell at the farmer to stop. He let them off, grinning, shaking his head as he drove away, and they stood beside the road laughing back at him, laughing at Bob when he said, in a stunned voice, "Jesus, we smell like chickens."

It was a long time, five years, but Jody knew the Greyhound still stopped at the filling station over on the highway south because Verna had gone to a funeral in Charlotte one day last winter and on his way to work Gurney had dropped her off to wait at the filling station. Jody thought about Verna waiting by the gas pumps in the cold early morning, and Bob McGee laughing and dancing in the red dust by the blacktop, and Billie Mae's mouth smeared black purple with berry juice and the day all still and warm, smelling of old trees and water and sun.

She stood up and moved away from the bed, her bare feet rustling quietly on the floor. Her clothes were laid across the back of a chair and she put them on, dark cotton pants to protect her legs from mosquitos— and chiggers, if she had to go in the woods—and a dark blouse that wouldn't show up at night like a white one. Then she took the small pile of things on the end of the dresser and slid them into a heavy paper bag from a downtown department store, making sure she had the neatly folded dress, shoes wrapped in newspaper, a change of underclothes, pajamas, toothbrush. In the darkness her hands moved quickly from one familiar thing to another, finding her purse on the dresser and the pair of tennis shoes on the floor beside the bed.

She was ready. But she paused with her hand on the knob and put her forehead against the door panel, resting it there a moment on the smooth wood. Behind her Billie Mae sighed in her sleep and the baby breathed in and out with little measured sounds, both dreaming, or maybe not dreaming at all but knowing only that sleep was a comfortable dark place with crib bars safely around it, and a big bed shared with Jody, and Verna in the front bedroom within call.

Jody slipped through the door and closed it gently. Marv wasn't home yet and the back door was locked only with a night latch, so she pulled it shut behind her and sat down on the steps to put on her shoes. It wasn't much cooler outside but it seemed so because the air was different, unused air that hadn't been caught and held inside a house with all the day smells of cooking and people and August weather. For a moment Jody remembered how it'd be if she had just come out to sit on the steps, glad to be free of the house and yet knowing it was there to go back into when she got tired of the dark and the hard steps and being by herself. But those other nights when she could have sat outside in the night and then gone back in to bed seemed to belong to somebody else, somebody different from her and already left behind, like the used stale air inside the house. Even the house had changed, closed and locked away from her, waiting indifferently for her to leave as if she no longer belonged to it.

She went off across the yard, not looking back. Her eyes were used to the darkness by now, and in any case she knew the path down the hill so well that she didn't need the small flashlight in her purse. Coming out of the stunted pines just behind the filling station, she hurried across the wide empty cement apron and paused at the corner of the station where a tall lattice fence screened the doors to the rest rooms.

When the station's big arc lights were burning they threw a brilliant white shadow far up the blacktop angling away from the highway, but now the only light in sight was the red neon sign at the truckers' all-night cafe a few hundred yards to Jody's left. She watched it bleakly, seeing how the red bulbs reflected in the highway, shimmering wetly on the cement. One large semitrailer had pulled up in front but there were no cars parked there and none moving on the highway. The silence and the darkness stretched on and on, out across the fields to the woods and beyond that to whatever waited in the night.

The trembling started again along Jody's arms and she swallowed to ease the dryness in her throat. For an endless moment of misery she thought longingly of Bob McGee, turning off the arc lights, whistling as he changed from his blue coveralls and locked the station, driving off in the dark to have a beer at the truckers' cafe up the road, then going home to climb into bed with a couple of smaller McGees.

High noon on a Saturday, he had said, but noon had passed several long hours ago and there was a whole long week of days until another Saturday. Tomorrow was Sunday and they'd all be home, Marv and Gurney and Verna, waiting in the kitchen for her, staring at her with their eyes, their voices going up and up, louder and harsher and surer than hers.

She wouldn't let herself turn to look back up the hill. Walking rapidly, almost running, she left the shelter of the station and crossed the highway to the other road. The asphalt, still warm from the heat of the day, was soft and pliant and silent under her tennis shoes. It was easier to walk down the middle of the road, and so she followed the pale white center line that went away into the darkness ahead of her.

But it was not as dark as she had imagined it would be. To the north, across an open field of broomstraw, a reflected glow from the lights of town fanned out against the sky. It was too far away to be of much help but it eased the depth of the night, somehow, outlining the trees and the edge of the blacktop and the weeds straggling over the ditches on either side of the road. Over her left shoulder, if she turned slightly, she could see an uneven chunk of moon, not much more than a half, pushing up over the bulk of the Hill. It was vaguely comforting to know that later, when she wasn't so afraid somebody might see her, there'd be plenty of light; too much, maybe, but by then she'd be at the filling station on the other highway and could keep out of sight.

The few houses she passed were dark and silent, and if there were dogs, sleeping in some warm spot left by the sun, they slept on without hearing her footsteps. There was so little sound anywhere that when she heard a flat thudding noise, dulled by distance yet carrying plainly in the stillness, she was startled enough to come to a complete stop in the middle of the road. She listened for a long time for the sound to be repeated. When it was not, she decided that it must have been a train switching cars somewhere in the town yards. She went on walking, but some of the uneasiness stayed with her.

She had gone another mile, maybe more than that, when she heard the loud pounding of feet on the road.

The uneasiness became a horror that stopped her breathing, her heart, her feet. For an agonizing instant she couldn't tell whether they were coming toward her or from behind her. Hugging herself with her arms and drawing in her shoulders as if she could make herself smaller and less exposed, she stood without moving and stared down the road.

Her breath caught suddenly, hurting her throat and making a small gasping noise that roused her to action. She ran toward the side of the road, jumped the ditch, stumbled along the edge of a field with plowed furrows and dark stalks that gave only slightly to her legs, and finally reached the tobacco barn a little way down the road. She put out both hands to guide her along the side of the barn until she had turned the back corner. Then, leaning her face against the rough siding, she took a deep breath and listened to the feet running on the road.

They came closer, hurried, incautious, thumping on the asphalt with an awful regularity that never paused or hesitated.

Jody edged to the corner of the barn and looked around it. The moon was higher now and her eyes were used to the shapes of the night, but the woods across the road darkened the shadows. She saw only a pale white blur that merged with the trees and faded into darkness, while the sound of its running grew louder and then lessened as it passed and went away from her.

She waited until there was silence. It was hard to leave the barn and still harder to walk down the road toward whatever the feet had been running from. But she went on, watching, listening, putting one foot stubbornly in front of the other along the white center line. The road finally left the woods and ran down one long hill and up another between open fields, and the moonlight was high and bright enough to cast a shadow before her. Just below the top of the hill the fence bordering the fields to her left came to an abrupt end in a tangle of vines, and she recognized the tall sycamore tree marking the dirt track she and Billie Mae had taken in search of blackberries that hot summer day.

When she had gone past the sycamore to the crest of the hill she paused to look back, not really thinking about it but merely wanting to reassure herself that she was still alone in the night.

In that brief moment she caught a glimpse of a flashing red light. It disappeared immediately and only the glow of the headlights remained, cutting toward the darkness at the top of the hill. Jody heard the faint smooth hum of a motor, but there had been no siren to warn her that she had only a precious minute or two to find a hiding place in that open spot of fields and moonlit road.

She ran back to the dirt track and scrambled across it to throw herself on the ground behind the fence. The vines grew thickly over the fence post and sagging wire, sufficient to hide her. She buried her face in her arms and lay without breathing until the car streaked by. She was still lying there, purse and bag crushed under her and her face hidden, when she heard the squeal of brakes as the car stopped somewhere over the hill. The doors slammed in the sudden quiet, and Jody tried desperately to remember what lay beyond the hill. Another dip and a bridge, she was almost sure, but she had no memory of any houses. Something had happened on the road then, maybe a wreck, maybe someone hurt, and that could be the reason for the feet running up the road, going for help.

So there was no hope of walking on down the road, and as she sat up slowly she realized that she couldn't stay where she was. She could see the part of the blacktop going up over the hill, and when the car came back its headlights would shine the whole length of the fence. She'd have to go back along the narrow dirt track and wait. If no one roused in the colored shanties and no dogs came out, she might follow it far enough to cut back to the blacktop farther along, beyond whatever had happened to bring a patrol car out in the middle of the night.

She left the fence to walk along the dusty ruts, past the sycamore and a thin strand of overgrown bushes that screened her from the road. There was a short stretch of open pine woods, then a shack set back from the track in a bare circle of hard dirt, then more trees. She kept on, trying not to hold her breath as she went past a dark cluster of little leaning houses, hoping the track wouldn't carry her too far from the blacktop. She didn't want to use her flashlight but it was very dark under the trees and she was glad when the path left the shadow of the woods to run beside open fields where the moon was bright from the east and she could see where the ruts were leading her.

He came out of the trees so quietly and unexpectedly that he was there, not more than six feet away, before she had time to feel anything more than the blankness of shock.

Even as she stared at him, he began to move again, his mind and his reflexes quicker than hers. The shock slid into terror and she turned instinctively to run back toward the blacktop and the patrol car. But she knew, despairingly, that it was too late.

When his hands touched her she thought she cried out, but it was only a gasp that burned in her throat. She tried to pull away from him and his hands tightened on her arms.

"Don't yell," he said in her ear. "I won't hurt you." Then he said it again, "Don't yell," and added, almost in a whisper, "please."

She stood motionless, listening to the voice, remembering how he had looked in that brief instant in the moonlight. Then she drew a long uneven breath and sighed it out. Closing her eyes, not caring about the tears, she wondered hazily if she'd fall when he stopped holding her up.

But he didn't let go. Seeming to feel through his hands that she wasn't going to scream or try to run, he turned her around. Jody opened her eyes, seeing him through a queer dazzle, and waited silently while he stared down at her.

"Jesus," he said then, on a flat note of disbelief. "Where did you come from?"

She shook her head wearily. Tay Brannon, that was his name, she remembered it as clearly as his face and the sound of his voice. But he looked different, somehow, even allowing for the pale moonlight that drained his face of color. His white shirt was gone, for one thing, and he was wearing only the jeans and leather jacket, the jacket hanging open across his bare chest.

"I thought you were with Marv," she said at last.

"I was,' he said shortly. He took his hands away and narrowed his eyes at her, frowning a little. "What are you doing out here? Anybody with you?"

She shook her head again, answering both questions. For another minute he looked down at her, thinking it over.

Then he said, "Listen, how close are we to your place? Where'll I come out if I keep going this way?"

He kept his voice quiet, the way he was holding himself, but she felt the tightness in him as surely as if she could reach out and touch it.

"On the blacktop," she said. "We're a long way from the Hill."

"Damn," he said without emphasis. "I thought I was getting away from the road, but it must curve back this way."

On an impulse she said, "A highway patrol car stopped over there a few minutes ago."

He thought that over, too, rubbing his chin with the back of one hand. He was still looking at her but not really seeing her, as if he had drawn away inside himself, alone again and wanting it to be that way, not noticing or caring that he was leaving her on the outside.

"Are they looking for you?" she asked softly.

He came back then, easily and all at once. "Not yet," he said, "but they will be."

She looked back at him steadily. "What happened?"

"Marv drove his car into a tree."

She frowned. "He doesn't have a car."

"I figured it wasn't his. If they'd been able to trace it to him there wouldn't have been any point in running." After a pause he went on, the words cool and even, not exactly hurrying but nudging each other along impatiently, "I was almost asleep so I'm not sure what happened. I must have tried to go through the windshield, the size of the knot I've got on my head. It knocked me cold, anyway, and, when I came to Marv was gone."

Jody thought of the running feet on the road. So it had been Marv, going past her in the night.

"Why are they looking for you?" she asked slowly. "You didn't have anything to do with it."

"Sure," he said. "I could just send 'em to Marv and he'd take the blame for the whole thing." He added flatly, "I've got other things to do besides getting myself locked up for wrecking a stolen car."

The silence grew around them. In the woods a night bird called sleepily, then subsided.

Jody said, almost whispering, "You'd better hurry."

"Yeah, I'd better. What happens back the other way?"

"This track goes over toward the river, but not all the way. It'd be easier to cut across the fields."

"What's at the river?"

"Another road. Not much of one, but I think it follows the river over to the highway south. There aren't many houses, it's back in the woods."

"It'll do," he said. "Thanks."

She waited for him to turn and leave her, but he didn't move.

"You going back home?"

"No."

"You haven't told me what you're doing, chasing around in the dark by yourself."

"You've got enough worries of your own."

"Sure, I do," he said absently. "Look, kid, I can't just walk off and leave you out here."

For the first time in long hours, Jody smiled. It wasn't much of a smile, no more than the corners of her mouth and eyes turning up, but she couldn't have kept it back. Not the way she was feeling, light and easy and relaxed, almost limp, with the weight of the night suddenly lifted away and trouble no heavier than the thin moonlight resting across her shoulders.

"Then let me go with you," she said. "They'll be looking for me, too, sooner or later."

The silence came back, lengthened. He stood there watching her, considering her words.

"I guess I don't have much choice," he said at last, and held out his hand. "Let's go. We'll chew it over later, when there's more time."

His hand was warm and hard and impersonal, taking her with him as he started off across the field. Uncultivated and neglected for years, it was choked with broomstraw and stray pine seedlings, a smooth level surface in the moonlight that broke up into rough clods and old eroded furrows under their feet. They stumbled across it, slowed down to a walk, and finally he gave it up and swerved toward the woods. Between the old field and the line of trees a wilderness of weeds flourished, but the ground was smoother and they made better time, almost running.

They slowed for a thin stand of second-growth hardwoods bordering the field and then pushed across another field that seemed to stretch on forever, grooved with broken lines of dry corn stalks that crackled loudly and prodded at Jody's legs. Beyond the corn the woods closed in, thick and dark and hidden from the moonlight.

Tay Brannon stopped there, under the trees, lifting his head to listen. But there was nothing to hear except Jody's quickened breathing, and she knew, from the feel of him standing so close to her, the instant he narrowed his attention from the rest of the world down to her.

"You okay? I didn't mean to push it so hard."

"I'm fine," she said quickly.

But he didn't go on at once, and she was glad of the chance to rest. The night was still and warm, and very silent; and the woods smelled of pine and a dry pungency that came from the dead musty leaves under their feet and the green sunbaked leaves over their heads. Closer, next to her face, she could smell his leather jacket and hear the small whisper as it moved out and in with his breathing.

"How much farther to the river?"

"I'm not sure. I've only been as far as the river once, and it seemed to take a long time." She added irrelevantly, remembering, "We were looking for blackberries."

"You and Marv?"

"No," she said, "not Marv." She paused, but felt driven to go on, "My little sister came with me."

He didn't speak.

"But we weren't in a hurry. It makes a difference, running."

"Running from the cops always makes a difference." He let the words stand by themselves for a moment. Then he said, "Let's get on with it. We'll have to take it easy till we get out of the trees."

"Can you see?"

"A little. I'm used to the dark."

Like his voice, the words held no particular expression. They were simply there, to take or leave, and Jody instinctively let them go by.

"I have a flashlight," she said, digging it out of her purse, "if it's safe to use it."

He took it from her. "Safer than breaking our necks. I'll go ahead and you hold on."

He didn't speak again. She kept close to him, held there by a sudden fear of being left behind while he went on without her, glad to be done with her, discarding her as a nuisance and a burden slowing him down. With her heart strumming in her throat again, she thought of how it would be to see the tiny flashes of light going away from her until there was only the darkness left, and the woods rustling around her.

But when she stumbled once, almost falling, his grip tightened swiftly and pulled her up, and she knew with gratitude that it was his hand, as much as her fears, that held her there close at his back.

At times the underbrush was thick and unwieldly, scrabbling at her clothes and her bare ankles. But his shoulders shielded her from the worst of it, pushing back the thin branches, restraining them, then letting them go to spring harmlessly into place behind Jody. She kept her head down, watching the place where her feet would be if only she could see them, and followed him blindly. The trees kept pace around them, separating to march past a twisting ravine or a small silent meadow open to the moon, then merging again into untidy ranks that seemed to stretch as far ahead as the night.

But the woods finally came to abrupt end at the edge of a field. Jody, her head down and her feet moving automatically wherever he led, bumped against his back when he stopped.

"Did you say there was a road this side of the river?"

She raised surprised eyes to stare at the moon. It was funny to think it had been there all along, growing brighter and bigger, waiting patiently for them to come out of the black woods and find it before them when they had left it behind on the other side.

"We ought to find it soon," she said in a whisper. "Maybe on the other side of that fence."

The fence at the far end of the field was overgrown with vines, hiding whatever lay beyond. Side by side they walked along the edge of the trees, staying in the shadows. Reaching a portion of the fence which had fallen under the weight of the vines, they detoured down a sloping gully and went through the break. On the other side was the dirt road, dusty and gravel-hard under their feet.

Jody wondered if he meant to take the risk of walking down the road as far as the highway. "It's not much of a road," she said hopefully. "There can't be many houses."

His hand closed around her wrist. Wincing a little from the unexpected pressure of his fingers, she looked up at his face and saw it set in hard narrowed lines, his eyes, mouth, the angle of his chin.

"Listen," he commanded.

Obediently, she listened to the silence. "I don't hear anything."

His hand tightened, slowing her blood.

Then she heard it, a distant scatter of sound that carried clearly over the silent woods and fields.

"I had an idea it might happen," he said. "They've got the dogs out after me."

They stood there together in the middle of the dirt road, Tay's hand still gripping her wrist, and listened to the deep mournful barking of a pack of hounds.

⊰{5}⊱

EVERYTHING visible in the moonlight, the dark
woods and the empty field and the road disappearing in a tunnel of black pines, seemed to stretch
out a web of silence to catch and hold the sound of the
dogs.

"It may take them a while to find the scent," Tay
said. "I went up a creek bed from the highway."

Jody looked at him curiously. "Did you know there'd
be dogs?"

"I didn't figure on taking any chances."

The barking had a bite to it, sharp and eager; you
could see them coming behind you, sniffing the ground
where you'd been, pulling hard at the leashes. There
was howling in it, too, from deep down in the throats,
a cold lonely howling that trailed out in the night to a
long whine. Jody felt a shiver begin in her shoulders
and tried to stop it. But it moved down her arms with
a quiet little ripple, and she knew from the way he
looked down at her that he had felt it through the
palm of his hand gripping her wrist.

"Maybe it's not so nice to hear them," he said, "but
at least you know where they are. The day I can't think
circles around a hound I'll quit." He waited, and when
she didn't speak he went on, "Do you have any breath
left? Because we've got to get moving or we've had it."

Jody asked slowly, "Are we going to run all night,
with bloodhounds after us?"

"The night's almost gone," he said. "Look, don't panic on me now. They may not get this far, and even if they do we've still got the river."

The river didn't seem much of a thing to count on, never very wide or impressive and surely, at this time of year, shrunken to a ribbon of muddy water not much wider than a creek.

"I don't know what they're like where you come from," she said, "but this one isn't a real river."

"Any kind will do," he said. "Come on, we're wasting our time."

He took her with him across the gullied ditch beside the road, hitting the other side at a flat run. The field lasted only a short way and then the woods began again, but here they had been thinned by storms and old age, letting in the moonlight. If he slowed his pace at all it was only to avoid the dead branches that littered the ground, rotting where they had fallen in twisted piles. Once they had to detour around a large tree, covered with vines and brush, that had gone over with such force that a crumbling layer of dirt had pulled free of the earth and still clung, dangling with roots, to the base of the trunk.

His hand had slid down from her wrist to get a better grip, and he used the other for the flashlight, turning it on as soon as they were out of sight of the road. When they left the woods and plunged headlong through a thicket of small trees, little more than seedlings, they almost fell into the river as they went over a bank suddenly and stopped, like the trees, just short of the water.

He turned the flashlight up the river and down it, and for a moment they both stood there without speaking and stared at the black water, moving so slowly that only an occasional eddy breathed in faint circles on the surface. Then he swung the light toward Jody's feet, letting it rest briefly on her tennis shoes.

"Good," he said. "They'll dry."

"So'll my clothes, I hope, if you're planning to cross here."

"I'm not going to cross it. Not here, anyway. No reason to make it any easier for those hounds than I can help."

He started out again, along the edge of the water, then stopped.

"Look, I'll need both hands for this. You walk behind me, and make sure you step where I step. Hold on to my belt."

She did as he told her, taking a tight grasp of his belt. She had forgotten that he wasn't wearing a shirt, but the unexpected feel of his bare flesh, warm and hard under her hand, was a reassuring contact. It was dark, with his body between her and the light, and the water was unpleasantly cold as it sloshed into her shoes.

The river was low, as she had expected, and the banks that filled to overflowing in the early spring sloped in dry runnels to the deepest part of the channel, less than six feet wide at best. Tangles of brush and dirt had gathered at each slight bend, forcing the channel toward one bank or the other, and there the trees dipped their branches in the surface water and ran great slimy roots across the muddy bottom.

Once her left foot slipped and she went into water up to her knees. But she didn't let go her grip on his belt and he immediately braced himself against her fall, reaching back with one hand to pull her up again.

"For God's sake," he said, "be careful. You want to break a leg?"

"No. I don't want to drown, either."

"It's not deep enough.'

A little flare of anger comforted her. "It doesn't have to be very deep."

"Take it easy," he said. "You aren't going to drown. Not tonight, anyway."

She resented the slight note of amusement in his voice. "I'm glad you're so sure about it."

"The only thing I'm sure about is that we've got to put those dogs off our scent and this is the best way to do it. If you've got a better idea, speak up."

When she didn't answer he turned and went on. Jody followed him silently, her brief flurry of anger already dying away into weariness. It was an effort to keep moving, to remember the importance of putting one waterlogged shoe in front of the other, exactly where he had put his, to worry about anything except her forlorn conviction that he intended to go on like this forever and that when the dawn came they would still be plodding down the river, down to bigger rivers, down across the Piedmont to the flat eastern fields, down at last to the sea.

She thought about that for a while, remembering the ocean and the hot white sand and the noon sun that cast no shadows except the hard unblurred lines of shade beneath piers and boat houses. They had spent a weekend at the beach once, Gurney, Marv, Verna, the babies, and Jody, renting a small cottage with broken screens, thin lumpy mattresses, and a kitchen stove so gummed with sand and grease that Verna spent most of the morning cleaning it. "I couldn't eat food cooked in a mess like that," she said with disgust. "How do you suppose folks get to the place they'll live like pigs?" She sent Jody to work on the bathroom, where the tub and bowl reeked of sulphur from the water supply that had stained them a dirty yellow-brown. "I brought along some Lysol, Jody, be sure and put it in your cleaning water."

"Leave it, why can't you," Gurney said impatiently. "I bring you on a vacation, I want you to take it easy, live it up, have a little fun. Come on and have a beer with me."

"It's not my dirt," Verna said, "and I'm not fixing to wallow in it, vacation or not."

"We ain't got time to reform the world," Gurney retorted. "Christ, it's only for a weekend."

But Verna and Jody worked on the little house until Verna was satisfied that it was clean enough to bring in the things from the car: the grocery store cartons full of sandwiches and fried chicken and potato salad; the case of beer and soft drinks; the laundry sack of clean towels and sheets; the suitcase packed with new bathing suits, suntan lotion, paper diapers for Neal. Then, while Gurney and Verna sat on the front steps drinking beer, Jody walked down the beach alone, barefoot, holding her dress up above the water as it rushed in shallow whirlpools around her legs.

She remembered that best of all, the being alone in the sunlight, tasting salt on her mouth, her feet cold in the water and hot on the sand, and the wind pushing her dress against her. And as far as she could see, the world filled with motion, blowing sand and restless water and sliding gulls, and at the hot quiet heart of it, the day at noon empty of shadows.

She remembered other things, too, but not with the same pleasure. Gurney and Marv in their tight swimming trunks, faces and necks brown above pale white skin that soon burned a deep painful red. Gurney, who couldn't swim, taking on the ocean with loud gusto, racing in and out of the water, shouting, carrying Billie Mae on his shoulders out beyond the breakers while she squealed and clung frantically to his neck. Verna sitting at the edge of the surf with Neal, her plump thighs as white and pink as the baby's in the white foam. Gurney and Verna coming back that night from a cafe down on the boardwalk, arms around each other, ignoring Jody as they walked unsteadily through the living room to the back bedroom. And then, at the tail end of the night, going out herself to get away from the stuffy house and the inescapable bedroom noises, wanting the wind against her and the clean salt taste and the being alone again.

But it had been different, in the night. She remembered it now, against her will, the way she had stood in the swirling water at the edge of the tide, holding herself stiff and silent while Marv called her name up and down the dark beach.

Stumbling behind Tay, she wondered if he'd ever seen the ocean. Probably not, he said he'd come from Kansas. It was all corn out there, or maybe wheat, she couldn't remember. But she'd read some place that it went on and on for miles, out across the land without a single tree or fence to hold it back. It must be quite a sight, wheat and corn growing as far as you could see; she had an idea it might move like the ocean, with the wind pushing it, but it'd be yellow, yellow as if the sun always shone on it.

"Pick up your feet or you're going flat on your face."

It took her a moment to realize that he was actually speaking to her.

"It's the mud," she said. "My shoes weigh a ton."

"We'll scrape them off, once we get across." He paused, swinging the light in a narrow arc. "You any good at broad jumping?"

Jody looked at the rough dam of debris and rocks that had caught along the exposed roots of a large tree. It formed a natural footbridge that cut the width of the river slightly, but there still seemed to be a great deal of water between the last rock and the opposite bank.

"I could have jumped it when I was a kid," she said, "without any trouble at all. But that was a long time ago."

"Yeah," he said, "I'll bet it was." Then, with the amusement back in his voice, he added, "Don't worry, I'll pull you out if you don't make it."

She smiled faintly. "Thanks."

"Don't mention it. I'll go first and hold the light for you. Stay where you are till I'm across."

She let go of his belt reluctantly and he walked out along the dam of dirt and rocks, moving slowly, testing its strength. It held firmly under his weight all the way to the edge of the channel, and he balanced there only briefly before jumping.

"No sweat," he said. "You won't even have to stretch."

It looked easy enough, the way he did it. But Jody hesitated, clutching her purse and paper sack under one arm, her feet feeling like heavy muddy roots chaining her forever to this side of the river.

"Don't think about it," he said, "just do it."

He was holding the light on the water at her feet, and in its reflected glow she looked across the river and met his eyes.

"You'll be okay," he said quietly. "I'll give you a hand from this side."

She took one small running step and jumped. Her feet hit solid ground and she threw herself forward, but it wasn't enough; she could feel herself slipping on a tangle of wet vines, losing her balance. Then, even as she braced herself against the shock of falling back into the river, his hands reached out for her and tightened on her shoulders, pulling her away from the edge of the slippery bank and the slow black water.

He waited a moment, holding her steady, before taking his hands away.

Then he said casually, "I thought you had taken root over there."

"I thought so, too."

She reached up and pushed back her hair.

"Give me your shoes and I'll do something about the mud."

"There isn't time. It'll wear off, just walking."

"When it dries you'll think you're lugging around a couple of cement blocks. Hand 'em over."

Obediently, she sat down and took them off.

"Here, hold the light on me."

Taking the flashlight, she watched as he knelt on the bank and dipped her tennis shoes in the water, scraping at them with a handful of dry weeds. He worked

75

quickly but without urgency, and for the first time in an hour or more Jody noticed that she couldn't hear the dogs.

"Do you think they've taken the dogs away?"

"No."

"I can't hear them."

"We're not so close now."

He didn't say it, but she realized that the trees and damp air hanging above the river might also muffle any distant sounds. She tried not to think about the pack of dogs crossing the fields in the silent moonlight, too intent on the scent to bark a warning, coming closer and closer in the night.

"They'll work up and down the road till they find something," Tay said, not looking up, "and that'll take time. Or maybe they won't find anything, and that takes time, too. Either way, we'll be far enough away so it won't matter."

Jody sighed. Her shoulders ached, as if she'd been holding them too high and stiff. She put her arms on her knees and rested her chin on them, letting go for a minute or two, watching him, thinking about him.

"Where do we go from here?"

He didn't answer at once. Standing up, he shook her shoes free of water and brought them back to her. They felt cold and clammy on her feet and the wet laces were hard to tie; he held the light for her while she struggled with them.

Then he said, "How far do you want to go?" and added, after a tiny pause, "with me, I mean."

"All the way."

As soon as the words were out she wished them unsaid. She searched desperately for something else to say but nothing came, and finally she put one hand behind her and pushed herself up.

He stood without moving, looking down at her. Waiting for him to speak, she felt the tiredness soaking into her, heavy and damp and burdened as the air above the river.

Then he said, "It's crazy, the whole thing. You ought to be at home, this time of night, not chasing around in the woods."

She felt almost sick with relief. He wasn't Marv, she kept forgetting that. He wasn't anybody but himself, and she didn't know enough about him to measure him by somebody else's size.

"No crazier for me than you," she said at last.

"I've got more reason."

"Reason or not," she said quickly, "I won't go back."

After a moment he said, "It can't be that bad."

"Look," she said despairingly, "I can go on by myself. You don't have to worry about being stuck with me."

He didn't say anything.

She went on, driven to set him free of her if that was what he wanted, "I planned to catch a bus south. Once I get to the highway I'll be okay."

"Do you have enough money for that?"

"Enough to get me as far as Charlotte."

"With any left over?"

She shrugged. There wouldn't be much left over, but none of it was his worry.

"What'll you do when you get there?"

"Look for a job. Woolworth's, maybe, or waiting tables some place." She added, smiling a little, "I'm pretty good at that."

He was watching her so soberly that she felt her smile slipping away. "You said they'd be looking for you, sooner or later. What for?"

"I left without telling anybody."

"You mean you ran away."

Something in his voice made her feel like a pouty kid with a pack on the end of a stick, running away because her mother wouldn't give her a nickel for ice cream.

"Yes," she said shortly, "I ran away."

"You're not that much of a kid. If you're over sixteen you can take off any time you please and nobody can stop you. Why sneak out in the middle of the night?"

"If you're a boy maybe they can't stop you, but it's different for me. There wasn't any other way to do it."

"Marv have anything to do with it?"

Startled, she glanced up and met his eyes.

He clicked off the flashlight. "I just remembered a few things," he said in the darkness. "Him staying behind at the house with you, and the way he acted later when he picked me up downtown."

She felt her face burning and was glad he couldn't see.

"Marv, then." He added softly, "Or was it your old man?"

Unable to find any words to hide behind, she stood there helplessly, grateful for the darkness.

Then she realized, too late, that the night was no longer a refuge. It had seemed dark when he first turned off the flashlight, but now that her eyes had adjusted she saw that the pale glimmer around them was not moonlight filtering through the trees but the gray beginning of day. She could see his face, faintly but clearly, and she knew that he could see hers, that he had been watching it all along.

"Okay," he said abruptly, "let's go."

They left the shelter of the trees for a wide flat expanse of weeds and thick grass that would be damp marshland in spring but that now, after the dry summer, held firm under their feet. It was easier going in the open, with the gradual lightening of day around them, although when they reached another patch of woods the night still lingered under the trees.

Jody wished he'd use the flashlight again, but didn't

want to ask; she narrowed her eyes, trying to see the ground under her feet. When a protruding root tripped her forward, she instinctively put out an arm to break her fall and stumbled against Tay's back, catching him unawares. For a moment she thought they would both fall, but he threw himself toward a tree and they came up against it with a jolt, off balance, grabbing at each other.

"Sorry," she said on a gasp of air, "I'll try to pick up my feet next time."

He didn't speak or move. She could feel him there against her, tight and stiff, holding himself so still that she wasn't sure he was even breathing.

"What's the matter?" she whispered, and stepped back, away from him.

After another silence he finally said, "My arm," and she heard him draw a deep breath that seemed to take a long time coming back.

"Did you hurt it?" she asked uncertainly, and said again "I'm sorry."

"Not now," he said. "Back when Marv wrecked the car." He straightened up, took another breath. "It'll be okay. We'd better keep moving."

When they came to the end of the trees and the gray haze of dawn again, she could see that he was holding one arm against his chest, cradling it slightly. But he dropped it, forgetting it, as he looked out across the field.

"People," he said. "Not so good."

The field was enormous, holding a good crop of tobacco that stood close to five feet high. At the far end Jody could see a frame house almost hidden by trees, and a hundred or more yards behind it a tobacco barn stood against the woods.

"That house must be on a road," Tay said thoughtfully.

Jody looked at the wide field, bordered by a distant line of black trees.

"Want to stick to the woods," he asked, "or take a chance on crossing here?"

She thought of going the long way around, through the dark woods, and said, trying not to beg, "They ought to be asleep, at this hour."

"That tobacco's ripe enough to prime," he said, "but I don't think they're curing now or we'd see the smoke."

Surprised, Jody looked at him. "How do you know so much about tobacco?"

He shrugged. "I worked enough tobacco when I was a kid to fill all the cigarettes I'll ever smoke."

She didn't have time to consider this new and different aspect of him, so unexpectedly shared with her.

"It's tall enough to hide us," he said. "Keep your head down and make for the barn."

He grabbed her hand and they started out at a run, crouching, following the straight rows of tobacco until even with the barn and then cutting through the tall plants. Jody's ankle twisted once with a sharp twinge of pain but she kept going, knowing that he was having to pull her along, using part of his strength to keep her with him.

When they finally reached the barn and paused behind it, Jody leaned against the siding and closed her eyes, breathing hard. His hand was still tight on hers and sweating slightly; she thought, with a childish wonder, that she could feel tiny beating pulses in each fingertip pressed against her palm. But the slippery damp of perspiration was oddly sticky, and she looked down, idly, to see his fingers black and wet on hers.

She stared blankly, a little bewildered, and when he turned to speak to her his eyes followed hers down.

"Damn," he said under his breath.

When he took his hand away she still stared down at hers, at the thick smear that was his blood.

"I thought the bleeding had stopped," he said. "It

must have broken open when we slammed into that tree."

Awkwardly, he slipped out of the leather jacket. Jody, seeing the cloth wrapped around his upper arm, knew at last what had happened to his shirt; the torn remains of it were black with blood.

"It won't take any more," he said. "It's soaked through."

"I have a white slip in my bag," she said, "if you don't mind using it. It's clean, I washed it just before I left."

He turned his head to look down at her. "You mind signing an affidavit? I always ask for one when I use a girl's clothes to keep from bleeding to death." Then he said, quickly, "I'm sorry. You'll be needing it later."

"Not as much as you do, I guess."

She dug in the bag, forgetting the blood on her hand, and when she pulled out the white cotton slip it was smudged with fingerprints.

"It was clean," she said ruefully. "Once."

"Same blood," he said. "Hold the light and I'll see what I can do with it."

"What if somebody sees it?"

He raised his head and looked around them. Nothing moved in the field or the trees at its far edge, but the eastern sky was flushed with a dull glow.

"A few minutes and we won't need a light," he said. "But we can't wait that long. Let's go inside, the door's open right around the corner."

The air in the barn was warm and close, and acrid with the lingering smell of cured tobacco. Tay, backing away from the oblong of gray light falling through the doorway, went down on his knees in the shadows.

"Keep the light away from the door."

She didn't take it from him. "You can't do any good with only one hand. Let me fix it."

"It's pretty messy," he warned.

"I don't mind."

It was true, she didn't mind the blood. But when she had undone the bulky knot he'd tied with the shirt sleeves and eased the wet cloth loose, she drew a sharp breath at the sight of the long ugly cut slashing his upper arm. There was so much blood still oozing from the wound that she couldn't tell how deep it went, but she knew with a sick certainty that it was much worse than he had let her think.

"Did you ram it through the windshield?" she asked finally.

"I don't know. It doesn't matter, it's done."

"There may be glass in it," she said, troubled. "It ought to be cleaned and sewn up."

"Sure, it ought. You got a needle and thread handy?"

She looked up quickly.

"You're wasting time," he said coolly. "Wrap it up if you're going to."

She tore the slip down one seam. Then, her fingers as gentle as she could make them, she folded half the material in a neat wad against his arm and wrapped the other half around it as a makeshift bandage.

"Not exactly sterile," she said, still anxious but following his lead and trying not to make a fuss. "I hope it doesn't get infected."

"It won't."

"I don't know how you can be so sure," she said irritably. "All sorts of awful things could happen to it."

"Gangrene," he suggested, "or maybe lockjaw?" Then he said, "Don't worry, I won't blame you."

When she glanced up this time he was smiling at her, and something coiled and taut in the pit of her stomach relaxed and let go. Surprised at the way his face changed, going warm and friendly and easy all at once, she thought wonderingly, It's the first time I've seen him smile, he doesn't give anything away for nothing. But even while she watched, the smile flickered out and his face was his own again, no longer shared with her.

"What business you got in my barn?"

Her heart jerked painfully, then stilled.

Beside her the flashlight clicked off instantly, leaving them in shadow.

Paralyzed, waiting in a panic for the voice to speak again from the doorway behind her, she suddenly realized that Tay was moving, without sound, easing up to a standing position.

"The light don't matter, mister. I can see you."

Jody turned her head toward the voice. For a moment she stared with horror at the man in the door, seeing nothing but a black bulk with no eyes or mouth, no features, shaped like a human but peculiarly inhuman except for the harsh threatening voice.

Then he stepped back, into the pale light of dawn, and she could see him clearly, a big Negro man wearing overalls and carrying a rake in his hands.

"Out," he demanded. "Now."

Jody stood up wearily, obediently. But she had taken only a single step toward the door when Tay's arm pushed her back.

He moved in front of her.

"Don't order me around," he said.

The big man lifted the rake. "You want me to, I'll come in after you."

"You might be sorry."

"You think I can't take you, man, you're a fool."

"I don't like being told what to do."

"It's my barn, my land. I tell you, you do it."

They were no more than six feet apart, the Negro man looking huge and black and stolid in the gray morning, Tay still only a shadow just inside the barn door. Jody, at his shoulder, could feel the tension rising in him; the muscles of his arm, touching hers, were knotted hard and tight.

"Okay, it's your barn," he said, "and we stopped in for a few minutes. You want to charge rent?"

The man gave a short humorless laugh. "Don't give me a hard time, mister. I ain't used to company before breakfast and it don't set too well." He stood with both feet separated, swinging the rake in his hand, lowering his head until it seemed to sink into his neck. "You coming out?"

Tay moved so abruptly that Jody, unprepared, felt suddenly bereft and vulnerable. But he only went as far as the door and stopped.

There was a silence.

"What the hell happened to you?" the man asked slowly.

"A little accident," Tay said. "We were just fixing it up."

"Gunshot?"

"A car."

Another silence.

"Hot?"

"It wasn't mine," Tay said shortly, "and that's all I know. I don't ask a lot of questions and I don't think much of answering them."

"That why you didn't wait for the ambulance?"

"Could be."

"You oughta be in a hospital, the shape that arm's in." The man paused, then asked carefully, "The law after you?"

"That's my business."

"It'll be mine," the man said, "if they find out you been hiding on my place."

Tay waited, motionless, silent.

"They got anything else on you?"

"No," Tay said, and added, "not lately."

"You're asking for trouble, man."

"Give a cop a chance," Tay said, "he won't ask any questions he hasn't already got the answers handy."

"Yeah," the Negro said pensively, "it happens that way."

He and Tay studied each other silently.

Then the big man lowered the rake. "You better come on up to the house," he said, his voice heavy and sad. "My wife'll take a look at that arm."

Tay hesitated. "One thing," he said. "They had the dogs out. We haven't heard them for a while, but they may try again."

In the hard flat light of dawn the man's face looked old and tired, tinged with blue. For the first time he glanced at Jody, standing behind Tay in the shadowed barn, and then his eyes moved on, not lingering, back to Tay.

"Raise a sweat on you, them dogs," he said. He waved his rake toward the house. "Let's go, I got tobacco curing in the other barn. That's how I come to see you. I been firing it all night."

Tay didn't speak for a moment. Then he said, in a queer drained voice, "Thanks."

The big man shrugged. "They get this far, we'll have to worry about it when the time comes."

Tay turned, picked up his leather jacket. Then he held out his hand to Jody. She took it, without speaking, and they walked out into the field together. The Negro stood aside for them to pass and fell in behind them as they went through the tobacco.

They could see the other barn now, smaller, set back in an angle where the field widened. They passed it and walked along the edge of the field until they reached the tall aged oaks shading the house. The Negro led them through the yard, hard-packed dirt worn to a smooth dark surface. A battered pick-up truck was parked by the back porch; they had to detour around it to reach the steps.

There was no light in the house, and as they went across the porch something inside the screen door scurried out of sight, a flicker of white in the dark room.

Jody stopped short, unsure, not wholly trusting. Then she heard a soft trickle of laughter, quickly smothered, and the man behind her stepped forward and opened the screen.

"It's okay, honey," he said softly. "Give us some light."

A lamp went on in the kitchen. Jody, going through the door first, saw it all in one hurried glance: the woman standing beyond the table holding a baby, her skin warm and brown above the baby's warm brown naked-ness, two pairs of eyes wide and black and startled in the lamplight; a little girl wearing only a white under-shirt, clutching at her mother's skirt, the laugh Jody had heard still trembling on her small round face; and on the stove a pan of lean bacon frying, a pot of coffee perking.

The woman said on a long rush of breath, "Oh, Eddie," but the words faltered and stopped and only the sigh remained.

"It's okay," he said again, his voice easy. "His arm's hurt, I told him you'd fix it up."

Her eyes rested on Tay, then moved to Jody.

"Belle had a coupla years in training," the man said proudly. "She's almost as good as a nurse." He went toward her. "I'll take the baby, honey. You go get your kit and see what you can do for him."

She handed him the baby reluctantly and left the room. The little girl, trailing after her, put her thumb in her mouth and looked over it, with wide shy eyes, at Jody and Tay.

"Sit down," Eddie said. "Make yourselves to home." He held the baby in the crook of his arm with care-less ease while he pulled two chairs away from the table. "Anybody comes through the field we can see from here. If they use the road we'll hear 'em in time." Looking at Tay, still standing by the door, he said quietly, "Go on, sit down. You're safer here than you'll likely be for a long time."

Jody sat down. Beside her Tay eased into the other chair, resting his arm on the table.

She saw him as she saw everything else, from the hazy distance of weariness. Propping her chin on her hands, she gave herself up to it, not fighting any longer but sliding further into it, relaxed, easy, not caring about anything.

The woman called Belle came back, and Jody watched idly as she put bandages and alcohol on the table and went to fill a small basin with water. Tay sat without moving, and Jody watched him, too. Then, drowsily, she turned her head to watch the big man by the stove, turning bacon with a fork. Over his wide shoulder she could see the top of the baby's head, wobbling unsteadily.

"Let me hold the baby," she said suddenly.

They both turned to stare at her.

"Please," she said. "I won't hurt him."

Belle gave her a slight, hesitant smile. "He may scream," she said, "but don't feel bad. He doesn't see many strangers. Eddie, get him a clean diaper."

But it wouldn't be the fear of strangers, Jody thought, so much as the fear of strange white skin, pale, queer, cold-looking. She took the baby and sat him on the square of diaper, holding him with gentle practiced hands.

They looked at each other solemnly.

"Hey," Jody whispered. "Hey, you."

The baby smiled. Jody smiled back. Encouraged, he grinned, gurgled with laughter. His little belly quivered, his head bobbled happily.

Jody put one finger above his tiny ear, feeling the smooth stubble of black curls. Then she moved it, light as a feather, down his cheek. He caught at her hand with his fist and held it tightly. Moving clumsily, he tried to put her finger and his fist into his mouth all at once, looking up at her with eyes round and black and bright as licorice drops.

The first rays of the early sun came through the window, shining at a slant across the table. The baby blinked, laughed again, grabbed at the bright light vainly and settled for a button on Jody's blouse. He pulled at it vigorously, talking to himself in contented grunts and sighs.

Later Jody vaguely remembered that Eddie had given them bacon and eggs to eat, and hot coffee. She knew that Belle had done what she could for Tay's arm, because the thick bandage was there as proof. But none of it was clear in her mind except the brown baby, laughing on her lap, and the way the sun slanted into the kitchen, fresh, new, and yellow as butter.

❧ 6 ❧

IN the big square mahogany bed Geneva Hackett
stirred reluctantly, coming out of sleep to the painful consciousness of old aching bones and drawn
muscles. For a while she lay there without opening her
eyes, trying to feel the time of day, listening for noises
outside on the street that would place the hour in its
proper context.

The milk truck, maybe, the Lord knows it made
enough noise to wake the dead; or Gurney stepping outside on the porch to get the morning paper, slamming
the screen door when he went out and slamming it
again on the way back in; or Mrs. Tucker across the
street putting out her dog at the break of day, silly
yapping little cuss, there ought to be a law to keep
people from being such fools over animals; or Addie's
alarm, going off earlier than anybody's on the street
and yet not early enough. Nobody, Mrs. Hackett reflected irritably, got up any more in the fresh of the
day to look things over and give themselves time to
smell and feel and think before the rest of the world
came rushing in on them.

She opened her eyes. The room was still quite dark;
looking down at herself she could see nothing but a
white blur of bedclothes and the small skinny hump,
getting smaller every year, made by her legs under the
sheet. It might be morning and again it might not. She
couldn't see the clock on the table by the bed, and the
pain in her bones was no longer a trustworthy guide

because she hurt all the time now and not just at the end of a long night's sleep. The only sound from outside came from a bird in the magnolia tree, and she'd heard it before she went to sleep. It'd probably been carrying on like that all night; there was nothing like a fool mocking bird to get day and night mixed up.

The bedroom, next to the kitchen, facing west and north, had always stayed dark long after sunrise, a fact not overlooked by Addie when she decided that her mother ought to be moved downstairs. But she was careful not to mention it when she first suggested the move, or the convenience of the dark green window-shades that could also be drawn to deceive Mrs. Hackett into sleeping past dawn.

"It'll be warmer in winter," Addie pointed out, "it's right over the furnace. And you know yourself how hot it can get upstairs in summer. It'll be a lot nicer for you, Mama, there's no getting around it."

"Like poor white trash," Mrs. Hackett said slyly, "sleeping in the dining room. I wouldn't have thought you'd ever come down to that, Addie."

Addie refused to be trapped. "Most people have a bedroom downstairs. It's not as if we ever used it now, eating in the kitchen the way we do. I always thought it'd make a nice bedroom, with those extra windows and being almost as large as the parlor."

"Extra windows don't help," said Mrs. Hackett, who knew very well how dark and cheerless the dining room was, facing the wrong way and shaded by the biggest trees on the lot. "It's always been like a grave. Times I've sat at the table and felt I was looking up outa my coffin."

"Mama, that's no way to talk."

"I never slept downstairs a night in my life," Mrs. Hackett went on. "Neither did your pa, even the nights he came in dead drunk and I had to drag him up those steps one at a time. Spent all our married life in that front bedroom, from getting babies to having 'em." She watched Addie's reddening face with bright bland eyes and added, "We got 'em all right up there in that mahogany bed and they was all but one born there."

"I know," Addie said. "You've told me about it."

"Anybody'd think that old bed would give up and fall to pieces, hard as it's been used. There's been two new mattresses, thank the Lord, and this last one ought to last my life out. Ain't nothing to wear it out, I reckon, with just an old woman sleeping by herself."

"Would you like to move it downstairs?" Addie asked patiently. "We could bring all your things down, the bed and dresser, and that old wardrobe, if you want it."

"Frame's still good," her mother said. "Solid mahogany, that bed, only lasting piece of furniture I ever had. Not a crack in it, I looked just the other day, and your pa was a big man." She gave a small cackle of laughter. "Springs fell down one night, slipped right off the slats, woke the whole house crashing down like that in the middle of the night. I couldn't do a thing with your pa, he just lay there hooting, head down and feet up, naked as a jaybird, laughing his fool head off."

"Mama," Addie said unhappily, "please."

"Please what?"

Addie sighed.

"Don't priss your mouth up at me," Mrs. Hackett said. "You was supposed to be a married woman once. The way a man's made ain't ought to be any big surprise to you."

"Sam wasn't like that," Addie said. "There's more than one kind of man, Mama."

"Not living and breathing, there ain't," Mrs. Hackett retorted. "I saw the preacher marry you, Addie, and you got Sam Steed's insurance money all tight and legal, but the Lord knows there's nothing else to prove you ever lived with a man. If I'd known when Sam was living what I know about you now, I'd have felt sorrier for him than I did."

"I didn't care for that kind of thing," Addie said with dignity, "and Sam never held it against me."

"Drove himself into a bridge, didn't he? Maybe he figured you'd like being a widow better'n a wife, I wouldn't doubt."

Addie's face paled. "The accident wasn't his fault," she said. "You've got no call to say things like that, Mama. He was my husband and you ought to respect the memory of the dead."

"Respect for the dead's one thing," Mrs. Hackett said, "but it's a mighty poor handout for the living." She looked at Addie's face thoughtfully, then shrugged. "All right, Addie, I'm sorry. I know he didn't do it on purpose, it was raining and the car skidded. I got no business making more out of it, and him dead and can't come back to call me a liar." She added, with a sigh, "It's too late to change the way you are, and I'm a fool for wishing it'd been different for you."

"Sam Steed was a good man," Addie said, "and he knew I was a decent woman when he married me."

Mrs. Hackett didn't answer for a moment. Then she said, slowly, "Being good and decent's got nothing to do with it, but I got no hope you'll ever have sense enough to see what I'm talking about."

Addie was sure it was no use talking about moving her mother. But she went on doggedly, hating to give up the idea, "It'd be nice for you down here, Mama. You'd be close to everything, not shut away up the steps when you don't feel like getting out of bed."

To her surprise, Mrs. Hackett didn't protest any further.

"I'll move down," she said abruptly. "It'll be easier for you, not having to climb them stairs all the time to fetch and carry for me."

"I'll run up some new curtains," Addie said, relieved. "We can take out that old carpet, it's so worn the flowers don't even show, and lay some throw rugs.

Maybe I could put some Kemtone on the walls, it'd brighten it up no end."

"I don't care what you do," Mrs. Hackett said. "Just don't bother me with it. I said I'd come down, now I don't want to hear any more about it."

But in the end she couldn't keep from meddling in the moving. She liked the old carpet, for one thing, and saw no good reason to roll it up and store it in the garage where it'd rot away, gathering dust and roaches and mice nests. She and Frank had bought it for the parlor with the first raise he'd got at the mill; she could still remember the day the Monkey Ward's truck brought it, and the way it looked when the colored men finished laying it, bright and warm with big splashy cabbage roses, every bit as pretty as the picture in the catalogue. Frank was working the second shift then and she could hardly wait for him to get home to see it. After supper she went in the parlor and turned up all the lamps so the colors would show up in the dark, and then she'd taken off her shoes and run her feet back and forth over the roses, as soft as velvet to the touch. Frank had laughed real hard when he saw her, but he was never one to hold back and spoil somebody else's pleasure; he kicked off his shoes first thing, and they came close to dancing a jig on the new rug. It was almost indecent, Frank had said, how good it felt on his bare toes, like something right out of a whorehouse. She gave him a good slap for talking like that, but it was all in fun; he'd never seen the inside of that kind of place, she was pretty sure, and the way he'd grinned at her she was just as sure he didn't feel that kind of need.

Back then they seldom used the parlor except when company came, and the rug stayed new and bright for a long time, as nice as the blue plush sofa and chair set Frank's mother had given them for a wedding present. But in time, with the kids growing and needing too much elbow space to keep one room shut off, they'd had to use the parlor for everyday living. The plush wore off the sofa in a hurry and the cabbage roses faded. Mrs. Hackett could remember staring at them the night before Frank's funeral when she had sat up all night in the parlor with the big oversized coffin; she had noticed how threadbare the roses looked with the back of the rug showing through and the colors all running together into a dull brownish-pink. As soon as Frank's insurance money came through she moved the rug into the dining room and bought a new one for the parlor; she'd been old and sensible enough to get a plain neutral color that time, and it would last for years to come with so little traffic on it.

So she kept the old carpet in the dining room when she moved down, and told Addie she'd no notion of breaking her neck on any throw rugs, little flimsy things made from cotton and cheap dye. Addie could throw 'em all over the upstairs bedrooms, if she'd a mind to, but when Mrs. Hackett put her feet out of the bed on a cold morning she wanted a rug under them, all the way to the corners of the room. What she didn't tell Addie was that it helped to warm her, somehow, to remember the roses and how bright and red they'd been in the beginning, back before they were all wore out with people and living.

It was the same with the wallpaper, and Mrs. Hackett lay in the big bed in the darkness and wished it was light enough to count the perky little bows that marched up and down the walls. She'd counted them times out of mind, lying there in bed, but she'd never gotten past six hundred before something happened to stop her, Addie turning off the kitchen light to go up to bed or Addie coming downstairs to start breakfast. Ugly old wallpaper, really. She'd put it on herself one year during the Depression, and Frank said it squirmed like it was alive, all them bows going up and down in straight and sidewise rows. She didn't know why she hadn't let Addie Kemtone the walls, it'd be a relief to have the paper covered up. But it'd been a help when she moved her things down, something she was used to, not strange and different like sleeping in the dining room instead of upstairs where she belonged. Not that she was so old and feeble she couldn't stand change, and the big bedroom had never been the same without Frank in the bed beside her, taking more than his share even there at the last, when he wasn't well and had begun to waste away. But still and all, it was like starting all over again, moving down, and the old wallpaper helped. You got used to things, even ugly things, they were a sight better than the emptiness inside where there wasn't anything to be Kemtoned or thrown away to make it better because what had been there was all gone, nothing left, all past and dead and gone.

Well, there was no point in lying in bed, moaning about what life had done to you. She raised herself, very slowly, and put her feet carefully over the side of the bed. Her toes just touched the rug and she slid over, taking a firm hold on the bedside table. Might as well get up and find her clothes, no sense in lying around half the day, waiting for somebody to come wait on her hand and foot.

Life always did what it pleased, the devil take the hindmost, and you didn't often have much to say about it. She'd known that for a long time; it was something most people had to learn sooner or later. Not that she was one of them Presbyterians, thought it was all laid out for you in a pattern before you was ever born, some little babies saved and some poor little babies damned right at the start. Foolish business. There was more crazy talk in churches than the good Lord could probably bear, with all the troubles he had that really mattered. Look at Addie, running down every whip-snatch to let the Baptist minister pray over her; she was a good woman, with all her faults, but it wasn't the church or that squint-eyed preacher made her good, it was what she had in her heart at the beginning.

It all came to you, whether you wanted it or not, whether you were good or bad, whether you wore callouses on your knees praying or spent a year of Sundays cursing. They didn't let you pick it over, like a mess of field peas, take what you wanted and throw the rest away. She had to laugh, sometimes, watching the girls on the Hill, all young and pretty and full of it, thinking they had the world flipped on its tail. Couldn't stand to look at old folks. They'd have it different, they would. Never catch them being dirty and old and broke, needing to be taken care of, just waiting around to die because everything else was gone and done with. Not them, they were too sassy and smart, they'd show you the way to live, pick and choose and take what they pleased. Oh, it was easy if you only knew how.

Mrs. Hackett found her cane, leaning against the wall. Hobbling painfully to the window, she pulled up the green shade.

There, she knew it was getting up in the day. The windows in the front of the Dowd house were fired with the early sun that slipped over the top of the Hill and under the leafy branches of Verna's oak tree.

Maybe they was right, the young ones. Maybe you had to feel that the world was made all fresh and brand-new for you, like it was this time of day, that you only had to reach out to get all the good things and none of the bad. Time you found out it wasn't so, you'd grown more layers of skin, tough old scar tissue, and nothing surprised you any more.

Everybody sleeping late at the Dowds, it seemed. She wasn't surprised at Verna and Gurney; likely they spent half the night working things out. Nothing permanent, she knew that well enough, but it made things easier during the day, having the night to think back on and another night to look forward to. Still and all, Jody ought to be up this late. There was usually a light on in the kitchen by the time the sun was up high enough to get over the Hill.

She opened the big wardrobe between the windows and felt along the row of dresses. Might as well put on her Sunday dress even if she didn't go to church. An old woman ought to keep herself up, not slouch around like she was sitting on the edge of the grave waiting to be pushed in. She took it off the hanger and went to the small dresser, feeling her way in the dim light. It took both hands to pour water from the pitcher to the basin and she spilled some, feeling it trickle down her feet. Well, let Addie mop it up, it'd serve her right for putting her sick old mother downstairs so far from the bathroom. She'd spent many a year without an inside toilet, but it was one thing to do without when you had to and another to use a chamber pot after you'd gone a year eating nothing much more than collards and fatback to pay for putting in a bathroom.

She took off her nightgown and washed, feeling a familiar pleasure in the coolness of the air against her damp skin. Let Addie come down, catch her bare as *September Morn,* there'd be the devil to pay all day. I'm just a sinful old woman, she thought with glee. It's a wonder I ain't struck dead where I stand.

It took her a long awkward time to dress, and when she had finished she sat back down on the edge of the bed to catch her breath.

She had to have her strength because there was so much for her to do. See how Gurney was taking it, that'd matter in the end. Watch for Marv, try if she could guess at his humor. But first of all, she had to talk to Jody. Verna might have tried, but Verna wouldn't be able to help much. Jody had been getting it fast and heavy lately, a lot more'n she could handle, and Verna didn't know half that was going on. Just as well she didn't and maybe never would, but it was that much harder on Jody, being alone with it.

Fumbling at the table, catching the clock just in time to keep it from going over the edge, she finally found the glass with her dentures. She snapped them in, then took her cane and pounded vigorously on the floor.

"Get up, Addie," she called plaintively. "You gonna stay in bed all day, let people starve to death? Addie!"

Verna went into the bathroom and snapped on the light. Turning the faucet full force, she waited patiently for the lukewarm water to run cool.

Drowsily, her eyes barely open, she glanced at herself in the mirror. She closed her eyes quickly, not wanting to see, wishing she'd taken time to cream her face before she went to bed. But she'd gone in the bedroom to talk to Gurney and there hadn't been a chance; he knew well enough how to make you forget everything else but him and what he wanted.

She washed her face thoroughly and reached for a towel. Then she brushed her hair with hard short strokes to get out the tangles, brushing it away from her forehead and pinning it back so it wouldn't look so tousled and cheap hanging down around her face. It was getting dark at the roots again; time for another bleach job. That was the way it went; she'd known when she started there'd never be any end to it.

Staring at her clean face, she noted with somber interest the faded brown circles under her eyes, the slight puffiness around her chin, the tiny lines radiating from her mouth and eyes. She smoothed them out but as soon as she took her fingers away they returned, looking like faint thin veins just under the skin. She'd heard there was a cure for it, just don't frown and laugh so much, but who could live any kind of freak life like that. It was the same crazy business as that face cream with bee jelly in it, or something; they said a queen bee never died and neither would you if you paid twenty bucks for a little jar of it. Or your face wouldn't, all creamed up with bee jelly.

There'd been a time, she thought ruefully, when she could look in a mirror any hour of the day and not be disgusted by what she saw. Even at dawn, the worst time. Or the middle of the night which was almost as bad, with your eyes full of sleep and no lipstick left. That was being young. Anybody could look that way, all smooth skin and clear eyes and sweet with sleep, when you were only a kid.

Like Jody. Verna thought of her, as always, with a surge of affection. Jody, almost grown now but still a kid. It was a good time, being seventeen, you never realized till it was all over just how good it was.

Verna smiled a little, remembering. Not that you didn't have problems. When she was seventeen she'd felt like she'd lived a lifetime, and maybe she had. She'd had to move back in with her mother and sisters that fall, when Jody was almost a year old and Ralph had left town for parts unknown. She hadn't heard from him for five years; even when the divorce was up in court he didn't bother to come back to town. When he finally came back for a weekend he hadn't cared enough about Jody to come by to see her. He had wanted to forget everything that went with being sixteen and crazy in love and getting married one Saturday night in South Carolina.

She put on her lipstick. Then, looking at herself critically, she added powder under her eyes and across her nose.

She'd had a hard row to hoe, back then, and she hoped Jody would never have to go through anything like that. But when you were seventeen and still had the whole world in front of you, you bounced back like a rubber ball. And some of it was good to remember, like the year she'd had with Ralph. She had always held on to that and tried to forget the bad times, and later, she'd realized it was better than nothing, just having something to remember. Something of her own, not touched by her mother's whining reproaches or her sisters' contempt, something private and apart from the crowded little house where eight people lived together in four rooms, something to keep her going. And then there'd been Jody, who made it all worthwhile.

She tied her cotton robe around her and left the bathroom. If only Jody had a room of her own. It wasn't right for her to be crowded up in that tiny back room with the kids. But Marv couldn't sleep with them, he had to have his own bedroom. There was no other way, but it worried her; a girl that age, it was important to have something of her own, if only a bedroom.

Verna paused by the kitchen table. It all came back to her from the hazy edges of her mind where she'd pushed it last night when she couldn't stand thinking about it any longer. Nothing she could do about it at midnight, she'd told herself, go on to sleep and worry about it tomorrow when it might do some good.

But here it was, morning already, no more putting it off.

The corners of her mouth drooped, and the soft pink skin of her face. For an instant she thought she was going to cry again; she could feel it right there in her throat pushing to get out.

She went over to the sink to fill the kettle with water. Putting it on the stove, she turned up the burner. Then she took a big can from the cupboard over the stove and measured coffee into the coffee pot.

In the back bedroom Neal was talking softly to himself. Not loud enough yet to wake Jody, Verna guessed, or she'd be up and have breakfast started by now; but then, he was a good baby and had never cried and fussed a lot. She might as well slip in and get him before he got to banging his toys on the crib, and that way Jody could get some extra sleep. She needed it, poor kid, the way Gurney'd flared out at her last night.

Verna stood by the sink, staring through the window at the quiet sunlight slanting across the driveway and the dry green-brown grass in the Hackett's front yard.

Oh, Lord, if there was only some way to work things

out. Some easy way that'd put a stop to all the quarreling and fighting and hurting. Some way she could think of to keep them all together without their sharp edges rubbing each other all the time, like they couldn't keep their elbows to themselves but had to keep prodding somebody's tender spot till it was raw and sore.

She sighed and walked softly across the kitchen to the bedroom door. It made a slight noise when she opened it and Neal's chatter stopped immediately. Seeing her there in the door, he smiled widely and stumbled to his feet, holding out his arms across the crib bars.

She had picked up the baby and started to tiptoe back to the door when she realized that Jody wasn't in the room. Billie Mae was still sleeping soundly under the window, but the other side of the bed was empty.

"For heaven's sake," she said aloud, "what's she up to this time of day?" Neal chuckled and clutched her tightly around the neck, and she murmured, "Where's Jody, Neal?" and kissed his cheek. "Sweet baby," she whispered, "you're Mama's sweet baby."

Carrying him back into the kitchen, she was a little surprised to see that the kitchen door was closed and locked. Jody often went outside and sat on the steps in the fresh air, waiting for the rest of the family to get up; this time she must have pulled the door shut, forgetting that it would lock behind her.

Verna opened it and went out on the steps. But Jody wasn't there, and the yard was empty and dark, still shadowed by the house from the sun.

With a little stir of alarm she went back inside and walked through the house to the front door. The porch was empty, the paper hadn't even come yet, and although she stood on the steps for a long time, she saw nothing moving on the street and heard nothing but the birds and the distant noise of a car starting up somewhere on the other side of the Hill.

She felt her mouth drying out, so that it hurt to

swallow. Grabbing up her robe, she went down the steps and across the yard. By the time she reached the driveway she was running, but she wasn't aware of hurrying until she got to the Hackett's backdoor and found herself too out of breath to speak. Neal whimpered in her arms and she loosened her grip on him, patting him on the back and bouncing him up and down a little, soothing him absently.

Addie opened the screen door.

"My goodness, Verna, you're up early today."

Behind her Mrs. Hackett sat at the kitchen table, her cup of coffee half way to her mouth. Verna looked at her helplessly, wanting to speak but unable to get the words out past the queer dryness in her mouth.

Mrs. Hackett asked calmly, "What's the matter?" and put her cup down without taking her eyes from Verna's face. "Somebody sick over to your house?"

Verna found her voice. "Is Jody here?"

Addie drew a sharp breath.

"No, she ain't," Mrs. Hackett said. "You lost her?"

"She's not in the house," Verna said. "I looked in the yard, too, front and back." She stood there indecisively, still patting Neal, her face so limp that she couldn't make any effort to pull it together. "Oh, Lord, I thought sure I'd find her over here. Where do you suppose she's gone?"

Addie was still holding the screen open, one arm outstretched, the other holding a crumpled paper napkin. "Maybe she went to walk, Verna. Just wanted to get out, nice as it is this time of day."

"She never took a walk before," Verna said, "so early, and breakfast not even started."

"Well, there's no telling what people'll get in their heads to do," Mrs. Hackett said shortly. "Come on in and put that baby down, Verna, he's too heavy to be lugging around. Addie, shut the door, no point to filling the house up with flies. Pour Verna a cup of coffee, she looks like she could use one."

Verna paid no attention. Without another word she whirled around, grabbing up her robe again, and ran down the steps and across the yard. She headed for the kitchen door, it was closer, but when she got inside the kitchen was just as she had left it, empty and still and dark. The kettle was whistling and she stopped long enough to take it off the stove and fill the coffee pot. Then she turned on the light and put Neal in his high chair, giving him a cookie to pacify him for a few minutes.

In the dining room she went straight to Marv's door and opened it quietly. He was lying diagonally across the bed with his head and arms hanging over one side, the sheet kicked aside and trailing on the floor. He was sleeping in shorts and T-shirt, and Verna's face wrinkled with distaste as her eyes moved from the bed to the dirty shirt and jeans in a heap on the floor at her feet.

She backed out and closed the door. Then, with a puzzled frown, she opened it again, not going inside, and reached down to pick up the shirt.

It was smeared with something, all across the front, and in the pale gray light filtering through the curtains the big splotches looked very black against the white cotton.

Verna reached out with her hand and snapped the light switch by the door. In the bright glare of ceiling light Marv stirred and muttered something, pushing his head deeper into the pillow. Verna stared at him blankly, then stared down at the shirt in her hands. The black splotches had changed color in the light; they were a dark brownish red, still damp to the touch.

She dropped the shirt and pressed the back of her hand against her mouth, biting into her finger until it hurt. Moving slowly and awkwardly, she turned and went through the living room to the front bedroom.

Gurney was also sleeping. He seemed to fill the bed, his bare shoulders and torso looking big and hard above the red-striped pajama pants. His face was buried in one pillow and his right arm was flung across the other; only a few minutes ago she had carefully slipped out from under it, smiling to herself because he always slept better when she was under his hand, pulled up tight against him or held down by the dead weight of his arm.

"Gurney," she said, "wake up."

He didn't move.

"Gurney, you got to get up, right now."

She could tell, from the different quality of his stillness, that he was awake. Then the muscles moved smoothly across his shoulders and he rolled over, flat on his back, looking up at her with his dark hair rumpled over his forehead and his eyes opened a narrow drowsy slit under the heavy brows.

"Morning," he said huskily. "What's with you?"

He turned his head and squinted at the luminous face of the small alarm clock on the chest.

"Judas, is that telling the truth? I oughta crown you one, waking me up this early, Sunday morning." He rolled over again, arms over his head. "Take the kids and go on to church if you got the urge, honey, but don't count on me, I need my beauty sleep."

"I'm not kidding, Gurney, you get up this minute. Jody's not here, I can't find her anywhere."

For a minute or two the room was so quiet she could hear his breathing.

He rolled over and sat up in the same quick motion. "Whadda you mean, you can't find her?"

"She's not in the house or in the yard."

His eyes were open now, all the way. "She's probably over to old lady Hackett's."

"No," Verna said, "they haven't seen her."

He stood up, reached for his pants. "You look in the can?"

"I was in there myself, Gurney. She's not here, she's not anywhere I can find her."

He dropped his pajamas and stepped into his shorts and pants together. "Maybe she went visiting. Why don't you call some of her girl friends? She's got a hell of a nerve chasing around this time of day."

Verna shivered and hugged her arms against her. "There's none I could call, offhand. She don't know any girls that well."

"Christ, she's gotta be some place."

He zipped his pants and slipped his feet into a pair of moccasins. Verna, watching him, felt a lump of nausea rising in her throat.

"You better go talk to Marv," she said without expression. "He's in there asleep, but there's blood all over his clothes."

Gurney stopped short.

"What'd you say?"

"There's blood stains all over his shirt," Verna said. She went on, her voice muffled and thick, "It's still damp."

"You crazy?" Gurney asked incredulously.

"I saw it with my own eyes. Go look yourself, I left the light on."

He stared at her. The look on his face chilled her; she could feel gooseflesh all over her body.

"You're off your nut," he said then. "It don't have to be blood, it could be anything."

She didn't speak. There wasn't anything else to say. She'd gotten it out and now everything had dried up again, her thinking and feeling and talking. She was afraid she'd be sick if she even tried to speak, and she put her hand over her mouth, biting it the way she'd done in Marv's room.

"You're crazy," Gurney said. "The whole thing's crazy."

But he was standing no more than two feet from her and she could see the faint sheen of perspiration on his face.

"Jesus," he said harshly, "it'd better be."

He brushed past her into the living room. Verna stood by the chest, putting out her hand to hold on to the edge, feeling it cool and hard under her fingers. Holding on with all her strength, she stood there and listened, without moving, to the sound of voices from Marv's room. Neal was calling her from the kitchen, banging on the tray of his high chair with growing disapproval, but he seemed far away and distant, no longer of any importance.

Then she heard Gurney say irritably from the living room, "Go on and get dressed, for God's sake, you gotta help us look."

Verna sagged against the chest.

"It was blood, all right," Gurney said behind her. "He got in a fight with that kid he had with him last night. Marv busted his nose for him, says the damn thing bled all over both of 'em. I could've told him not to get mixed up with some strange guy, bumming around looking for trouble."

Verna swung around. "You believe him?"

"Sure, I believe him." Gurney scowled at her, his face still pale and damp. "What the hell, you think he'd lie to me about a thing like that?"

"Yes," Verna said baldly, "he'd lie about anything to save his own skin."

The color surged back into his face. "Dammit, I oughta know if he's lying or not. He was over to Ashton, he never laid an eye on Jody all night."

"He tell you that for sure, Gurney? He didn't see her when he came home, after we was in bed?"

For a minute she thought he was going to hit her. "You never had any use for him, did you? You think he's that rotten, you jump to blame him first thing, anything that happens."

"I'm not blaming him," Verna said sickly. "I just don't know what to think. Gurney, where's she gone to? You think anything bad's happened to her?"

He drew a long breath and put his hands on his hips,

frowning down at her, and gradually the dark flush died out of his face.

"I don't know," he said finally, "but don't worry, we'll find her. I told Marv to get dressed. He's gonna cover the Hill, see if he can get a line on something. Maybe she's just walking around, you know what screwy ideas she gets sometimes."

Verna shook her head silently, despairingly.

"Come on, let's get some coffee. Marv can't find her, I'll call the cops. She ain't a little kid but they'll put out a call, missing person and all that."

He put his arm around her and led her toward the kitchen. Neal, still banging on his tray, was beginning to cry with honest anger, and Billie Mae suddenly appeared in the door, her eyes twisted shut against the light.

"I'm hungry, Mama, where's my oatmeal? Jody promised me oatmeal, she said I could have brown sugar on it."

"You can eat corn flakes and like it," Gurney said. "Go wash. I'll fix it for you."

Verna sat down at the kitchen table and put her face in her hands.

"I want oatmeal," Billie Mae said, whining the words. "I don't like corn flakes."

Gurney slammed a cupboard door. "Eat what you get or go without."

He put a frying pan on the stove and took a package of bacon from the refrigerator. Marv came into the kitchen, still buttoning his shirt, his face pale and blank with sleep. He glanced at Verna and then looked away quickly.

"Where you want me to start looking?"

"Up and down the street," Gurney said, "around the block, down on the highway. Don't run your mouth, tell everything you know, but if you see anybody she knows you might feel 'em out. Somebody musta seen her, and you can bet they wouldn't forget it, a girl out

107

chasing around at break of day. Probably figure she'd had a big night and was just coming in."

"Yeah," Marv said. "Well, I'll take a look."

He went out the back door, letting it slam behind him.

"Where's Jody?" Billie Mae asked. "We was going to Sunday school, Jody and me."

"Shut up and eat," Gurney said. "Verna, you want two eggs or one?"

Verna didn't answer. The tears from her closed eyes wet her fingers and ran in slow runnels down to the sleeve of her robe.

"I hate corn flakes," Billie Mae said loudly. "Mama, why don't you fix me some oatmeal? Where's Jody, she promised we'd have oatmeal for breakfast and then go to Sunday school."

Neal cried shrilly, his face red and strained.

"Jesus Christ," Gurney said savagely, "I'm gonna strangle both of you. Eat them corn flakes, Billie, or I'll ram 'em down your throat. I can't be bothered with you, I got to do something about this baby or he'll choke a gizzard."

He took Neal out of the high chair and gave him a piece of bread. The screams ceased instantly, and Gurney held him firmly in one arm while he put a cup on the table before Verna and poured coffee in it.

"Drink some, honey," he said gently. "You'll feel better, get something hot in your stomach. Don't you worry about the kid, I'll find her."

He turned back to the stove and the pan of bacon, but it held his attention only briefly. Carrying Neal, he went to the sink and looked out of the window, bending his head to see through the plastic curtains. Then he walked to the back door, and stared out at the morning and the long shadows cast by the house across the small square of back yard.

O N the porch, shaded by the magnolia tree from the warm morning sun, Mrs. Hackett sat in her rocker and watched the Dowd house.

A police car, parked in the driveway behind Gurney's car, blocked her view of the Dowd porch, but she had seen the neighbors going in and out for the past hour, scurrying past the police car with their eyes averted as if it might reach out and snatch them up if they dared to look at it with open curiosity.

She fanned herself leisurely with one of the oval cardboard fans Addie had brought back from the church. On one side it was printed with a colorful picture of Jesus holding a white lamb and smiling down at a crowd of children; the white of His robe and that of the curly lamb was very white, the blue of the sky a hard bright blue, the green of the grass as brilliant as green enamel. Mrs. Hackett always used it on Sundays because it seemed more fitting to use a Baptist fan on the Lord's day, but her sense of pleasure in it derived purely from the clear vivid colors that looked like nothing on earth, which was as it should be, and the gentle smile on the face of Jesus. It had often occurred to Mrs. Hackett that no man living could wear such ridiculous clothes, like an old sheet draped endwise, hold a smelly lamb, be surrounded by a mob of noisy kids, and at the same time look out at the world with such an unconcerned air of kindness and compassion. Mrs. Hackett was not entirely convinced that the living Jesus had been so much a saint and so little a real man, but it was comforting to look at the picture on the fan and imagine how it would be if life was as full of Heavenly love as the preachers and the men who drew the Bible pictures seemed to think it ought to be.

I love Thee, Lord Jesus. Well, there wasn't much comfort anywhere today. She had an idea Addie wouldn't find much in church, either, it wasn't likely she'd have any revelation from above telling her where Jody was.

It was hard to sit and wait, not knowing what was going on next door. If anybody had a right to know it was her, she'd started it all with her big mouth and her notions of getting things straightened out for Jody. Not that she could figure there'd been any other way to go about it, except to tell Verna. Keeping quiet was just what Marv Dowd had counted on, he'd thought he could go on doing what he pleased to torment Jody because she'd be too scared to tell on him.

Gentle Jesus, meek and mild. The old woman rocked to the refrain, spacing it out in an even rhythm. GENtle . . . JEsus . . . MEEK and . . . MILD. Pigs' feathers, there was such a thing as being too meek and mild. Not everybody could be a saint, you had to live in this world and not the pretty one on the church fan.

Jody and Verna had a problem, always had. They were butter-soft, woman-soft, looking out at life with big wondering eyes and never seeing trouble till it slapped 'em in the face. Marv knew it, oh, he knew from the start they was as easy to torment as baby kittens. He knew just how to poke his finger where it went in the deepest and hurt the most.

She saw Addie cross the driveway between the two houses. It was hard not to call out that she didn't have to take all day; but Addie looked so solemn and unhappy that Mrs. Hackett wasn't sure, for a moment of agony, that she wanted to hear the news in such a hurry.

When Addie reached the steps she climbed them heavily and sat down in the swing.

"Let me borrow your fan, Mama," she said. "It's going to be another scorcher, looks like. I wish I hadn't put on my good dress till later, it's so hot in Verna's house I got right faint."

Twisting her rocker around, Mrs. Hackett handed the fan to her. "They heard anything yet?"

Addie shook her head. "The policeman just came out to get any information he could. What she looks like, more than anything. He said he'd like a picture if Verna had one. It'll be in the paper, probably. He said that helped sometimes."

"Verna have one?"

"That one Jody gave her for Christmas last year. But she's wearing her hair different, you know how short it is now." Addie dropped the fan in her lap and looked blankly out across the yard. "He wanted to know what she was wearing, if Verna could tell from her clothes what was missing." Her voice choked. "That's a good way to identify people, he said."

"I expect it is," Mrs. Hackett said calmly. "Somebody sees the picture and reads about what she's got on, they may remember seeing her some place."

Addie drew a deep breath and began to fan again.

"Verna didn't know," she said, "but I did, right off the bat. It was that green one I made her, remember, with the little jacket." Her eyes filled with tears. "No telling where she is or what trouble she's in, and she picked one of my dresses to wear when she left."

"Then they don't think anybody carried her off?"

"I reckon not," Addie said, "but I don't know how they can be sure. The policeman went in her bedroom, poked and plundered around everything that was hers, but what does that tell anybody? No sign of a struggle, he said, and who's to say she was in the bedroom when it happened?"

"When what happened?" Mrs. Hackett asked tartly. "Don't go making nightmares for yourself, Addie, it's plain as day what it was. Jody was tired to death of it all, tired of Gurney and Marv and even you and me, I don't doubt, and she just got up and left. I had a notion it might happen but I didn't have enough sense to see when it was coming, and that's to my eternal shame. I just wish to goodness she'd come to me first, she ought to know I'd do what I could."

"After last night," Addie said, "I don't know why she'd think so." Her face was as reproachful as her voice; for a moment she looked at her mother with an undisguised bitterness. "You should have left well enough alone, Mama, and maybe this never would have happened."

Mrs. Hackett ignored the words as if they'd never been said. "How's Verna taking it?"

"She's lying down, I only talked to her a minute or two. Can't stop crying, you'd think nobody loved Jody as good as her."

"Maybe that's so," Mrs. Hackett said, and Addie gave an audible sniff. "What's Gurney doing?"

Addie didn't answer for a long while. Then she put the fan flat on her lap and looked down at it, moving her fingers gently over the bright colors.

"When I went over he was in Jody's room. Just standing there by the dresser, not moving or doing anything, staring at the wall."

"That don't sound like Gurney. Wasn't yelling or cursing, anything like that?"

"He looked queer," Addie said. "I'm scared of him, Mama, the way he's acting." After a pause she added, slowly and reluctantly as though she hated to say the words but hated more to keep them inside, unsaid, "When I went to look through Jody's clothes for Verna I turned around and he was there in the doorway watching me. He didn't say anything, or even look like himself. He just stood there the way he was doing when I first went over, staring at Jody's things till you'd think he'd never seen them before."

Mrs. Hackett was silent. She began to rock again.

"I saw him take a bracelet of hers, Mama. Stole it, and me standing right there seeing him. You know that silly jangling one she wears, with the little charms on it? He picked it up and jingled it back and forth, I tell you my nerves were on edge, and then he put it in his pocket. I was looking straight at him and he knew it, and he just stared through me and put it in his pocket and walked out."

Mrs. Hackett sighed. "It's not exactly stealing, Addie. He probably paid for it."

"He gave it to her for her birthday," Addie said. "Last time she wore it I thought, that's Gurney for you, it's already turning green."

Mrs. Hackett leaned her head against the tall back of the rocker and looked up at the shiny green magnolia leaves brushing the porch gutters. Addie began to move the swing back and forth, and the chains clinked faintly with the motion.

"And Marv," Mrs. Hackett said at last, "I suppose he was sitting there as innocent and nice as you please, bird feathers all over his mouth."

"I didn't say a word to him, nor him to me, but he looked sick enough to be in bed."

"Might be sick over Jody," Mrs. Hackett said thoughtfully, "if he was anybody else. But not Marv, I wouldn't believe it if he swore on a stack of Bibles."

"No doubt he was out drinking most of the night," Addie said with contempt. "I know how these young people behave on Saturday nights."

"Do you, Addie? Imagine that now, you knowing about any such kind of wickedness."

"They're not in church Sunday morning, I know that."

Mrs. Hackett started to speak, then changed her mind. She kept looking at the magnolia leaves, slick and heavy, dark green in the shade.

"I'm going to be late myself," Addie said, "if I don't get a move on." When her mother said nothing, she stood up, straightening her dress automatically. "Where do you suppose she went? It don't sound like Jody, running off without saying a word to anybody."

"Only way to run," Mrs. Hackett said. "Say a word here, say a word there, first thing you know somebody'll put a kink in your plans."

Addie looked at her curiously. "You sound like you're glad she ran away."

"No, I ain't glad. She'll have her hands full when they catch up with her, nothing'll be better and most of it worse."

Addie stood by the swing, still fanning absently. Then she dropped the fan on Mrs. Hackett's lap and went to the door.

"I'll go in and get my hat. Will you be all right, Mama, while I'm gone?"

"I reckon," Mrs. Hackett said, as she did every Sunday morning. "I can't go far on my own and nobody's offered to carry me."

She watched the policeman walk down the Dowd steps and cross the yard to his car. He sat inside for a time, writing on a pad, before slamming the door. The black car backed out of the driveway and idled slowly down the street; as it turned the corner another car passed it and drove up the street to stop before the Dowd house.

Addie came out on the porch, hat in place, carrying white gloves and a spotless white lace purse.

"I'll be back, Mama. Please don't try to go next door while I'm gone. There's nothing you can do now and I'd worry all through the service if I thought you might walk around and fall and I wouldn't know a thing about it."

"Go along," Mrs. Hackett said. "You're gonna be late."

She waited impatiently for Addie to reach the end of the walk and turn to the right along the uneven sidewalk. Keeping her eyes on the old green car in front of the Dowd house, she smiled a little to see it start up again and pull across the driveway to the edge of the hedge bordering the Hackett yard.

Bob McGee got out and looked up the street after Addie. Then he vaulted the hedge and detoured around a flower bed, coming across the yard with an easy slouching walk.

At the foot of the steps he took off his ball cap and grinned up at Mrs. Hackett.

"How come you're not going off to church with Addie? Seems to me you're the one needs it."

"Smart aleck," Mrs. Hackett said. "How come you're not?"

"I've been already. Early Mass, first thing this morning."

Mrs. Hackett snorted. "Heathen Catholic. Idolater. Worshipping golden images instead of the good Lord."

"Sure," Bob said, "that's the way it is. Sin and a shame, ain't it?" His grin still flickered across his face. "You're getting to sound just like Addie."

Mrs. Hackett smiled back at him. "Come up and set a spell, Bob. Heathen or not, you're a good boy."

He took the steps two at a time. Balancing himself on the railing, he hunched his shoulders and looked down at her soberly.

"What's this I hear about Jody?"

"She's gone. You heard it mighty quick."

"Marv was out looking around."

"Marv," Mrs. Hackett said, spitting out the word as if she couldn't stand it in her mouth. "I'd like to wring his skinny neck."

"Yeah." Bob looked thoughtful. "I had an idea it might be that."

"You wouldn't happen to know anything about it, would you?"

Bob met her eyes directly. "I wish to hell I did. Just last night I told her I'd be glad to help any time she got the urge to take off. Give her a ride, money, help her find a job some place, anything I could do."

"I don't know why you thought it'd help," Mrs. Hackett said indignantly. "When did running off ever help anything?"

He shrugged. "Whatever the kid wanted to do, I'd be for it."

Mollified, Mrs. Hackett said, "You're a good boy. Give her time, she'll see it."

"Time's run out, looks like."

"She'll be back. No need to doubt it, they'll turn over every rock in the county till they find her."

"Maybe she's not in the county."

"Unless she robs a bank she won't get much farther. She had ten bucks when she went to bed last night and I don't know where she'd find any more in the Dowd house."

Bob laced his hands together and stared at them. "Saw the police car leaving next door," he said casually. "The place is sure lousy with them this morning."

Mrs. Hackett stopped rocking.

"Had a couple of deputies down at the station, soon as I opened up."

"How come?"

"Seems there was a bad wreck over on the blacktop last night, three miles or more from the intersection."

"Lord, I haven't read the first line of the paper this morning, what with everything else. Anybody we know?"

"Nobody we know, or the deputies either. Nobody, period."

"I'm not gonna bite," Mrs. Hackett said, "so you might as well go on and tell it straight to, not keep me hanging."

"Somebody called and reported it, said a man was hurt bad, but when the highway patrol got out there nobody was around. Plenty of blood, though, and they radioed the sheriff's department to bring out the hounds."

Mrs. Hackett's eyes sparkled. "You don't say. My word, all that going on right down the road and me sound asleep. I never heard a thing."

"They traced the scent a little way down the road, then lost it. They figured he must've come in this direction, so they were up and down the highway this morning, asking a lotta questions."

"Anybody hurt, you'd think they'd be looking for help."

"The car was stolen," Bob said. "Some poor guy down town, eating at a restaurant, came out and it was gone. The deputies said it was really tore up, went off a curve and wrapped itself around a tree." He put one foot on the railing and rested his arm on his knee. "They asked me had I seen any suspicious characters around, looking like they didn't belong to the cars they were driving."

Mrs. Hackett leaned forward. "Well, had you?"

"Nope, not lately. But when Carl came in, the fellow owns the station, I heard a right interesting little piece of news." Bob raised his head suddenly and smiled at Mrs. Hackett. It was a cold small smile, not reflected in his eyes. "Carl saw Marv Dowd down town last night, nine o'clock or so, driving a new black Chevie. He wondered if Marv had struck it rich, bought himself a car."

Mrs. Hackett let out her breath in a long whistling sigh. "He tell the law about it?"

"Not yet. He says it's none of his business, he hates to get a guy in trouble."

"Addie saw Marv today," Mrs. Hackett said, frowning, "you saw him, too. She said he looked sickly,

Bob, but if he'd been in that kind of mess you'd think he'd have more to show for it than that."

"You'd think so." After a pause he said, "What about that fellow he had with him last night? You ever see him before?"

"I ain't seen him the first time. He came to the house with Marv, I saw that, but it was too dark for me to get a good look. He went off with Gurney later on. Down town, I guess. It was about time for Gurney to pick up Verna."

"Carl said there was some guy in the car with Marv, he didn't know who it was. I figured it was the same one Marv had with him down at the Greek's, earlier."

"They could've met down town," Mrs. Hackett said. "You think it was his car?"

'Maybe," Bob said. "Only thing, he didn't look to me like he owned anything but the clothes on his back, and they weren't much to speak of."

Mrs. Hackett rocked slowly, shaking her head. "Trust that Marv, he's always floating around with a bunch of trouble makers. Well, looks like he's made a peck of it for himself this time."

"I don't know," Bob said slowly. "This guy wasn't a tough. Oh, tough enough, I guess, he looked like he'd been around. There was something about him, y'know. I sure as hell didn't have any urge to tangle with him, not without a damn good reason. But the first thing I thought, seeing him at the Greek's, was what on earth a guy like him was doing hanging around with Marv Dowd."

"It could've been him who stole the car," Mrs. Hackett pointed out. "Maybe it was Marv hanging around him, he can be like a leach. Ask Jody, she knows."

"I wish I could," he said coolly.

Mrs. Hackett sighed. "Marv was madder'n a wet hornet when he left here last night," she said. "He might have done anything the way he was feeling."

Then she added reluctantly, "Whoever did it, there was somebody got hurt, and from all that shows it wasn't Marv. It must've been the other fellow, and maybe he's learned his lesson, taking up with anybody as worthless as Marv."

Bob grinned slightly. "You reckon Marv's learned a lesson?"

"Not him," Mrs. Hackett said emphatically. "Well, Bob, you gonna call the police?"

He slapped his cap against his leg a couple of times, then put it on and pushed it to the back of his head.

"I'm thinking it over," he said, and the cold little smile came back to his face. "It's a handy thing, sometimes, knowing something nobody else knows."

"I'm somebody," Mrs. Hackett retorted, "and I know."

"Sure, but you wouldn't spoil it for me, would you, first time I find a good big stick to hold over Marv's head?"

"What about that other poor boy, hurt and maybe dying, and nobody knows where he is unless it's Marv?"

Bob's face sobered. "Yeah, I thought about that. But he looked like a guy who could take care of himself, and Marv, too, without much sweat. It's Jody I've got on my mind now." He stood up, putting his hands in his pockets, hunching a little. Looking down at Mrs. Hackett he said coldly, "Once we get her back, I'm gonna see Marv leaves her alone. Gurney, too, he's just as bad. This stick's a big horny one, I'll beat the both of 'em with it if I need to."

"We got to get her back first," Mrs. Hackett said.

Bob stood on the edge of the steps, rocking back and forth restlessly, frowning out across the lawn. "Yeah," he said, and was silent for a long minute.

Then he turned abruptly to Mrs. Hackett. "Let me know if there's anything I can do to help. I'll keep my ears open, maybe I can pick up some kind of clue. Thought I might drive down to Charlotte tomorrow and take a look around, she said something about it once."

"You're a good boy," Mrs. Hackett said.

He touched one finger to his cap and went off across the yard. Mrs. Hackett watched until the green car had started, on the fifth try, and jolted slowly down the street.

Then she picked up the fan and fanned herself briskly. It was going to be another scorcher, Addie was right about that.

8

BELLE made Jody go to bed that morning before she'd finished eating, and Tay didn't argue about it. "She's about to drop, look at her, can't keep her eyes open just sitting there." Belle frowned at Tay reproachfully. "No place you can go with her dead on her feet, might as well let her sleep a while."

Belle went into the bedroom and Tay could see her through the open door, stripping the bed and putting clean sheets on it. Jody didn't pay any attention; she sat with her elbow on the table, her face propped on one fist, and looked down at the plate of food as if she'd like to eat it if she could only figure out a way to get it to her mouth. She didn't protest when Belle came back and said, "Why don't you come lie down, honey, I fixed the bed nice and clean," but got up silently, so docile she might already have been moving in her sleep, and started for the bedroom. She stopped in the door long enough to say to Tay, in a low tired voice, "You won't go off and leave me?"

"Don't worry," he said quickly, "I'm not going any place."

There wasn't any question about her needing to sleep. He'd known, as far back as the river, that she was pushing herself too hard; he'd managed to give her a few minutes to rest when he cleaned her shoes, but it wasn't nearly enough. She was tired clean through, he could see that; he'd figured they'd have to find a place to hole up for a few hours, and here it was, handed to them free of charge. He wished there was some way of letting Eddie and Belle know how he felt about it; it'd been a long time since he'd been so grateful to anybody for a favor.

It was safe enough, he was pretty sure of that. He hadn't heard the dogs again and there was always the chance they'd gone after Marv; wherever he'd run to he'd gone on foot, leaving a clear scent of his own. Still, Tay couldn't be sure the cops wouldn't be checking around; he knew how they worked. Even if their dogs didn't pick up anything they'd stake out most of the county roads in the neighborhood, just keeping their eyes open and asking a lot of questions. But you had to take a risk, now and then, and this one had to be worth it, they needed a break too badly not to take it.

Then Belle came back to the kitchen and began clearing the table. She glanced at Eddie, standing by the screen door with the baby in his arms, and said, "You better eat something yourself, Eddie. Give me that child and I'll put him in his crib, it's past time he had a bottle."

Eddie said hastily, "No hurry, I'll grab a bite later."

Tay knew what it was. He'd been away for a long time, but not that long.

"It's your table," he said, "sit down and eat. If I don't like it I can get up and leave."

Eddie didn't speak for a moment. Tay knew, without looking, how blank and expressionless his face would be while he worked the words over in his mind and tried to decide whether it was safe to take them as they stood or if he'd better turn them over and look behind them, not trusting his instinct, not trusting Tay even when he sat at his table and ate his food and took shelter in his house.

"You from around here?" Eddie asked finally.

"Yes," Tay said. "Sorry if it spoils your appetite." He stirred his coffee, then said patiently, "Maybe it's where I've been that counts."

"Man, you must've been a long way from here."

Tay looked up and met Eddie's eyes. "I guess so," he said, and let it go at that.

After a minute Eddie shrugged. He took a plate of bacon and eggs from the back of the stove where Belle had left it for him and poured a cup of coffee. Sitting down at the table opposite Tay, he ate without speaking again. Belle came back without the baby and started to wash dishes; she glanced at Tay and Eddie once, then busied herself at the sink with her back to the room. When Tay said, "Thanks, that tasted better than any food I can remember," she turned and gave him a quick bright smile. "Food always does," she said, "when you're hungry."

Then Eddie said, "Find him one of my shirts, Belle. He's gotta keep that arm covered up, the next few days." He grinned at Tay. "Not to mention you'll look more ordinary with clothes on. Pants ain't enough, man, people liable to get curious."

"I've got a bag at the bus station," Tay said. "Didn't figure I'd need it so soon or I wouldn't have left it behind."

"Maybe I can pick it up for you later. It don't take long to drive to town, and Belle can keep an eye on that tobacco for me."

"I'm an old tobacco hand," Tay said. "I'll do it."

Eddie stood up, taking a pack of cigarettes from the back pocket of his overalls. "You keep out of sight. Nobody's gonna look for you here, inside the house." He laughed a little, down in his throat. "Not in a colored house, man, you're as safe as in church."

"Yeah," Tay said. And then, "That's the way it goes."

Neither of them spoke for a moment, and Tay kept his eyes carefully away from the cigarette in Eddie's hand.

"Better grab some rest yourself," Eddie said finally.

"That arm don't look good to me, it's gonna be trouble-some if you don't watch it."

It was already aching, with a dull pain that had moved up to his shoulder and down to his fingertips. But Belle had given him a couple of aspirins when she dressed it and he figured there wasn't anything else to be done for it except to forget it and hope it'd start healing on its own.

"You go sleep a while," Eddie said, "there ain't any need to go chasing off half-cocked. Belle and me, we'll watch out."

Tay watched Eddie stride across the back yard, and the weariness he had been fighting almost got out of hand when he thought about letting go, even for an hour or so.

"It's cooler in the living room," Belle said. "You can stretch out on the couch, and I'll keep the kids quiet."

He looked at her, knowing he ought to say, sure, he'd use the couch, the kids wouldn't bother him.

But he left it too long, and after a pause she said softly. "Go on in the bedroom. She'll feel better, know-ing you're there."

Tay didn't think she'd feel anything about it, one way or the other; she was sound asleep, lying on top of the sheets with the faded chenille spread folded back neatly over the foot of the bed. But when he lay down beside her, moving so carefully not to wake her that the springs didn't even squeak, she stirred and opened her eyes.

They looked into his for a brief moment. Then they slanted with her smile and closed again, and he felt her hand slip into his.

"It's nice," she said, "having a bed to sleep on." Her eyes didn't open again but the smile deepened. "The way you were going, I'd given up hope of any-thing softer than the ground."

She was asleep again, just like that, he could tell

from the sound of her breathing. Her mouth still held the smile, though, and he lay there and watched as it gradually faded away, leaving only the corners of her mouth turned up slightly. He didn't figure it'd be that easy for him, with all he had to think about and the pain beating in one big solid pulse up and down his arm. But he hadn't counted on the way it felt to just lie there quietly, watching her face and feeling her hand in his and knowing she was glad he was there next to her.

When he woke up he knew instantly that he'd slept most of the morning. His arm was easier for one thing, and when he looked through the tiny back window to the yard and fields he could see the shadows standing straight up with the sun at noon.

Jody hadn't moved, except to put one hand under her cheek, and he turned his head back and lay very still, looking at her. Her skin was warm and the short dark hair around her face clung together in little damp points, like commas; he blew on one, gently, and it lifted slightly with his breath and drifted back to separate into soft brown feathers. Her lashes were also dark and pointed, and he was so close he could see the way each one rested against her cheek and then curved away. His eyes moved down to her mouth, clean and pale as a kid's without makeup, not smiling now but relaxed all the way and parted a little, warm and crumpled and tired.

He looked away from her and stared at the ceiling. The roof had leaked some time in the past, and there was a big discolored circle in one corner; the wallpaper was pulling away in ragged strips and several cracks wavered out from it across the ceiling. He kept his eyes on it for a long time, waiting patiently until he was thinking again and not just feeling. When he had it under control he eased his legs off the bed and stood up.

His whole arm felt stiff and it hurt when he moved

it, but Belle's bandage was still neatly in place and it wasn't stained, which meant the bleeding had stopped. There was no way of knowing yet if it was infected, but maybe his luck would hold that far; if not, he'd have to take the risk of looking up a doctor some place. Maybe in Charlotte; it was a big enough place to get lost in if you'd had as much practice at it as he had.

He went to the window and looked out at the yard. Hands in his pockets, he leaned one shoulder against the wall, careful to stay in the shadow where he couldn't be seen.

The little girl was playing on the hard dirt close to the house, and he watched her for a long time. Squatting on her heels, she put one chubby finger on the ground in front of a large red ant; whenever it scurried in another direction she moved her finger to block its escape, chuckling to herself. Finally she tired of the game and left the ant alone. Taking a doll from the steps, she clutched it tightly in her arms and sang to it. The doll was dirty and broken, missing one leg, but the child was very tender with it, smiling down at it and crooning quiet unintelligible words. A chicken made its way across the yard, pecking indifferently at the hard ground, and drew her attention; she dropped the doll in a grotesque position, body doubled over its head, and stared at the chicken. For a few silent minutes she stood there watching it, absorbed, thumb in her mouth. Then, suddenly, she waved her arms and squealed loudly, and the startled chicken flew around the corner of the house with a flurry of squawks and flapping wings.

Tay grinned. From the back door Belle said softly, "You leave them hens alone, Lucy, or I'll warm your bottom for you."

The house was getting hot and stuffy as the day wore on, and Tay felt sticky with perspiration. The yard looked cool in the heavy shade of the oak trees, but he knew better; on a day like this there wasn't any place you could escape the heat, even if you went in the deepest part of the woods looking for relief you'd find nothing but sour air and the hot heavy smell of summer that had followed you in.

It'd be worse out at the barn, where Eddie was curing his tobacco. He was killing it out now—he'd have to watch it constantly to be sure the temperature stayed just right; no matter if it went up to a hundred in the shade, he'd still have to stay in the open shed by the barn, feeding the fire and nursing his tobacco along until it was finished. Then he'd be out in the fields again, priming till he had another barnful of ripe tobacco, and the whole slow hot process would be to do over again. Nothing had changed about it since the first time Tay had stayed up all night to do his share of watching the fire for his father. He'd heard some farmers had changed over to oil heat, but the long hours of watching must still be the same; nobody had invented a way of curing tobacco from a comfortable bed.

Tay's gaze moved from the shady yard to the tobacco field beyond, green in the glare of the sun. If he narrowed his eyes slightly he could almost believe he was home again. He'd grown up in a house like this, a little larger but not nearly so clean; there'd been a yard of cement-hard dirt and a towering oak tree and tobacco fields that reached almost to the house. He used to jump out of bed in the mornings, when he was a little kid, to see if the tobacco had crept up to the back porch in the night when he wasn't looking.

He turned away from the window, swinging his other shoulder around so that his back was flat against the wall, and looked at the girl on the bed. She was lying on her side, her head turned toward him, one hand caught under her face, sleeping like a baby without moving or dreaming, her breath going in and out with a quiet regularity.

He knew there wasn't going to be any question about

what he'd do next. He had some plans of his own, but they had waited a long time and a few more days wouldn't matter.

She moved slightly, sighing to herself.

Tay waited, his back still against the wall, hands in his pockets, watching her.

When she opened her eyes they widened gradually, staring at the ceiling, the chest across the room, the bed. She held herself so motionless that she might not have been breathing at all.

Tay said quickly, "Feeling better?"

Her eyes focused on him and the wide fixed look went out of them. "For a minute," she said, "I didn't know where I was."

She sat up, pushing her hair back from her face and holding it up off her neck.

"It's hot," she said. "Did you sleep any?"

"Too much," he said. "It's late, we've got to get moving."

She stood up at once. "I'm sorry, I didn't mean to hold you up."

"We both needed the sleep."

"How's your arm?"

"Good as new. If you want to wash your face there's a bathroom off the back porch."

She walked to the chest of drawers and picked up her purse. Looking in the small mirror on the wall she said ruefully, "It'd help, maybe. The way I look, nobody'd doubt I'd been wandering around in the woods all night, falling in rivers and getting chased by bloodhounds."

"You look fine to me," he said, and immediately wished he hadn't. He had an idea she didn't remember how it'd been when he lay down beside her; she'd been too groggy with sleep and knowing she was safe inside a house for a little while. But it hadn't seemed to bother her at all to wake up and find him there in the room with her, watching her sleep, and he could kick himself for giving her a chance to draw back inside herself, the way she'd done a couple of times during the night, not sure whether she could trust him or not.

He said casually, "It's nice to see what you look like in the daylight, for a change," and thought angrily that he'd better shut up, he was making it worse instead of better.

But her grin was like a boy's, easy and amused and uncomplicated. "Pig in a poke," she said. "You'll be more careful, next time, who you pick up in the dark."

She left him and went through the kitchen, and he heard her speaking to Belle out on the porch. Going back to the bed he stretched out on his back and waited, staring at the ceiling again, until the familiar discipline had cleared his mind of everything but the immediate problem of where they'd go next to keep out of sight until dark, and how he could get her to Charlotte without both of them being picked up by some suspicious deputy.

When she came back she was carrying a blue cotton shirt, starched and freshly ironed.

"Belle sent this to you," she said. "She thinks we ought to wait till Eddie comes up from the barn before we leave. It'll only be a few minutes, and she's fixed lunch for us."

"You hungry again?"

She gave him a quick little smile. "It looks wonderful. Corn and butterbeans and tomatoes and iced tea."

"You twisted my arm," he said. "A few more minutes ought not to matter, one way or the other."

He remembered that Eddie had said something about picking up his bag at the bus station, but he didn't think they should hang around long enough for that. He wanted to see Eddie again, though, and ask if he knew a less conspicuous route to Charlotte than the superhighway, and it wouldn't hurt for Jody to have another meal under her belt before they took off.

"They're nice people," she said. "Why do you suppose they've been so good to us?"

"I don't know," he said soberly. "Some people are made that way. It could have been anybody in trouble and they'd do what they could to help."

When you were on the bum you learned not to ask why when somebody did you a favor. He remembered the time a big fellow pulled him up into a boxcar somewhere in Georgia, one freezing December night with a hard sleety rain driving out of the north; the train had stopped at a water tank and was picking up speed, and Tay'd never have made it if the guy hadn't given him a hand. But that wasn't all he'd given; he'd shared a can stopped at a water tank and was picking up speed, and when Tay had lain down on the hard rattling floor to sleep, feeling lonelier and younger than his fifteen years, the guy had talked in a low companionable voice for a long time. He'd still been talking when Tay finally dropped off to sleep. Then, when he woke up in the cold dawn, he'd discovered he was covered with the big fellow's heavy overcoat. He'd never forgotten how he felt, too choked up to say thanks, but the man had only grinned and said, "We'll soon be in sunny Florida, kid, I keep my blood warm just thinking about it."

Tay never saw him again, or expected to, after that night; and there was no way of knowing what had driven the man to put out his hand to a strange kid and then help him through a bad night.

Jody asked, "Do you suppose Eddie's ever been in trouble with the police?"

"Could be," he said briefly. "Don't ask him."

She looked surprised, as if doing such a thing had never occurred to her. "He wouldn't tell me, anyway. Colored people keep to themselves, they don't trust anybody who's white."

Tay shrugged. "Do you blame 'em?"

He reached for the blue shirt. It fitted well across the

130

shoulders but the sleeves were too long and he rolled them up to his elbows.

"You're like that, too," Jody said.

He looked up quickly from buttoning the shirt. She was watching him from the foot of the bed, her eyes grave and thoughtful; they were a funny color, he thought irrelevantly, not dark or pale but a shade in between, a sort of light clear brown with tiny flecks of green.

"You don't trust anybody, I mean," she said. "You keep all of you to yourself."

He turned his back on her and walked to the window. Unzipping his jeans, he stuffed the shirt inside and zipped them up again, then put his hands in his pockets and stood there silently, looking through the window. Eddie was coming across the yard; his overalls were wet with sweat and his dark face glistened in the sun.

"Time to eat," Tay said. "Eddie looks like he could use a big tall glass of iced tea."

When she didn't say anything he turned around, already sorry he'd cut her like that. But she wasn't there. She'd gone into the kitchen, and he could hear her talking to the little girl.

He leaned against the wall wearily, conscious of a sudden urgent need to get outside, on his way, going some place even if it was wrong. He felt trapped and helpless shut up inside the stuffy little house, waiting for something but not knowing when and how it'd come at him, not even sure enough of what it'd be to get ready for it. You might sleep and forget for an hour or so, but the rest of the world kept moving. The dogs and the deputies were still out there in the glaring sun, somewhere; they didn't forget, damn 'em, they had memories like elephants. His face prickled with sweat, then his whole body felt damp with it.

But he stood without moving, back against the wall, and fought the fear stubbornly, knowing he couldn't let it get out of hand. Jody might sense it, for one thing, and she scared easy. For another, he'd had enough of losing his head. He'd cut loose and run too many times when it was wrong. He had to learn, he had to, that if he held on long enough he could whip it, he could fight it inch by inch and it was only a matter of time before he'd be okay again, that there was nothing he couldn't handle if he kept his head and his patience and the sense he was born with.

By the time Eddie came to the door and said, "You want something to eat, man?" he had it under control.

He knew he'd be okay, at least for a while, when he found himself agreeing with Eddie that they'd be crazy to take off for Charlotte that afternoon.

"I been thinking about it," Eddie said at the table, "and it don't seem like a smart move to me. They'll be watching the highway, they know a guy gets in a jam the first thing he thinks about is getting out of town. Then you gotta figure there may be something about it in the papers, and even if you catch a ride without any sweat it's liable to be with some joker who read all about it and can't wait to drive you to the nearest police station."

"Yeah, I know all that," Tay said. "But I thought maybe we could keep off the main highway. There's more than one way to get to Charlotte."

"Sure," Eddie said. "There's more than one way to get to jail, too." He put his elbows on the table and leaned forward. "Listen, stick around here today, nobody's gonna bother you. If them dogs had picked up your smell, we'd have 'em sniffing around my back porch right now. They got no idea where you went to, and there's a lotta territory to cover this side of town. Let 'em look. Even if they come down this road they ain't gonna bother old Eddie Thompson."

Tay listened without comment, watching Eddie's face.

"Oh, they might stop and ask if I seen anybody in the woods or on the road, but that'll be all. I used to work at the courthouse, they think I'm a good honest nigger." Eddie grinned at Tay, his mouth pulled back against his white teeth. "Yeah, that Eddie's a good nigger, don't give you no lip, knows his place. 'Course he used to drink a little whisky now and then, cut a man up a little now and then, but that's a spook for you. He don't get into trouble much now, he's a hard worker, got a farm he works himself. You know a good nigger's always a good plowhand."

Belle sighed, a small sharp sound, and picked up her tea. The ice rattled against the glass and she put it down again, staring at it, her underlip caught between her teeth.

Tay glanced at her and then away. "Looks like you got a lot of influence down at the courthouse," he said easily. "Maybe if I took you down with me they'd let me off, not even make me put up bond."

Eddie laughed, a deep amused laugh that reached his eyes this time. "Yeah, man, they liable to make you mayor, any friend of Eddie's gets red-carpet treatment."

"I don't want to make trouble for you," Tay said, and added deliberately, "or your wife."

"No trouble," Eddie said. "I ain't lying, nobody's gonna look for you here. Belle don't mind having you, she likes company."

Jody said quickly, "Maybe we'd better not stay. You've done enough for us already."

Belle looked at Jody and smiled. "If it'll help," she said, "I'm glad to have you stay."

"Look," Eddie said, "wait till dark, anyway. You got your mind made up to go to Charlotte, I'll run you down in the truck. It'll be easier at night, they can't stop every car on the road."

"They won't stop any," Tay said, "I'm not that important."

"You oughta see a doc, too, before you take off. I know one can keep his mouth shut, I could take you by after dark and let him fix you up. Then we could swing

into town to get your bag and be on our way. No
sweat, easy as breathing."

Tay, trying to find the right words to say what he
had to say, pushed his plate back and rested his arms on
the table. But there weren't any words, he knew, just as
there wasn't any right way to turn down a guy like
Eddie.

"Thanks for offering," he said finally, "but you'd better keep your nose clean. Anything went wrong, they'd
throw the book at you."

"I can look after myself, don't worry about Eddie."

"I'm used to trouble," Tay said.

"You think I'm not?"

"No point in asking for more."

Eddie looked down at his hands, big and dark and
calloused. He put them flat on the table, palms down.
"Anybody can't help when you're in trouble, man,
they might as well give up trying to be decent."

Tay said quietly, "You don't have to prove it to
me."

Eddie raised his head and looked at Tay, his eyes
black and somber. "I want to do what I can. Don't
mistake me, I got plenty of room for hating, there's
nobody can hate as big and hard as I can. But there's
been a white man or two helped me out when I needed
it, now maybe I can pay some of it back. I never
wanted to before, not till you come along."

Nobody spoke for a moment or two.

Then Tay smiled. "It's your funeral," he said.

Eddie lifted his glass, drained it, and pushed his
chair back. He grinned cheerfully. "I gotta get back to
that tobacco. You take it easy, rest up for tonight."
Then, with no expression in his voice, he added,
"Maybe I ought to mention it, he's a colored doctor."

Tay shrugged. "So long as he's got a license."

Eddie's grin came back. "Man, you're not a bit particular." At the door he paused. "Too bad you in such
a hurry. Best thing you could do would be lay up a

week or so, let 'em get tired and ease off looking for you."

Tay, thinking of the agony of staying shut up inside the small house for an entire week, shook his head.

"Don't say it again," Eddie said. "You want to get to Charlotte. But I know a good job open, last maybe a couple of weeks, any guy didn't mind hard work."

"You must think that doc of yours can work miracles," Tay said. "Nobody's going to hire a guy with a bum arm."

"It's field work, you could do it. I primed and handed a whole crop of tobacco one year with one finger split open and tied up like a sausage. This fellow I know, he wouldn't push you too hard."

Belle looked at Eddie inquiringly. "Mr. Causey?"

"Yeah, he's been after me all month to help him out. He ain't got much of a crew this year and his crop's gonna get outa hand if he don't watch it."

Tay considered it for one long moment of weakness. Then he said reluctantly, "It wouldn't work, Eddie."

"Okay, just a thought. He's not a bad fellow, lives by himself, wife dead and his kids gone from home. But whatever you say, man, you're running this show."

"I'm trying," Tay said, "but you keep twisting my arm."

Eddie laughed and went out, and Tay pushed the idea of a job away resolutely. He needed the money, for damn sure, but he couldn't risk it. There was Jody, too, he couldn't just turn her loose and say, sorry, I've got other things to do, you'll have to get to Charlotte the best way you can. He hadn't figured out exactly what he'd do with her, anyway, once they got there; she couldn't have much money and he had all of two bucks, left over from pawning his watch in some little town in Tennessee. Even if she found work right away, she'd run short before her first pay day; nobody rented you a room without getting their money

in advance, and she'd have to keep enough to eat on
for a week.

He wondered if she'd thought any of it out for herself before she left home; probably not, she'd taken off
in a hurry and when you were desperate you didn't stop
to bother with practical problems, you went ahead with
what you thought you had to do and hoped it'd all
work out, somehow, with a little luck. Well, he was all
the luck she'd had, so far, and he'd do the best he
could for her. That wasn't saying much; God knows his
best wasn't going to be good enough.

He didn't let any of it show in his face. Jody and
Belle were clearing the table and he went back in the
bedroom to keep out of their way, stretching out on the
bed with one arm behind his head, glad of a chance
to think it through before Jody got to talking again
about going off on her own so he wouldn't be stuck
with her.

But she didn't give him much time, and when she
came in and sat down on the edge of the bed he knew
from the way she looked at him that she'd been doing
some thinking for herself.

"You didn't say anything before," she said, "about
going to Charlotte."

He was prepared for that. "Didn't you tell me that's
where you wanted to go?"

"I didn't think—" She stopped, looking worried and
anxious and guilty all at once, then started over. "I
don't want you to feel you have to see that I get there.
I can go on the bus, I told you I had enough money
for that."

He gave an inward sigh. "This way you can save
your money. Eddie said he'd take us down, and even
paying for the gas it'll be cheaper than the bus."

"But you hadn't planned to go to Charlotte," she
protested. "I don't want you to do it, just for me."

They were getting nowhere fast. He knew several
things he could tell her if she'd been a couple of years

136

older, say, and had been around enough to hold her own; but if she'd been that kind of girl he wouldn't be wanting to say them, which left him exactly where he'd started. Nowhere, with no place to go. Except Charlotte, maybe, for a beginning.

He thought it over and said finally, "You remember what you said to me last night?"

She waited, her eyes questioning, the worry settling on her mouth so that it looked sort of sad and forlorn.

"I asked you how far you wanted to go with me, and you said all the way."

Her skin was so clear and pale he could see the warm flood of color pushing up under it.

"I figured that meant we were going to stick together," he went on calmly, "at least till things got straightened out for both of us. What's happened to make you change your mind?" He added, making a good case of it while he had the chance, "Maybe you think it's too dangerous, hanging around with me, and if that's it I guess I can't blame you for wanting to cut loose."

But she didn't rise to the bait. "You know it's not that," she said soberly. "I said that last night because I was scared of the dark and being in the woods, and I didn't want you to go off and leave me. But it's different now."

"Sure," he said. "It's daylight and you're out of the woods and you figure you can do better on your own."

"It's not me I'm worrying about."

"If it's me," he said, "you're wasting your time."

"I know you can take care of yourself," she said levelly. "Maybe I can, too, only you don't seem to give me credit for any sense at all."

He couldn't help it, he grinned. "I'm not saying you can't," he said. "It's just that I haven't seen any signs of it lately." He regarded her with an open amusement. "I give you credit for a lot of things, kid, but offhand

I wouldn't say you had enough common sense to come in out of the rain."

She didn't look offended. "I admit I haven't had much practice at this kind of thing, but maybe I'm learning."

"Maybe," he said, unimpressed. "You don't seem to have learned much in your life so far."

That got her. The dark lashes swept up, widening her eyes, and he watched the flecks of green merge together until they almost obliterated the clear brown.

"That's only your opinion," she said coolly.

"I'll name you reasons, if you want," he said, still amused.

"Don't bother."

"No bother," he said. "Nothing I like better than pointing out somebody else's faults."

To his surprise the green look faded out of her eyes and she smiled at him. "Can I play this game, too?"

"Don't be crazy. That'd take all the kicks out of it."

She doubled her legs under her and clasped her hands around one knee. "I'm used to have my faults pointed out," she said. "You don't scare me."

"That's what I mean," he said. "You're scared of all the wrong things. The dark. Dogs chasing you. Crossing rivers. Running from the cops."

"And the right things?"

"People, for one. Do you go around trusting everybody, just for the asking?"

"No," she said slowly, "that's one thing I've learned."

"Not so anybody'd notice."

After a long pause she said, "Anyway, you didn't ask."

"I asked you not to yell," he said ruefully. "Why didn't you?"

"I knew who you were."

"You mean you'd seen me once, for a couple of minutes, with Marv. Was that enough for you?"

"Yes," she said, almost inaudibly.

He realized then how far he'd brought her, not intending to, not looking ahead from one word to the next. For a minute he couldn't speak at all, his throat filled with something warm and choking and unmanageable.

"Well, there you are," he said finally, as casually as he could. "What you need is a keeper, kid, and it looks like I've been elected."

She was silent, leaning her head back against the maple bed, her eyes almost closed. Then, unexpectedly, she asked, "You wanted that job Eddie was talking about, didn't you?"

Taken unawares, he could only shrug and say, "I can find a job in Charlotte."

"They may be looking for you there."

"It's easier to get lost in a town."

"It may be harder to find a job."

"I won't have any trouble. I've done a little bit of everything in my time."

There was another silence. Tay could hear Belle in the other small bedroom, putting the kids to bed for a nap. He didn't think they'd sleep much, the heat was so heavy in the house you could almost see it and the flowered plastic curtains at the window hung limp and motionless.

"Eddie said that farmer lives by himself," Jody said, her eyes still closed and hidden. "Maybe he'd give me a job, too. I'm a pretty good cook."

For the second time he found it hard to speak.

"If we're going to stick together," she went on, "we ought to work things out together and decide what's best to do." She opened her eyes suddenly and looked at him directly. "We don't know yet that anybody's looking for me, so it can't matter much where I go. It doesn't have to be Charlotte, I only thought about going there because I knew I'd have to get some kind of a job and a big town seemed better for that."

He just lay there, watching her and saying nothing.

"But we're pretty sure they're looking for you, and that's what ought to count. Eddie thinks you'd be smart to keep out of sight a week or so, and so do I."

"Working tobacco for some farmer isn't exactly like hiding in a closet," he said. "If he can read there's a chance he'll see something about it in the paper and get suspicious."

"You and Eddie can think up a good story."

"It'd have to include you," he said carefully. "I'll lay odds he's a good church-going Baptist who wouldn't think highly of you and me chasing around together when we just met for the first time last night."

She didn't look away. "He doesn't have to know that."

"Look, kid, we'd probably have to tell him we're married or it'd be no go, good story or not."

It didn't seem to throw her. "I guess it won't be the last lie we'll have to tell," she said, "before it's over."

He started to draw a deep breath and stopped before he'd finished, not wanting to give himself away.

"You said you'd worked in tobacco when you were a kid," she said then. "I didn't know they grew tobacco in Kansas."

"They don't, so far as I know."

He hesitated, but he knew it wasn't enough. He didn't want to cut her again, or shut her out so she'd go away; he wanted her to stay there, curled up on the bed beside him, talking to him with that funny solemn honesty that made her seem such a kid, yet looking back at him no matter what he said with her eyes so quiet and old you'd think there was nothing left in the world that would surprise or frighten her.

"They raise wheat, mostly," he said. "I followed the harvest up from Texas. It was good money, if you liked working outside." Then, with an effort, he added, "It was the first time I'd been west of the Mississippi. I grew up on a little farm down east of Raleigh."

He hadn't said those words aloud for longer than he could remember and it was queer how empty he felt inside now that they were out, and how little it seemed to matter.

"You see," she said on a note of triumph, "I knew you weren't a stranger."

He grinned. "I've been gone a long time, so you can't exactly call me home folks."

"Is that where you were heading? Home, I mean?"

"It's not there any more," he said steadily. "That's why I left."

She didn't say anything, and he knew somehow that she wouldn't pry no matter how many openings he gave her.

"They thought I was going to a basketball game," he said, looking at the ceiling, "but I grabbed a fast freight and headed south. Just took off, without telling anybody, and never went back."

"Like me," she said softly.

"Like you."

He could feel her watching him, but he didn't speak again for a long while. He kept his eyes on the tattered wallpaper on one corner of the ceiling, then he narrowed them until he could see only the uneven stain where the rain had leaked through.

"Why don't you go back?" he asked her then, very quietly.

She didn't answer.

"I know what it's like," he said to the ceiling. "You think you'll go nuts if you don't leave, you're so fed up there's no other way out. You think you'll have it made, once you get so far away you can forget everything behind you like you'd wiped it off a blackboard."

He stopped and turned his head so he could see her face.

"A long time later you find out it's not that easy. If it was you'd have a lot of company, every poor bastard in the country would be on the bum."

"Are you sorry?" she asked slowly. "Do you wish you hadn't done it?"

"I don't know," he said. "I've gone over it a hundred times, maybe ten hundred, and it always comes out the same. How can you figure what's right and wrong, or how things might have been if you'd done them a different way?" He added wearily, flatly, "I haven't had anything but trouble since the night I left. Maybe I didn't learn anything else but running, once I started. I don't know, I can't add it up."

He felt her hand touch his, light and easy, as if she'd moved it by accident and found his in the way. He turned his hand over, palm up, and closed his fingers around hers.

For a long time they didn't speak, lying there on the bed with their hands touching, listening to the quietness of the house and beyond it to the silence of the afternoon baking in the hot sun.

9

VERNA went in the back bedroom to find a clean sunsuit and diaper for the baby. But she hadn't had time to do a washing and most of his clothes were soiled, crowded into one of the chest drawers; she looked through them hastily, remembering with sadness how Jody always kept his things in tidy piles, sunsuits in one, shirts in another, diapers stacked neatly on top of the chest, everything clean and ironed and sweet-smelling.

Finally she found two clean diapers and an old faded sunsuit Neal had almost outgrown, and she took them into the living room. Lifting the baby from his playpen, she hesitated for a minute, her eyes going to Marv's closed door. Then she turned toward the front porch, hurriedly, leaving the door open, running down the steps and across the yard with the baby held tightly in her arms and her head bent over his.

Mrs. Hackett watched her from her rocking chair. "She was scuttling," she told Addie later. "Scuttled right out of that house like the Devil was after her, hot on her heels. Well, maybe that's Gurney's name, big and mean as he can be, I tell you it wouldn't have surprised me any to see him chasing after her, right up to my door. She was looking for some place to hide, no doubt about it."

But when Verna reached the porch she sat down in the swing with Neal in her lap and her face as composed as though she had nothing on her mind but the hope of finding a cool spot to sit and rest.

"My goodness, it's hot," she said, "and it's only ten o'clock. We'll all be melting before the day's over."

"Not much of me left to melt," Mrs. Hackett said. "You take some of that fat off you, Verna, hot weather wouldn't be so hard on you."

Verna looked vaguely apologetic. "I know it, I ought to get a job where there's no food in sight. But I don't eat much when it's hot, anyway, you'd think I'd lose weight instead of gaining."

"It's a cross you'll have to bear. Some women are made that way, just look at a potato and gain a pound. Might as well be glad you got some flesh on you, Verna, if I was a man I wouldn't give a hoot for a dried-up scrawny piece of woman." Mrs. Hackett gave a cackle of laughter and then asked, "You going to work the usual time today?"

"I guess so. One of the girls is out on vacation, and one's sick. I hated to ask for time off, short-handed as they are."

"You want Addie and me to keep them kids?"

"That's why I came over, to ask. Billie Mae's down the street playing, she'll be home by lunch, then the two of them oughta go in for a nap." Verna hesitated, looking down at Neal. "I know it's a lot of trouble, but I just didn't feel like I could ask anybody else around here, people being so curious and all."

Neither of them spoke for a moment. Mrs. Hackett glanced at Verna and saw that the composure had left her face; it was soft and miserable, almost frightened, and her eyes glistened wetly.

"No trouble at all," Mrs. Hackett said. "Me and Addie want to help any way we can, you know that. You hear anything more from the police?"

"Not a thing." Verna's voice broke slightly. "It seems like she's just gone off the face of the earth, nobody can find a sign of her any place."

"I don't expect she's gone that far," Mrs. Hackett said soothingly, "but you got to figure it'll take a while to locate her. Nothing's easier than to lose yourself where nobody can find you, especially if you don't want to be found."

Verna frowned, little lines of anxiety pulling down the corners of her mouth so that they drooped unhappily.

"I don't believe Jody'd do a thing like that, I just don't. It's not like her, you know she never caused me a minute's trouble in her whole life before."

"There's always a first time."

"It's about to drive me crazy, worrying about her, not knowing where she is or if she's all right. There's no telling what could happen to her, she's only seventeen." Verna put the back of her hand against her mouth. Then she went on rapidly, "I tell you if you'd seen all the dirt I have you'd have nightmares thinking about all the terrible things she could run into and not know how to take care of herself."

Neal looked up at her face and his own began to crumple. He gave an experimental cry, his mouth turning down until he looked as unhappy as Verna.

"Do something about that boy," Mrs. Hackett said, "or he's gonna start hollering." She watched as Verna found a pacifier in her pocket and put it in Neal's mouth. "Jody's no baby, Verna. When I was seventeen I was married and so was you, with a baby of your own. Besides that, girls grow up quicker nowadays, it's right foolish to think Jody don't know a horse's head from his tail."

"She's not like other girls," Verna said. "It's my fault, not letting her get out any more than I have. But you know how it is when you work all day, you can't let a kid run loose. Not on the Hill, anyway, there's too many girls been getting themselves in trouble." She sighed deeply. "She don't know what people are like. I've kept her too close to home, thinking I was doing the right thing, and now look what it's come to."

"Gurney had something to say about that, too,"

Mrs. Hackett retorted. "He's done his share of keeping her shut up, worse'n any prisoner."

"He didn't want her to get in trouble."

Mrs. Hackett snorted. "Well, you may think Jody's different, but she ain't. Lotsa things go on under your nose, Verna, you oughta open your eyes now and then."

Verna stared at her. "You mean Jody's been in some kind of trouble I didn't know about?"

"No, I don't mean anything of the kind. All the trouble she's had was right to home, where you and Gurney kept her so she wouldn't be running loose, seeing all the dirt in the world."

"Marv," Verna said, hardly above a whisper, and the tears in her eyes overflowed and ran down her cheeks. She made no attempt to wipe them away but sat there silently, motionless, staring at the floor.

"Don't go to pieces," Mrs. Hackett said, "you've stood up real well so far. Come inside, there's some coffee left from breakfast. Or maybe you'd like a nice cold glass of tea, hot as the weather is."

She took her cane from the arm of the rocker and stood up slowly.

"I expect the baby'd like a cookie. Addie baked the other day, made a whole batch of them thin little things with sugar on top." She looked down at Verna and her face softened. "Bring the baby, Verna, and come on in the kitchen with me. You don't want Gurney to see you carrying on like this." Then, struck by a sudden thought, she asked, "Isn't he over to the house?"

After a moment Verna said unevenly, "He's out riding around, looking for her. He's been at it since yesterday some time, only slept about half the night."

She stood up, shifting Neal's weight to her hip, and wiped her face with the back of her hand.

"A cup of coffee would taste good, if you've got

some made. I didn't take time to eat breakfast, seems like food just won't go down and stay down."

She held the screen door open for Mrs. Hackett, who moved with patient dragging steps down the hall. Addie came to the kitchen door, wiping her hands on her apron, her square plain face flushed and damp.

"Hello, Verna," she said, and asked quickly, "Any news yet?"

Verna shook her head silently.

Addie's look of expectancy faded away. "Well," she said, awkwardly sympathetic, "well, it's still early in the day."

"Put the coffee on to heat," Mrs. Hackett ordered briskly. "And get out them cookies, Addie, give Neal one to chew on."

Addie smiled fondly at Neal. "Come to Addie," she said, holding out her arms. "He's Addie's baby, Neal is, she'll give him a cookie."

Verna relinquished him gratefully. "He's getting too heavy to be carried around, but it don't look like he'll ever start to walking."

"You'll be sorry when he does," Mrs. Hackett said, sitting down at the kitchen table. "He'll run us all ragged, just like Billie Mae did. That pesky kid was into everything. There was no way of holding her still short of putting her on a leash and tying her to the clothesline."

The kitchen was hot with heat from the stove oven and the heavy scent of roasting chicken. On the table a pie sat cooling, its meringue tall and golden, and the sauce pans on the stove bubbled their lids gently with steam that smelled pleasantly of vegetables and potatoes. A small fan on the window still hummed steadily, oscillating in a semicircle.

"You're doing a lot of cooking for Monday," Verna said.

Addie put the coffee pot on the stove. "Well, I didn't

get much done yesterday, with so much going on, so it was here to be done today. I bought this chicken Saturday, and you know how quick they spoil if you don't cook them up."

Still carrying Neal, she put two cups and saucers on the table and went into the large pantry off the kitchen. Coming back with a plate of cookies, she pushed the pie out of the way and put the cookies on the table.

"Why don't you stay and have dinner with us, Verna, help eat up some of this food? I know you never eat heavy in the middle of the day, but it might do you good, I'll bet you haven't eaten a thing today."

"I'm not very hungry," Verna said. She frowned, staring down at the empty coffee cup, turning it in the saucer.

"Well," Addie said, then stopped. She sat down at the table with Neal and gave him a cookie. He smiled up at her, then turned his attention to the cookie, examining it with solemn care before biting half of it off.

"I believe he's got another tooth," Addie said. "He's not going to be a baby much longer, the way he's growing. You still give him those vitamin drops, Verna, the doctor told you to?"

Verna sighed. "I've been out of them for more than a week, but the next time I stop by the drug store I'll pick some up." She smiled faintly at Addie. "You'd make a good mother, Addie, it's a shame you never had any kids."

"Oh, she'd like having a baby fine," Mrs. Hackett retorted, "if she could find it under a cabbage leaf and then keep it from growing past six months."

Addie flushed. "You get those vitamins, Verna, the doctor never would've said anything if he didn't think they were important."

"I'll try to remember," Verna promised. She got up and went to the stove for the coffee pot and poured the two cups full. When she sat down again she picked up her cup but didn't drink, and a frown settled back on her face.

Mrs. Hackett put two heaping spoonfuls of sugar and a generous amount of milk in her coffee and stirred it rapidly; it slopped over the edge and she drained the saucer back into the cup.

"Gurney'll be home soon," she said, "wanting some lunch. Why don't you let Addie slice you some chicken and maybe cut a piece of that pie, then you won't have to worry about fixing anything."

"Yes, he'll be home before long," Verna said.

Her face changed, the frown smoothing away into blankness. She bit her underlip sharply with her teeth, but her mouth still trembled.

"You look scared to death," Mrs. Hackett remarked. "Tell us what you've done, Verna, may as well get it out before Gurney comes after you."

Verna put down her cup and it rattled against the saucer.

"I called the police," she said. "Oh, Mrs. Hackett, Gurney's liable to kill me when he finds out."

"Not in my house, he won't."

"I had to do it, I couldn't stand thinking about it any longer. What if Marv had done something to her, all that blood on his clothes, and I just took his word and never checked to be sure he was telling the truth or a lie?" The words came out in a rush, unsteady and slurred with tears. "Gurney believes him but I'm not sure, he's not mine and Jody is. I'd never forgive myself if he'd hurt her and I believed his lies."

She paused to draw a deep shuddering breath.

Addie and Mrs. Hackett stared at her. Then Mrs. Hackett said slowly, "What blood, Verna?"

"It was all over his shirt, I saw it, and he told Gurney it was only where he'd hit that boy in the nose and it bled on him. I don't know, maybe he's telling the truth. But when I woke up this morning and Jody was still gone, after another whole night, I knew I had to do it. I called the police and told them."

Addie made an odd choking sound and put her cheek against the top of Neal's head. She closed her eyes, her face so pale it seemed tinged with green.

"Told them what?" Mrs. Hackett asked.

"That he might have done something to Jody. I saved his clothes for them to see the blood."

"What'd they say to that?"

"The policeman I talked to seemed pretty upset. He said they'd come out right away to see Marv, probably take him down to the station."

Verna put her face in her hands.

"Well," Mrs. Hackett said, her eyes sparkling, "imagine that, the police taking Marv Dowd off to jail!"

"They didn't say they were going to put him in jail," Verna said from behind her hands, "just ask some questions."

"It's the same thing. He won't like their questions and they won't like his answers, you'll see, and first thing he knows they'll pop him right behind bars." Mrs. Hackett's dry chuckle slid into laughter. "No wonder you're hiding from Gurney. My Lord, Verna, it wouldn't surprise me if he don't try to skin you alive when he finds out."

Verna didn't speak. Neither did Addie. Mrs. Hackett studied them for a long moment, her face sobered.

"No need to get yourselves in a tizzy about it," she said finally. "Marv didn't hurt that girl. Not that he couldn't, if he put his mind to it, but I got an idea he had his mind on other things Saturday night."

Verna looked up quickly. "What makes you say that? Do you know something about Jody I don't, Mrs. Hackett?"

"I know a lotta things you don't, but that's not saying I know where she is. I'm talking about Marv now, it's easy to accuse him of being mean when any-

body can see he is, but I still don't think he did anything to Jody Saturday night." Mrs. Hackett drank her
coffee noisily. "If he's lying, it don't have to be on
Jody's account. Marv Dowd's got more'n one thing he
might not want to let the whole world know about."

Verna bit her lip and looked at Mrs. Hackett with
her eyes filling again. "I don't know what to think any
more."

Mrs. Hackett laughed again. "The police won't,
either. Marv says he hit somebody in the nose, but
where's the man and the nose to prove it? He can
swear where he was Saturday night till he's blue in
the face, but they ain't about to take his word for it
without finding somebody was with him and don't
mind saying so."

"I ought not to have called the police," Verna said
dully. "When Gurney gets home I'll have to tell him,
and what's he gonna say, with Marv in jail and me the
one who put him there?"

"It won't hurt Marv none," Mrs. Hackett said cheerfully. "Might shake him up a little, the Lord knows he
needs it."

Verna shook her head slowly. "D'you suppose
they've come to get him yet?"

"I hope not," Mrs. Hackett said indignantly. "I sure
would hate like sin to miss seeing them cops dragging
Marv Dowd off to jail. Why didn't you tell me before
we come in, Verna? I never would've left that front
porch till I saw it with my own eyes."

Addie stood up abruptly and handed Neal to Verna.
She went to the stove and stood there a moment, her
back to the room.

"I knew it," she said, her voice tight and hoarse.
"I knew all along something awful had happened to
her. It was Marv, I should've known it."

"You don't know any such thing," Mrs. Hackett said,
"so stop working yourself into a fit."

"Blood on his clothes," Addie said to the wall. "I knew it, I just felt it in my bones."

Verna's eyes closed and her face paled again.

Mrs. Hackett said irritably, "If you don't shut up, Addie, I'll knock a knot on you. The two of you oughta be in Dix Hill, you're crazy as bedbugs. If Marv had done anything to Jody, you think he woulda come home and gone to bed just like that, leaving his bloody clothes all over the place for anybody to find? He's mean and sneaky, but he ain't stupid. Besides that, he don't have that kinda guts."

The front door slammed with a jolt that shook the house.

The three women jumped involuntarily, so that when the shout came it was too much of an anticlimax to elicit any reaction beyond the sudden stiffening of Addie's back.

"Verna, you over here?"

They were silent. Mrs. Hackett stood up, using the table and the back of her chair for support.

"Somebody answer me or I'll tear this house apart! Mrs. Hackett, you seen Verna?"

Verna clutched at Neal, one hand groping out, holding to the table so tightly that the soft dimpled flesh on her fingers showed red and splotched.

"Oh, Lord," she whispered, "he knows. They must've come for Marv already."

Mrs. Hackett, reaching the door, said, "You don't have to holler, we ain't deaf."

"You seen Verna?"

"I ain't blind, either. 'Course I've seen her, she's right here in the kitchen drinking coffee. You can come in and have a cup, too, if you're a mind to quit yelling."

"Yeah, I'll quit," Gurney said, his voice dropping, going soft and dangerously pleasant. "Now I know where she is, I don't need to waste my breath."

He loomed in the door, towering over Mrs. Hackett.

Looking over her head, he stared at Verna, his eyes narrowed in a glittering line, his chin jutted forward.

"Okay, let's go. I gotta few things to say to you, Verna."

Verna said hurriedly, "Gurney, I had to do it, I couldn't—"

"Shut up," he said harshly. "Shut up and come on home."

"She's gonna finish her coffee," Mrs. Hackett said, but she was pretty sure that he wouldn't hear anything she had to say unless she screamed first.

"Get a move on," he ordered Verna.

Mrs. Hackett cocked her head and looked up at him. "She's not going anywhere till you calm down. The cops take Marv off yet?"

That got to him. He lowered his head slowly, as if it hurt to move it, and stared down at her with his face dark and set. Then his eyes went back to Verna.

"Damn you," he said savagely. "Goddamn you for a sneaky lying bitch."

In the brief silence Verna stood up. "Go home, Gurney," she said, low. "I'm coming."

He didn't move. "I oughta beat the living tar outa you," he said, his voice as low as hers, cold and flat with fury. "Send my boy to jail, will ya, tell a lotta lies about him to the cops, then run your mouth telling lies all over the neighborhood. You oughta be whipped up and down the street, let people see what a lousy little bitch you are."

"Gurney," Verna said in a broken whisper, "don't talk like that. Please go on home, I said I'd come."

By the stove Addie twisted her apron in her hands.

"Get out of my house," she said. "Get out or I'll call the police."

His eyes flicked her contemptuously, disregarding her words.

"Yeah, you're coming all right," he said to Verna. "Now, with me."

153

Mrs. Hackett sighed audibly. "Sit down, Verna, I don't aim to let you go with him till his blood cools." She looked up at Gurney with a calm defiance, folding her arms. "You can sit down and behave yourself, or you can go home. I don't care which, it's no skin off my nose if you want to make a fool of yourself, carrying on like a wild man. But I'll tell you one thing, you ain't dragging Verna outa my house till she's good and ready to go."

"I'll call the police," Addie said, her voice going up, high and wavering. "You got no right to come in my house, threatening and cursing, talking to decent people any such way!"

Mrs. Hackett didn't take her eyes from Gurney. "Be quiet, Addie, there's been enough calling the police for one day."

"Yeah, shut up, Addie," Gurney mocked her. He gave Addie a brief furious stare and added, "The phone's here in the hall. You wanta try getting past me?"

When she was silent he turned his anger to Mrs. Hackett again.

"You ain't telling me nothing. Better get outa my way or you're liable to be sorry."

He put one hand on either side of the door, hunching his big shoulders forward, but Mrs. Hackett didn't move.

"I'm warning you, old lady. Come between a man and his wife, dammit, you're gonna get hurt."

"Loud mouth," Mrs. Hackett said rudely. "You don't scare me."

For an instant he didn't speak, his big hands clenched, his body held very still.

"Gurney," Verna said quickly, "be careful."

Her warning came too late. Gurney glanced down at Mrs. Hackett, muttered, "I warned you," and swept her aside with the back of his hand.

Pushed back against the wall, she began to crumple. She lost her balance, grabbed at the door to steady herself, and then slid slowly down, piecemeal, legs buckling, arms sagging, her head dropping against Gurney as she fell.

He caught her before she hit the floor.

"Christ," he said, looking stunned, "I didn't hit her that hard."

Holding her against him with one hand, he slipped his arm under her legs and lifted her easily. For a moment he stood there staring at her in his arms, her head falling back and her thin legs dangling helplessly, seeming to have grown very small and shrunken with her eyes closed and her voice silenced.

"Oh, Gurney," Verna whispered, "look what you've done."

Addie came across the kitchen at a run, crying, "Don't touch her, keep your dirty hands off her!" She raised her hand and struck at Gurney's face with the open palm of her hand; even as he turned his face, trying to escape her, she hit him again with the back of her hand. "Put her down, you've killed her!"

Gurney, defenseless while he held Mrs. Hackett, watched Addie with wary astonishment. Then, as she started to hit him again, he ducked his head and tried to move by her.

"My God," he said, "get her off me, Verna, she's gone off her nut."

Verna came around the table, but she still had Neal in her arms and could do nothing but say, "Addie, let him put her on the bed. She'll be all right, he didn't mean to hurt her."

Addie was beyond hearing her. "I'll have you hauled off to prison for this," she said, almost screaming, pulling desperately at his arm. "You're evil, Gurney Dowd, you and your son, too, there oughta be a law keeping you away from decent people! You take your evil hands off my mother and get outa my house.

Don't ever come back or I'll have the police put you away like they've already done Marv!"

"Shut up, Addie," he said calmly, "and get outa my way."

He lifted his arms, using Mrs. Hackett's limp body as a shield, and pushed past Addie to the bedroom door.

Laying Mrs. Hackett gently on the bed, he leaned over her and unbuttoned the neck of her percale dress.

"Put that baby down, Verna," he said, "and get me something cold and wet. A wash cloth'll do, look over there by the basin."

Addie, at the foot of the bed, repeated in a high monotonous chant, "Don't touch her, take your hands off her or I'm gonna call the police!"

Gurney ignored her. Standing there quietly, his face still red with the imprint of Addie's hand, he held Mrs. Hackett's wrist, his fingers searching for her pulse. When Verna handed him the wet cloth he took it with his free hand and laid it on Mrs. Hackett's forehead, not letting go of her wrist.

"Her pulse is okay," he said then. "She ain't dead."

Verna said softly, "Thank the Lord." Addie's shrill voice trailed off into silence. Tears streaming down her face unchecked, she clutched at the mahogany bed and bent over it as if she were caught there by some agonizing inner pain. Verna put a sympahetic hand on her arm but Addie paid no attention; she stared down at her mother, her mouth twisted awkwardly, making no effort to hold back the tears or the choked grunting sobs that shook her body.

Mrs. Hackett opened her eyes.

"No, I ain't dead," she said crossly. "For pity's sake take that wet rag off my face, Gurney, you wanta drown me?"

Without a word, Gurney reached for the cloth.

"Stop that bawling, Addie," Mrs. Hackett said then. "I never thought you'd go to pieces like this, you oughta know by now I'm too mean for Gurney to kill me that easy. Verna, take her in the kitchen and get her some coffee, see if you can't calm her down."

Verna picked Neal up from the floor, where he was poking his fingers happily at the faded roses on the rug. Then she took Addie's arm and led her around the bed past Gurney. Addie went silently, not looking at Gurney or Mrs. Hackett, wiping her face with the corner of her apron.

The bedroom was very still.

"Close the door, Gurney," Mrs. Hackett said wearily, "and pull that chair up to the bed."

He did as she told him. Sitting down beside the bed, he leaned forward with his arms on his knees, hands laced together, dark head bent.

The silence lengthened.

Then he said, low, not raising his head, "Christ, I'm sorry, you know I didn't mean to do any damn fool thing like that."

"I know it," Mrs. Hackett said, watching him. "I egged you on."

He looked up briefly, tried to smile. "I always had a lousy temper."

"It's getting worse."

"Yeah," he said. The smile, not very successful, faded away.

"You never have been a man easy to get along with, Gurney, but you didn't used to be so ugly about it."

"I used to be able to handle it, that's all." He stared down at his hands. "Jesus, I don't know what's the matter. I can't handle anything lately, everything's gone wrong."

Mrs. Hackett studied his bent head thoughtfully. "You figured out why yet?"

"Hell, there's no way to figure it. Marv in trouble. My wife calling the cops to put him in jail. Jody gone, nobody knows why or where." His face darkened again. "I ain't to blame for all of it, I know that."

"Not for all of it, maybe," Mrs. Hackett said, "none of us but can look back and see our mistakes. But you got to take your share, no doubt about it."

"Listen, I've done the best I can." He scowled at her. "You tell me how I could've changed things."

"You sure you want me to tell you? I don't know as you're ready to hear, it's not easy to take a good look at yourself."

There was a blaze of anger in his eyes, but he only said bitterly, "Okay, get it over with, say your piece. I ain't a kid, I never asked for it to be easy."

Mrs. Hackett thought it over, searching for some way to begin.

"There's no sense in listing all the things you done wrong," she said slowly. "Wouldn't do any good, that's past and over with. But what's still to come, Gurney, you ought to be prepared for it." She met his smouldering gaze directly, not flinching from what she was determined to say. "Take Marv, for instance. If you don't start facing the truth about that boy he's gonna be ruined for good, probably spend the rest of his life in and out of jail."

"You're all down on Marv," he said tightly. "The whole lot of you, sitting around smirking while you wait for him to do something so you can say 'I told you he was no good.' Well, dammit, there ain't a kid worth his salt don't get into a little trouble growing up. I tell you, he'll settle down."

Mrs. Hackett sighed. "I know how it is, he's yours and you don't want to see any faults in him. But the time's coming, Gurney, when somebody else besides you is gonna have the say about whether he's full of mischief or just plain rotten."

He glared at her, his heavy brows meeting in a straight line.

"Lay off Marv, I already know you got no use for him. Maybe I'm to blame for his faults, I ain't denying that. I've tried to be as good a father as I know how, but nobody's perfect. I can tell you a hell of a lotta mistakes I've made you never even thought about yet." His voice grated a little. "I didn't ask you that, no old woman needs to tell me how to raise my son."

"You asked me how you could've changed anything, I was just trying to tell you."

"You said it was all my fault. Well, make up your mind, is it mine or Marv's?"

"It's all of a piece, you ain't too dumb to see that."

"Marv had nothing to do with Jody running off," he said grimly. "What he did was wrong, okay, but thanks to your big mouth he got found out. We all knew about it, he couldn't get away with anything like that again."

"I doubt Jody was that sure about it."

"Don't hand me that. She's not crazy enough to be scared of a kid like Marv, hell, she's lived in the same house with him for years."

"Maybe it wasn't only Marv she was scared of."

"She wasn't scared of me. Sure, I yelled at her, told her off a few times. But you got to keep after a kid, they all need to be straightened out now and then."

"It wasn't your yelling scared her," Mrs. Hackett said carefully. "You know what it was, same as I do."

"The hell I do. Quit talking in riddles, make some sense."

"The way you feel about her ain't no riddle, except maybe to Verna. I got sense enough to see it, have for a long time, and Jody was beginning to."

Trying to measure the depth of his rage by the length and shape of his silence, she wondered what she'd do if he hit her again, and her already on the bed with no way of stopping him this time by fainting dead away in his arms. Well, it had to be said, might as well lay it on the line good and straight.

"You're gonna have to face up to it, Gurney, not keep pushing it down inside where you think it don't show. It shows, all right, you're the only one can't see it. Something like that's bound to come out one way or another, you wouldn't be human if it didn't. It wouldn't surprise me none if that's the very reason you've got yourself in such a state, mean as a snake and twice as hard to live with."

He tried to speak but no words came. Closing his mouth so tightly that a muscle jumped in his cheek, he kept staring at her with his eyes thinned out and almost shut, a queer blank look on his face.

"It ain't exactly a sin," she said softly, "she's no blood kin to you. But if you don't watch out Verna's gonna catch on and be hurt mighty bad, and that'll be worse than sinning."

He was so white around his mouth that he looked ill. He met her eyes for a long silent moment. Then, with an abrupt gasp of breath, he put his face in his hands, leaning his head against the edge of the bed so that she could see nothing but the crisp black hair and the rigid set of his shoulders.

"Jesus Christ," he said, his voice muffled and rough, "she's only a kid."

Mrs. Hackett felt old and tired, close to being sick herself. She put out her hand, then drew it back. For a long while she didn't speak; if it'd been her, she knew she'd want some time to be left alone with it.

Then, at last, she said, "The Lord knows she's grown up a sight the last few years, Gurney, a person'd have to be blind not to see she's got something about her can drive a man crazy if he's around her much, day in and day out, the way it's been with you."

"It's never been like she was my kid," he said, his face still hidden. "Even at the beginning it was like having two of Verna, one grown and one just starting out."

Mrs. Hackett said, "I know."

"I tried, dammit, I tried. When Billie Mae come along I figured it'd be easier to treat 'em both the same, but it didn't work. I couldn't forget she didn't have none of my blood, I couldn't make a daughter out of her."

"She and Verna come out of the same pod," Mrs. Hackett said. "They can't help it, neither of 'em, they were born more woman than the law allows."

"Christ, you don't have to tell me that."

"No need to blame yourself too much, Gurney. Jody can't help being the way she is and a man can't help what it does to him. But you gotta be careful, try if you can't work it out for yourself so all of you ain't hurt worse'n need be."

He straightened in the chair and stood up. For a moment he was motionless, looking down at Mrs. Hackett, his face open and exposed, letting her see all the close private pain that was so new he hadn't learned to hide it.

Then, while she watched, he pulled himself together until there was nothing showing but the paleness and a weariness that seemed to come from too deep inside him to hide.

"There's no way to work it out," he said heavily. "You know so much, you oughta know that, too."

He opened the door and went into the kitchen. She heard him say, "Come on, Verna, we better be going home." There was a slight pause before he went on, in the same spent voice, "You got a right to be sore, Addie, I'm sorry as hell it happened."

There was no answer. In a minute or two the front screen door slammed in the silence, and the only sound left was the gentle whistle of steam from a saucepan on the stove.

From the door Addie said, "You feel like eating, Mama?"

"I reckon," Mrs. Hackett said. "After you done all that cooking it'd be a downright crime not to try."

Addie sat down in the chair Gurney had left beside the bed. Her hair was unkempt and rumpled, straggling down the back of her neck, and she had twisted her apron with her hands until it looked like a damp rag.

"You sure you don't want me to call the doctor, have him check you over?" Addie's voice trailed off. Then it began again, vague and subdued, "I never saw you faint before, it liked to scared me to death."

"That was plain enough," Mrs. Hackett said tartly. "My Lord, Addie, you should've figured I had to do something, the way Gurney was carrying on."

Addie's eyes widened. "You did it on purpose?"

"Fooled the lot of you," Mrs. Hackett said with satisfaction. "Don't ever give me up, I always got one more trick up my sleeve. Woman's a fool if she can't get the best of a man, that's why God give her brains instead of muscles."

Addie stared at her incredulously. Then she put her arms on the bed and dropped her head on them. She cried quietly this time, her face against her hands and the tears seeping through her fingers to soak a round wet circle on the counterpane.

"Oh, Mama," she said despairingly, "I don't know if I can stand much more."

Mrs. Hackett stifled a sigh. There was never any end to it, if there were only two people left alive in the world one of 'em would be hurting and the other getting hurt, one laughing and the other crying, neither one knowing what to do about their troubles or able to reach out to the other with understanding or help.

She put her hand on Addie's hair and stroked it gently.

"You can stand what you have to," she said. "None of us get let off, Addie, we're all of us carrying some kind of burden."

The house was warming up, despite the shade trees and the drawn window shades that kept out the worst of the glare. Mrs. Hackett's dress stuck to her damply and her stomach was queasy from the smell of food. She felt drowsy and tired, and was annoyed by such a weakness; things had reached a pretty pass when she couldn't have company without getting all wore out before dinner time. But she didn't intend to give in to it, there was no time for napping now.

"That chicken smells some good," she said cheerfully. "I believe my appetitie's come back, now I've rested a while. Nobody can cook like you, Addie, it's a shame you ain't got but one skinny old woman to waste that good food on."

Addie lifted her head and dried her face with her apron.

"I baked another lemon pie for you," she said, "but the meringue fell a little, it's so hot and sticky today."

Mrs. Hackett put her legs over the edge of the bed and sat there for a minute, trying to find the strength and energy to get up and cope with a heavy midday meal when her stomach felt tied in a knot. It'd give her a burden to carry, all right, she'd be taking Pepto-Bismol all afternoon. Well, it was there to be done, no sense in putting it off.

"Nothing I like better'n a lemon pie," she said, "even in hot weather."

Because it seemed the right thing to do at the moment, she allowed Addie to help her into the kitchen.

❧{ 10 }❧

IT was hot in the open shed attached to the barn. Hot and getting hotter by the minute, despite the occasional breeze that gusted across the field and whirled small dust devils up and down the straight rows of tobacco.

Jody, her blouse sticking wetly to her back, longed to wipe away the perspiration trickling down her forehead into her eyes. But she had learned that any pause, however brief, might break the monotonous rhythm of her hands, an acquired rhythm she had struggled most of the morning to master, and throw the other two people in the shed out of stride. She was determined not to stop again.

Hers was an easy chore, they told her, usually assigned to children. Wade Causey had said, with an amiable smile, that handing was the best way for a new worker to learn what was going on. At first she hadn't understood why, feeling awkward and inept as she tried to learn the knack of grabbing three or four tobacco leaves of approximately the same size to give to Belle, then getting another hand of leaves ready by the time Belle reached for it. A young white boy named Clay, who lived down the road and had obviously been handing tobacco since he was in diapers, stood beside her, talking constantly, his hands moving with such steady and automatic skill that he seldom looked at them, the tobacco leaves seeming to jump from the table to his hand, all neatly sized and ready for Belle without any

164

conscious effort on his part. Jody watched him carefully and imitated him as closely as possible, but it was some time before she could manage the unwieldly leaves well enough not to slow down the whole process.

Belle kept her at it, politely and firmly, and Jody began to see the wisdom of turning green hands over to an experienced stringer. Belle, who had been the kindest and gentlest of women in her own house, was an entirely different person in the shed beside Wade Causey's tobacco barn. A good stringer, Jody discovered, was prodded by pride to keep ahead of the men in the field who pulled the tobacco and sent the loaded slides to the barn in constant rotation, and since Belle's speed depended upon the speed of those handing the tobacco to her, to be looped with twine and flipped on alternate sides of a long stick, it was up to Belle to keep the assembly line moving at a satisfactory pace.

"You're good at this," Jody said admiringly, when she could manage to speak without unconsciously slowing her hands. "Do you think I'll ever get over having five thumbs on each hand?"

Belle gave a superior smile. "I can keep three people handing," she said proudly, "but it tires me out more, in the long run." Her brown fingers, supple and quick, never seemed to pause. "I hardly knew what a piece of tobacco looked like till after I married Eddie. My folks owned a drug store in town and I didn't have any kin in the country to visit, like most kids. But I learned in a hurry. Eddie says some people just have a knack for it."

"Handing's easy," the boy named Clay said with mild contempt. "So's stringing, there ain't nothing to it but being fast with your hands. It's curing that's hard. My pa says you don't know nothing about tobacco till you can kill it out the way it oughta be done and then sell it for top grade."

Belle shrugged. "My part's getting it in the barn, then I leave the rest up to Eddie."

"Yeah, but I gotta know it all," Clay said "from planting to market. There's two farms coming to me and my brother, some day, my uncle's and my pa's."

"You talk like you know it all already," Belle said, and Clay grinned.

"I reckon I know enough to string more'n you, if you'd only let me prove it. Wanta bet I can keep ahead, and you and Jody and Lacy all handing?"

Belle laughed and glanced at the boy bringing another slide of tobacco toward the barn. "You won't get Lacy off that tractor," she said, "to do any handing."

Clay flushed. "He's only a year older'n me," he said desolately, "you'd think Mr. Causey would trust me with his old tractor once in a while."

"I'm glad you're working with us," Jody said quickly. "It's hard to get the hang of it without having somebody to watch who really knows how."

The flush faded from his face and he said, diffidently, "You caught on quick, for a girl."

He began to whistle, keeping time with his hands, and Belle looked at Jody with a solemn face and a tiny amused smile wrinkling the corners of her eyes.

"Girls always catch on quick," she said. "Mr. Causey ought to pay her time-and-a-half."

"Mr. Causey ain't gonna pay nothing he don't have to." Clay looked at Jody, then away. "You and your husband fixing to stay with him, here at the house?"

"I guess so, as long as he needs somebody extra."

"He'll be needing help right on through September. There's another ten primings, anyway, and me'n Lacy got to go back to school the first of the month."

"My goodness, Clay," Belle said, "I thought you were already finished with school."

"I oughta be," he said, disgusted. "I got behind. Last year pa kept us out, there was too much to do at home."

He subsided into an unhappy silence. Jody, seeing the smile in Belle's eyes again, returned it faintly.

"I just got out of high school this year," she said casually. "Sometimes you get to feeling that you'll never finish."

"I'm eighteen," Clay said. "Much more of it and I'll just quit, to heck with finishing."

"You're older than I am," Jody said, not looking at Belle. "I won't be eighteen till October."

He grinned at her, straightening his long thin height. "How about that," he said, and began to whistle again.

Lacy, stopping the tractor outside the shed, was as tall and tow-headed as his younger brother.

"Time to eat," he said. "Belle, Mr. Causey said for you and Jody to go on up to the house, see what you can find to put on the table." He swung down from the high seat, pulling on his shirt, "Let's go, Clay, Ma'll have dinner waiting."

Clay's grin widened. "See you later," he said to Jody, and started off at a run. Lacy joined him, racing him up the sandy road that followed the edge of the field to the asphalt highway.

Belle shook her head. "It's been a long time since I had that much energy. Makes me tired, just watching."

Jody followed her out into the hot sun. She could feel her own tiredness, a sort of heavy limpness that spread slowly up from her hands to ache across her shoulders. They had been working without a break since before six o'clock, and the day was only half done; she tried not to be dismayed, wondering if she'd last till quitting time.

"The first day's always the hardest," Belle said with sympathy. "Wait till you eat, you'll feel better."

Jody looked across the field. Tay was still pulling, working steadily down the field with Mr. Causey and Eddie. Early in the day he had pulled off his shirt, and she could see the bandage on his arm, stark white against his brown skin.

"Don't worry," Belle said. "He's doing okay."

Jody, suddenly aware that she was frowning, looked

away from the field. "I thought he was going to take it easy, but he hasn't stopped once all morning."

"You know how men are, honey. He probably figures he's got to show Mr. Causey he's earning his pay." Belle laughed a little. "Some men, anyway. Eddie's like that, even when he's doing his own work. He says he grew up the hard way, back when people had to grub for every penny and then weren't sure they could keep it, and it's too late for him to change. I don't reckon I'd want him to, even if he could."

"Do you like farming," Jody asked, "better than living in town?"

"I like working with Eddie," Belle said, "and I like knowing he's close by, somewhere around the place, most of the time." She shrugged. "My family thinks I'm crazy, not going on to finish my training. But I don't have to go out nursing, not so long as I've got Eddie to take care of me."

Her voice softened, the way it always did when she was speaking of Eddie, and Jody remembered the things she had said the evening before when Eddie and Tay had gone off in the truck to see the doctor and then pick up Tay's bag at the bus station. Jody had sat down on the front steps, watching the red tail-lights disappearing down the road, wishing they had taken her with them; waiting was harder than anything else in the world, even without the loneliness that cramped inside her the instant Tay climbed up in the truck beside Eddie and slammed the door shut.

"It's better this way," Belle had said, sitting down beside her on the steps. "If you went along it might draw somebody's attention, and that's one thing they can do without."

"I know it," Jody said ruefully. "I'm a coward, anyway, I'd be shaking like jelly the whole time." She took the baby from Belle and put him on her knees, holding his head cupped in her hands.

"I feel that way about Eddie," Belle said. "I can't

always go with him, but I sure hate to see him going off without me, out of my reach. I think of all the things that could happen to keep him from coming back, worrying myself sick all the time he's gone. Then he gets home and nothing's happened, and I have to pull myself together so he won't guess how crazy I am."

Jody had said nothing, but something in her silence as she sat on the steps with Belle, holding the baby on her lap and staring out at the warm darkness, must have reached Belle across the gap that separated them.

"Right before we planned to get married," Belle said, very quietly, "he went to Georgia to visit his mother. She was dying, and he hadn't been back for a long time, not since he was a kid. I was glad he went, we both knew it might not be easy for him to get down later."

She paused, watching Lucy run across the dark yard after a lightning bug that flew just beyond her reach in a lazy erratic pattern of yellow light.

"He got into some trouble with a white man outside a tavern and cut him up, and they put him in prison for five years. A prison camp, really, he was on the road gang."

Jody moved her knees back and forth, rocking the baby gently. She didn't speak, there was nothing to say.

"His brother wrote me," Belle went on, her voice still quiet and soft. "I didn't know where to turn or what to do. Lucy was on the way, you see, we'd known that before he left. Five years seemed like the rest of my life, or near enough."

Jody looked at Lucy and listened to her small exasperated cries as she stalked the lightning bug.

"But Lucy's only—" she began, then stopped abruptly.

"Three," Belle said calmly, "last April." Then she went on, hugging her arms against her, "He came back, the week she was born. He was out with a crew, working on a highway, and he knocked out a guard and just walked off. They're still looking for him down there, I guess, but his mother died while he was in prison and his brother left for Detroit, and nobody else knew where he'd come from."

Driven to offer some comfort, however small, Jody said, "Maybe they'll never be able to trace him up here. It's a long way from Georgia."

"Maybe," Belle said. After a pause she said, "My father gave us the down payment for this place. Eddie's got part of that debt already paid off, doing his own work and hiring out to Mr. Causey whenever he can spare the time. He'll amount to something, Eddie will, if they'll just leave him alone."

Now, walking up to Mr. Causey's house in the glaring noon sun, Jody wondered whether Belle would always regret her confidence of the night before, if she would never be free of the added worry that she'd said too much to somebody who couldn't be wholly trusted. But if she felt that way, she didn't show it. Her face was calm and serene, smooth brown and black, unwary, unworried, even smiling.

"That doctor did a good job," she said, "stitching up his arm. It'll mend, I expect, even with him pulling tobacco. Don't you fret, honey, if it starts to hurting bad enough to do any harm he'll quit using it. Mr. Causey knows about it, he won't push him too hard."

Jody said, "I'm not fretting, he can take care of himself," and was careful not to look back again when they turned the corner of the house.

It was narrow and white and old, with a tall red brick chimney on each flank and a red tin roof sloping to the eaves in wide faded strips. The trees around it were older than the house, and Jody, coming into the thick quiet shade, gave a small sigh of pleasure. The grass was clipped and green under the trees and there seemed to be an acre of it stretching down a hill to the highway; she wondered how Mr. Causey managed to keep the place so tidy, living alone the way he did, and remembered Clay saying that he and Lacy took turns mowing the lawn.

"He's not very young," she said to Belle, "It must be hard on him, trying to do everything himself."

Belle stood at the sink on the screened porch along the ell of the house and scrubbed at the black tobacco gum on her hands. "He's got a married daughter in town who's been after him to sell and move in with her. But he's held out so far, says he was born here and plans to die here. Mr. Causey's right hard-headed about some things." Belle chuckled. "So's Eddie, when you come down to it. Must be a man's just born with his mind made up he's not going to let any woman tell him what to do, come what may."

Jody smiled. "But it doesn't always work that way."

"Hardly ever," Belle said. "That's what makes life interesting."

She winked at Jody and went into the kitchen, humming under her breath. Jody, taking her turn at the sink, rubbed her blackened hands with the bar of strong soap and tried not to think about what Mr. Causey would do and how he would feel if he knew the truth about her and Tay. She hated it because he didn't know, because they'd had to lie to him. She hadn't seen enough of him yet to like him or dislike him, but he'd been kind enough so far and she couldn't help feeling grateful to him for taking them in without asking any questions.

At least she supposed he hadn't asked any that Eddie and Tay couldn't answer. When they came back the night before Eddie had said cheerfully, "Well, we saw the doc and got his bag, and nobody even looked at us twice. Then we stopped by Mr. Causey's and got everything fixed up. He can use both of you, he's priming tomorrow, and you can stay there at the house with him." Then he had grinned and added, "He's a hard man to bargain with. Me and Belle, we go along with the deal."

He and Belle had seemed more amused than anything else, not greatly concerned about leaving their own work. Eddie said that it wouldn't hurt to put off their next priming for a few days and anyway they could use a little extra money; Belle said she'd leave the kids in town with her folks and it'd be a nice change all around. Then Eddie and Tay had gone off to the barn to finish killing out the Thompsons' tobacco and had stayed the rest of the night, so that there hadn't been any chance then to ask Tay what he had said to persuade Mr. Causey to give them a job and a place to stay.

But when she'd mentioned it to him in the truck coming over that morning he'd only said, "I told him we were on our way south and ran out of money."

"That much was true, anyway."

"He wasn't very curious."

She had been a little puzzled. "You'd think he'd be more careful, letting strangers stay in his house."

Tay had grinned. "I guess I've got an honest face."

Maybe he hadn't been forced to lie, outright. Maybe he'd only told that small part of the truth and left the rest unsaid; he was good at that kind of thing. He knew how to keep quiet when there was something he didn't want you to know, and he made it hard, somehow, to ask a lot of prying questions. Still, even if Mr. Causey hadn't asked him, she knew he hadn't been able to avoid one plain lie; upstairs, in the front bedroom, her paper sack of clothes and his battered suitcase lay on the chest of drawers side by side, and Clay had called him her husband.

"Don't go to sleep standing up, honey."

She looked up at Belle, her eyelids feeling heavy and warm, unable to remember for a queer dazed moment what she was supposed to be doing and why she was standing at the sink.

Belle's laugh was quiet and amused. "You'd better not look at him that way," she said, "or he won't be able to finish out the day."

Jody tried to tighten the muscles in her face, to erase whatever look was there that shouldn't be seen. But it was no use, she couldn't manage her face any better than the rest of her.

"I feel like warm butter," she said helplessly. "It doesn't have anything to do with him, it's just me."

"You're tired," Belle said comfortably. "Handing tobacco's a long hot job, even when you're used to it."

That was it, of course, she was only tired. A good kind of tiredness, the way you felt on the edge of sleep when you began to drift, drowsy and content, vaguely aware that life went on at a distance and not caring, giving it up gladly. Once you were awake it was hard to remember exactly how it was, sliding into sleep, but she didn't think it was very different from this moment, now, a moment as round and heavy as the transparent drop of water clinging precariously to the spigot over the sink, which might, if she kept very still and didn't jar it, hold her mirrored in its center while it reflected the rest of the world with a gentle curve of distortion. In the same way, her mind caught and held all the images of the day around her. The thick green shade under the old trees, the glare of sun on the tobacco fields. The border of petunias around the old well, pink and white and lavender, drooping in the heat, and the water from the well that poured cold and bright over her hands. The stillness. The heavy hot silence of noon. The kitchen, cool and dark and old-fashioned, and Belle's quiet humming as she moved from the pantry to the stove to the big round table in the dining room. The smell and look of green beans and yellow corn and salty red ham, and the sound of ice rattling in the frosted pitcher of tea. And then, breaking the silence, Eddie's laughter in the yard and Mr. Causey's answering voice, the clatter of a tin dipper in the bucket at the well. Tay, pouring water over his head, letting it run down his shoulders until the wet drops spun and glittered on the smooth brown skin, drying so carelessly with his shirt that it stuck to him damply when he put it on again.

She was careful not to look at him for more than a brief instant when he came into the kitchen, but it wasn't easy. He checked a moment in the doorway, and his eyes, not yet adjusted to the cool dimness of the house, were narrowed and a little wary. Then they flickered around the room, found her, focused suddenly. He smiled, his whole face changing, losing its wariness, opening up.

Mr. Causey saved her. Stepping around Tay he said in his slow nasal voice, "I knew it, I could smell hot biscuits before I got to the yard. Any time you want to leave that worthless Eddie and get a regular job, Belle, you can come over and cook for me."

Belle laughed. "You've got a new cook now, Mr. Causey. Treat her right and she'll cook you all the hot bread you can eat."

He took a biscuit from the pan on the stove and asked, "How about that, Jody? You know how to stir up a good buttermilk biscuit?" Holding the pan toward Tay, he said, "Have one while they're hot, son, there's nothing better."

"I can try," Jody said, "but I'm afraid I don't have Belle's touch."

"Takes practice, you'll learn. How'd you do with that tobacco this morning?"

Belle answered for her. "It didn't take her long to get the hang of it. She kept up with Clay right along, I didn't have to stop for her once."

"She'll start dragging, come three or four o'clock." He looked down at Jody with the beginning of a smile in his faded blue eyes. "Probably have to put you to bed and cook supper myself."

She smiled back at him, thinking he was somebody

you could begin to like in a hurry. "There'll be biscuits for supper," she promised rashly. "I'll have my second wind by then."

"Fourth or fifth, more likely," he said mildly. "I never hired a pretty girl yet who could last out the day."

As the afternoon wore on, stifling and bright, she was afraid more than once that he'd been right and she'd never manage to keep going until the barn was filled and they could quit for the day. But when they had gone back to work after dinner Mr. Causey had told Tay to exchange places with Belle, saying calmly over Tay's protest that he'd do well to stay out of the sun for a while and make sure he'd be around to work another day; and somehow the time passed more quickly and the handing was easier when Tay was at the barn stringing instead of Belle. He worked steadily, not seeming to be bothered by his arm, and kept up with the pace set by Mr. Causey in the field; but whenever Jody fumbled, her hands growing stiff and awkward from weariness, he slowed down until she had recovered herself and then went on without a word, not urging her to hurry or acting as if he'd noticed that Clay was giving him two hands of tobacco to Jody's one.

"I didn't know a barn could hold so much," she said once. "How long does it take to fill it up?"

"Too long," Clay said, "when no more'n a handful's working at it. My uncle's got thirty acres or more, he works a big enough crew to do two barns a day, maybe three." He grinned at her tired disbelieving face. "Gets it done before supper, too, then sends everybody out to pull suckers till dark."

Jody, not sure she knew what pulling suckers meant but very sure she didn't want to know, said nothing more. It took too much effort and energy to talk, anyway; it was easier to listen while Clay's high eager voice went on and on endlessly and Tay's low one made an

occasional remark that set Clay off again like a dime
dropped into a jukebox. It was even easier not to
listen at all; for the last hour or so she concentrated
on the table of tobacco and her numbed hands, black
and sticky with gum, and stubbornly willed them to
keep moving.

To her surprise, she lasted out the day. She also
baked hot biscuits for supper, and a peach cobbler that
smelled so sweet and buttery it erased the last bitter
tang of tobacco from her nose. Then she washed dishes
and carefully put them away without breaking anything, and swept the kitchen and back porch before
going out on the front porch to join Tay and Mr. Causey.

Sitting on the steps beside Tay, feeling pleasantly
clean from her bath and cool in her green cotton
dress, she wondered curiously if her body would keep
on working, slower and slower, until finally it simply
gave up and collapsed in a heap like a skeleton of
bones falling apart at the joints.

Mr. Causey, his chair tipped back and feet on the
porch railing, was reading the morning paper. Jody
watched him from under her lashes, trying to guess
from his face if he'd read anything about a wrecked
stolen car that might make him suspicious. But she
finally gave it up, too tired to worry about it, seeing
that Tay didn't seem in the least concerned about the
paper or anything Mr. Causey might read in it.

He sat a couple of steps below her, leaning back
on one elbow. When she first came out he had given
her a faint smile, then turned his head back to look
out across the lawn again, his eyes almost closed and
his face quiet and withdrawn. She wanted to ask about
his arm but decided not to; he had changed the dress-
ing himself when he took his bath, not asking for any
help, and if it was paining him he wouldn't like her to
draw attention to it.

He was used to being alone, she thought, he had

gotten out of the habit of sharing anything, even trouble.

Mr. Causey let his chair down with a thump. He folded the newspaper carefully and slowly, the way he did everything.

"Well, Jody, you ready for another day of handling tobacco?"

"Yes," she said, and sighed. "Not right now, but maybe by tomorrow morning."

"I reckon I'm going to have to apologize to you."

"For not having to carry me up to bed?" She smiled up at him. "I'm not sure it won't come to that yet. It's a long way up those stairs."

"For having just the right touch with a biscuit," he said. "Tay's a smart boy, he knew a good thing when he saw it. Marry a girl can cook, that's the ticket, it's not so hard to put up with the rest of it."

She didn't know what to say. It wasn't easy to lie, even in fun, but it was just as much of a lie to keep quiet and let him go on thinking something that wasn't so.

"You're getting old," Tay said easily into the silence, "or a biscuit wouldn't count for so much. I never gave it a thought, whether she could cook or not."

Mr. Causey chuckled. "I'm getting old, all right, but you're still pretty young." He struck his leg idly with the folded paper. "Saw a little lightning there, to the west. We could use some rain, but I'd like it better if it held off to the end of the week."

"You ought to be glad any time it comes," Tay remarked. "I never saw things so dry, this time of year."

Jody listened while they talked about the weather, the crops, the price of tobacco at the markets, the latest government regulations, the advantages of curing with oil instead of wood. Their voices were quiet and slow in the blue dusk, pausing, falling into a comfortable silence, picking up the conversation with no hurry or constraint. Then they left her to walk down to the barn; Mr. Causey, who cured with oil, had said there would be no need for anybody to stay at the barn through the night, but farmers with barns full of curing tobacco were a little like mothers with sick children, and she suspected that this wouldn't be the last time he would go down to check on it before morning. She watched them go, Mr. Causey walking slowly, hands stuck in the bib of his overalls, Tay keeping pace, his hands in his jeans' pockets. They were still talking when they went around the corner of the house, Mr. Causey pointing at the vegetable garden beyond the driveway where the bean vines hung thick and motionless on their sticks in the still air.

Jody sat on the steps for a long time, watching the lightning bugs under the trees, gazing out past the road at the bottom of the lawn to the open farmland rolling up a hill to the sky. The fields looked deceptively damp and green with the dew rising above them and their boundaries of trees looming a darker green, distant and unreal, softened by the pale white mist of night; and in all that space of fields and trees and sky there was no sound and nothing moving. She had never known such stillness before, and she closed her eyes, letting the silence soak in.

Tay found her like that, head on her knees, almost asleep.

"Wake up," he said. "Do you think you can make it up the stairs to bed?"

She raised her head and gave him a drowsy smile.

"I suppose. Is it time?"

"For you."

"But it's not even dark yet."

"Haven't you ever gone to bed before dark?"

She shook her head. "Not since I was a little kid."

"Maybe you've never worked this hard before." He sat down on the step beside her. "Sorry we didn't go on to Charlotte?"

She hadn't got her eyes all the way open; they curved

down in a dark arc of lashes, the eyelids seeming too heavy to lift. Her voice wasn't awake, either, it stayed down in her throat, low and husky and warm.

"No, I'm not sorry," she said, "I like it here. Don't you?"

There was no point in denying it. She'd know, anyway, she saw a lot more sometimes than you wanted her to.

"Yes," he said briefly. "I was looking for something like this, it's why I came back."

After a moment she asked, "Where's Mr. Causey?"

"He had some chores, out back. I tried to help but he told me to wait till my arm loosens up."

"How's it feeling?"

"Fine. The doc gave me some pills for it, but I haven't needed any today."

"Take one before you go to bed, it ought to help."

He smiled. "I won't need a pill to put me to sleep tonight."

"You know a lot about farming," she said thoughtfully. "Did your folks raise tobacco?"

"Tobacco and cotton. Cotton one year, peanuts the next. It wasn't a very big farm. My dad didn't own it, he only worked it for another man and got his share on the crops."

She didn't make any comment. Maybe she didn't know what it meant, she wasn't exactly a country girl.

"He wanted to have his own place. He was saving what he could, every year. It wasn't much, you don't make enough tenant farming to save any big pile, but he hired out when he could and tried to put that aside."

Tay stared down at his hands. He was talking too much, he ought to shut up now while there was still time.

But Jody asked, "Did he ever get his own farm?"

She wasn't being curious, he knew her better than that now, she was only interested because he had brought it up.

"No," he said, "he didn't get it. My mother saw to that." He tasted the old bitterness, thick and sour in his throat. "She took what money he had for alimony, and then she tried to take me. When he wouldn't let her, she had him thrown in jail."

Jody said, "Oh, Tay," and he heard the sharp intake of her breath.

"Maybe it wasn't all her fault," he said then. "Her folks egged her on, they had a big dairy farm and thought they were better than anybody else. I used to wonder why they let her marry him in the first place, but I found out they didn't have much to say about it. My dad took her off to South Carolina one weekend, it was as easy as that."

"My folks got married in South Carolina, too," Jody said softly. "Only it didn't work out the same, it was my father who walked out."

He glanced at her, surprised. "Then you know what it's like."

"I don't remember anything about it. I never even saw him, I was just a baby."

They were silent for a long while. The dusk was receding slowly, blue into black, leaving big dark patches of shadow under the trees.

"I guess I didn't know much about it either, at the time," he said finally. "I thought I did, it's easy for a kid to take sides. She didn't take me when she left, I don't think she wanted a baby at the start and she was sick for a long time after I was born. I was only ten when she went back to her folks and I wanted to stay with my dad anyway, so I didn't hate her for that."

Jody looked at him, waiting, her eyes dark and soft in the fading light, wide open now.

"I hated her for not sticking it out. She knew he was trying to make things better for her, but she couldn't wait, she didn't have enough guts to help him out."

"Maybe she didn't know how," Jody said. "Maybe she'd never had to wait for what she wanted."

"She was sick," he said, low. "Sick from more than having me. She died while my dad was on the roads, working off his sentence. He never saw her again after she went home."

"I'm sorry," Jody whispered. Then, as if she couldn't bear the silence, she went on, "Did he want to see her?"

"I guess he never stopped wanting it, no matter what she did to him."

It was funny how easy it was to talk about it, almost as though it'd happened to somebody else. But then he'd never tried before, he'd never had anybody like Jody to listen. He could tell she cared about it, even cared what it meant to him. She'd had enough trouble of her own to know how you could carry something inside you, heavy and hard as a stone, and it didn't matter that what had happened was over and done with a long time ago, you still couldn't seem to let go of it.

"He gave her what money he had when she went home to her folks and I thought that was the end of it, she'd leave us alone and we'd get along fine without her, my dad and me." He shrugged, looked down at his hands again. "Her old man decided my dad wasn't fit to raise me. For a couple of years he tried everything he could, almost drove my dad crazy, then he talked my mother into taking it to court. The judge said she could have me, and they sent a deputy out to take me away from him."

Jody sighed. She put her hand on Tay's arm, and he tried to relax the tight muscles under her touch.

"My dad beat him up and ran him off the place. He knew better, he'd always lived by the law, but I guess he was past caring about anything by then."

"Except you," Jody said. "You were all he had left to care about."

"He didn't have me very long after that," Tay said evenly. "They sent a carload of deputies out to pick him up and throw him in jail. They had enough charges then, contempt of court, resisting an officer, assault. He got a year on the roads, and the Taylors got me. She'd already named me Taylor after her family, so I guess they thought I belonged to them as much as any of their pedigreed cows."

"They probably loved you," Jody said, her voice groping out to him in the darkness. "You were their grandson, after all."

"They didn't even want me. I found that out as soon as I went to live with them. They were just getting back at my dad." He could tell she didn't know what to say to that, so he went on quickly, "When my dad served his time I decided I'd take off and find him. My mother was dead by then, and there didn't seem to be much point in staying around where I wasn't wanted. But it took me more than a year to find out where he was, and by then it was too late. He'd hired out on a farm close to Raleigh, and he let a tractor roll over on him one day."

"Let?" Jody said on a small rush of breath.

"He wasn't careless," he said. "Not about things like that."

Along the horizon he could see an occasional flicker of lightning. Heat lightning probably; it didn't feel like rain. Another hot day of it tomorrow, but he didn't mind, it was too good to be working again.

Close beside him, Jody said, "Clay said Mr. Causey'll need somebody to help him for the next month or so. He'd be glad to keep you on, I'll bet, if you asked."

"We can't stick around that long."

"Why? Do you think they'll come looking for us, even here?"

"Sure," he said, "only if we're smart we'll be gone by then."

She seemed to be thinking it over. Then she said soberly, "There isn't any end to it, is there?"

"I tried to tell you," he said, feeling a surge of pity

for her. "You ought to go home where you belong and stay clear of all this."

"Why don't you go back? It's only Marv's word against yours, after all."

"Marv's a home town boy," he said coolly. Then, knowing he might as well get it over with, "And he doesn't have a record."

That stopped her, all right. He could see on her face, as clearly as if a light was shining on it, the struggle between wanting to know what he meant and not wanting to ask tactless questions.

Finally she asked carefully, "How could they know anything about you?"

"They could check, easy enough, unless I lied about where I've been the past few years." He forced himself to go on, so there wouldn't be anything left that she didn't know about. "But I couldn't lie about the two years I spent in the service. That part's okay, I got along fine with the Army, but they've got a record of everything that went before."

"Was it bad, what went before?" Her voice was troubled, apologetic for asking.

"Bad enough, I guess," he said, remembering the first months after he'd left the Taylors, when the only important thing had been surviving without money or a job. It'd been the top of tourist season, and everybody and his brother seemed to be looking for a job in Florida; besides that, he'd been a thin scrawny kid of fifteen and nobody wanted to take a chance on hiring a runaway who might get picked up any time. So he'd lived the only way he could, stealing food in the supermarkets and clothes from the dimestores, rolling drunks on the beach, earning a few bucks now and then at odd jobs, sleeping in the bus station and on the ground, anywhere he could stay put for a couple of hours at a time without running into a cop. But there was no point in telling her all that, he had more on his conscience than petty larceny.

"I got a job doing construction work, there's plenty of that in Florida." He smiled slightly. "Digging ditches was what it mounted to, putting in sewer lines." Then, keeping his voice even, "I started running around with a bunch of guys I thought were pretty cool, I was just a dumb kid who didn't know any better. We got away with everything short of murder, and it might've come to that sooner or later if we hadn't gotten caught drag racing one night. The cars weren't ours, you see, we used to get them out of parking lots down town and take them back when we got through."

She didn't say anything.

"Big joke, getting picked up for dragging when we'd done a lot worse things without even thinking hard."

She didn't ask him what things. She didn't ask anything.

"I got off with a suspended sentence. First offense, and I was old enough for the Army by then and didn't mind giving it a try." He wondered what she was thinking, if she was wishing she'd never come with him. "I was in Texas and Kansas, in the service, and I got a kick out of the kind of farming they do out there. So I just stayed on, when I was discharged, and worked the harvest gangs for a while."

Down on the road a car went by, throwing gravel under its tires from the edge of the asphalt, headlights going out in front and a trickle of dust behind.

"Why'd you come back?" Jody asked at last.

He shrugged. "Homesick, I guess. Tired of moving around."

"And you ran into Marv first thing," Jody said. "No wonder you didn't want to get caught in a stolen car."

He couldn't tell much from her voice, it hadn't changed any. But whatever she was feeling about him, he'd had to tell her, she deserved to know.

"When I was in jail down in Florida," he said, "waiting for my case to come up in court, I thought about my dad a lot. Being locked up can do things to a man, rotten things. You try to figure where things started going bad, and how you got yourself so fouled up, but It's not easy, sometimes none of it makes sense. You wonder if maybe it would have happened no matter what you did or how hard you tried, and you get to feeling you might as well give up, what good does it do to try." He paused a moment and then said, "I think that's what happened to him, it wasn't the tractor." He tried to keep the words from sounding as rigid as his mouth felt. "I was scared it'd do the same thing to me, if I ever had to serve time."

"But you didn't have to," Jody whispered.

"There's still a damn good chance," he said, "if they catch me. They won't even have to think twice about it."

There was a sharp click behind them and light streamed across the porch from the hall.

"You kids may be young enough to stay up all night," Mr. Causey said, "but I think I'll turn in. Lock the front door when you come."

"We're coming right now," Tay said quickly, wondering how long he'd been there and how much he'd heard.

But he didn't act any different, standing in the hall with Tay to watch Jody climb the stairs. He looked up at her, amiable as always, and said, "You want us to catch you if you fall?"

"I'll make it," she said, "all the way."

"If you do I'll have to take back everything I said about pretty girls." Then, winding his big watch, he smiled at her as she reached the top. "Sleep well, young lady, and I'll wake you in plenty of time to bake up some biscuits for breakfast."

She laughed and said, "I'll be ready," and disappeared in the dark at the top of the stairs.

Tay gave her as much time as he could. He went to the back porch and had a cold drink of well water, then waited while Mr. Causey locked up. But there wasn't any way he could manage to stay behind when Mr. Causey turned out the downstairs lights and started up the stairs. He didn't know whether she'd thought much beyond just going to bed, tired as she was, and all the talking he'd done would have kept her mind off the subject. But he was pretty sure she'd had a bad moment or two when she went in the bedroom and remembered it, on top of the way she was probably feeling about him right now.

Well, he'd spent half the day trying to think of a way out of it and hadn't succeeded; they'd come too far to foul things up now.

In the upstairs hall Mr. Causey said, "Hope you get a good night's sleep, son. Let me know if you have any trouble with that arm."

"Thanks, it's okay," Tay said. "Goodnight."

He couldn't stand there, waiting, so he opened the bedroom door and closed it behind him quickly, just in case Mr. Causey was watching.

She was already in bed, wearing faded cotton pajamas, the sheet pulled up over her. The headboard was big and dark, towering over her head, and she looked small and lost, lying there with her eyes slanted and almost closed and her face very pale.

He stood still for a moment, getting his bearings. It was an old-fashioned room with a lot of heavy dark furniture and white ruffly curtains and a lamp on the chest of drawers by the door, round and plump and covered with pink china roses. Tay reached out for it, thinking it was better, all things considered, to turn it off right away. Then he told himself savagely that he didn't have any guts, it wasn't going to be any easier for her to take it in the dark because he was too chicken to let her see his face.

He hesitated, his hand dropping away from the lamp.

"Listen," he said, "it's okay, you don't have to worry."

It sounded all wrong, dammit. How the hell could he say it and make her believe him, he was crazy to think he could get away with it.

"I tried to think of another way, but I didn't have much luck." He smiled at her, but it was hard to do. "Not enough practice, I guess."

She still didn't say anything. With something like despair, he snapped off the light.

"You want me to sleep on the floor?"

"No," she said, sounding faint and faraway, "don't be silly."

He undressed quickly, down to his shorts. Then, as casually as he could, he stretched out on the bed beside her, his heart drumming somewhere up in his throat and perspiration crawling down his face.

"Don't worry," he said again. "Go to sleep."

"You're the one doing all the worrying," she said in the darkness.

Her voice was low and careful, but there was laughter in it. He couldn't believe it, but it was there.

"Anyway," she said, "I figured you'd be so tired you'd go right off to sleep."

Tired but not dead, he could have warned her, but he didn't. For a moment he considered how it'd be the next night, and the next, and the one after that. Then he deliberately shut it out of his mind.

He wanted to reach out and find her hand, but decided he'd better not.

"I'm already asleep," he said. "See you in the morning."

Lying there quietly, relaxing, listening to the steady sound of her breathing, he wondered with amusement if she'd kept awake long enough to hear him. And when he dropped off to sleep himself, a minute or two later, the amusement was still with him, and the wonder.

{11}

MARV lay on the bed, hands behind his head, and stared at the ceiling.

In the kitchen Addie was doing a load of wash in Verna's old washing machine; he could hear the wringer clattering and vibrating every time she tried to put any clothes through it. She'd been pulling it in from the back porch when he came home, but she didn't ask for his help and he hadn't offered it. She had no business there, she oughta be home where she belonged, her and old lady Hackett both. They were supposed to be looking after the kids for Verna, but that was a laugh, what they was doing was looking after everybody else's business but their own.

He lay without moving, wearing nothing but his pants, and still the perspiration ran off his body and soaked the sheets beneath him.

He had troubles, no question about it. The damn cops didn't believe him, and he was beginning to doubt if Gurney did. That was Verna's fault, the dirty sneak, calling the cops behind his back, letting them take his clothes so they could see every last drop of blood and think up a million tricky questions to throw at him. Give her time and she'd fix him, but good, maybe even turn Pa against him; it wouldn't surprise him any if she'd been waiting for a good chance like this since the day she married Gurney. She didn't like him, Marv knew that, and never had; well, that could work both ways, he didn't think much of her, either.

He hated her. Her and Addie and Mrs. Hackett. Jody, too, the lying little bitch. He wished he knew where she'd disappeared to, he had a thing or two to settle with her. She must have known she'd get him into trouble, leaving like that, but she couldn't care less, it was just what she wanted. She was like Verna, they both thought they could fix it to get rid of him, and if they didn't watch out that was exactly what was going to happen. He had half a mind to take off and never come back, and it'd serve 'em right. If they ran him off, Pa'd come, too. He'd never sit back meek as a mouse and let 'em get away with it. And they'd get along okay, him and Pa, they did okay for themselves before Verna ever come along.

Only he couldn't leave. Not now, with the law after him and every damn cop in town sure he was lying about a fight and a bloody nose that had bled all over his clothes.

He couldn't figure where in the hell Tay Brannon had got to. He'd been hurt bad, out like a light and bleeding all over the place, and he hadn't moved a muscle when Marv pulled him over to the driver's seat. There'd been an awful moment when Marv couldn't tell whether he was even breathing, then Tay'd groaned a little and Marv took off down the road, sure he wasn't dead but just as sure he wouldn't be able to move around much before somebody found him. It hadn't taken the highway patrol long to get there; Marv had called from the telephone booth outside the filling station where Bob McGee worked, hanging up before they could ask for his name, and he'd waited on the Hill, at the back of the Dowd yard, until he heard a siren and the screech of tires as the car turned off the highway down below.

Damn, he'd done some quick thinking, had even been sort of proud that he could work things out so well in a jam and not get rattled. When they found Tay in the car they'd have to take him to the hospital, and by the time he came to it wouldn't matter what his story was. Marv would be asleep in bed and he'd deny having anything to do with it. Sure, he'd say, he'd ridden over to Ashton with Tay, he figured the car was Tay's and didn't ask any questions, why would he think it was stolen? Then, when Tay started to drinking, Marv decided it wasn't safe to ride back with him and he thumbed a lift with a truck driver, and went straight home to bed. It was a good story, there was no easy way to check on all the trucks that came through during the night and if there had been, the police knew that not many truck drivers would admit to picking up a hitchhiker against company regulations. Besides, he'd counted on his father sticking up for him; Gurney hadn't thought much of Tay when he met him, and if things got rough he might even say he'd heard Marv come in earlier and knew for sure he was home in bed when the car was wrecked.

And so what if Tay insisted he hadn't been driving and it was Marv who turned up with the car; the cops would only think Tay was lying to save his own skin. He was a bum, he'd just hit town the day before, nobody knew anything about him. He was a cold customer, too, the cops would spot that right away, and it might be he already had a record some place else they'd find out about once they got his fingerprints. The whole thing was made to order, it couldn't have worked out slicker if Marv had thought it out beforehand.

But something had gone wrong, it hadn't worked out at all.

He had suspected it when the cops didn't come around Sunday to ask him any questions about the wreck. It was a good thing, maybe, because he'd had to change his story in a hurry when Gurney and Verna found out about the blood on his clothes; but it'd been a bad day, not knowing what had happened and having the cops all over the place because Jody was gone.

Then in Monday morning's paper he'd read that they hadn't found anybody in the car, and later, when he learned it was all over the Hill that the sheriff's deputies had the dogs out and lost the scent, he'd been so relieved he was almost sick with it. It was plain Tay Brannon didn't want anything to do with the law, for reasons of his own, and he wouldn't be fool enough to show his face around town again. There was nothing, absolutely nothing, to connect Marv with the stolen car, and as long as he kept his mouth shut he was in the clear.

Then Verna, damn her to hell, spoiled everything. If he hadn't been so beat that night he'd have hidden his clothes, remembering she was the kind to sneak around and spy on him. But he'd been so glad to get home he'd fallen in bed without thinking about anything but getting rid of his shakes and working out his story of what had happened.

He was still getting the shakes, off and on. He had them now. It was queer to be cold inside and dripping wet with sweat on the outside.

The telephone rang and he jumped, the cold taking his nerves until they felt all curled up and quivering.

Mrs. Hackett answered it and he lay very still, listening to her voice in the dining room beyond his closed door. After a minute or two he decided it wasn't anything important, like the cops wanting him to come back down town; it must be somebody asking about Jody, the way Mrs. Hackett was gossiping on, telling everything she knew and probably making up a lot she didn't know to go with it.

Jesus, he'd like to wring Jody's neck. Wherever she was she'd be laughing her damn head off if she knew how much trouble she was causing him.

They thought he'd done something to her. Killed her and cut her up in little pieces, maybe, then stuffed her in a hole some place. Well, just let him get hold of her again, he didn't know but he might not be tempted to spill a little blood when he thought how careful he'd been and how he'd held off from her all this time, and then the first time he touched her she acted like he was trying to rape her. It was all of a piece, if he hadn't been so mad at her he wouldn't have picked up the car in the first place, or drunk so much, or gone off the road into a tree. It was her fault, the whole damn fouled-up mess.

But he couldn't tell the cops any of that. He'd stuck to his story of going to Ashton with Tay Brannon and then leaving him when he got to drinking, and he'd added the bit about having to bloody Tay's nose for him when he got ugly in a parking lot outside some beer joint. They didn't believe him, he could tell that from the way they looked at him, damn sneering bastards, thought they were better'n anybody else because they wore little badges and had the law on their side. He had stopped 'em, though. They might not believe him but they didn't have any proof or they never would have let him come home.

Still, if Jody didn't show up pretty soon he was going to be in real trouble.

Funny, Gurney seemed more cut up about her being gone than anything else. He'd come down to the station with Marv, all right, and said he'd get him a lawyer and see nobody railroaded him to jail for something he didn't do. But he hadn't said much to Verna, the way anybody would expect, for calling the cops in the first place; and so far as Marv knew he was still driving around every minute he wasn't at the garage, just looking for Jody, when he might better be spending his time doing something to get his son out of trouble.

He was pretty sarcastic, too, about the way Marv acted in front of the cops. "Christ," he'd said on the way out, "you want them jokers to think you grew up with a switchblade under your pillow? You better learn to say 'yessir' and 'no sir' to them boys, and smile when you say it. It ain't healthy to be smart to a cop, he'd just as soon throw you in jail as look at you."

"They don't scare me," Marv had said. "They can think what they want to, if they got enough brains to do any thinking." The shaking hadn't left him and he was still a little rocky from the effort of keeping his story straight with two lousy cops throwing questions at him, but Gurney didn't seem to care about that. "Small-town cops, my God, they make me sick. They push me around much more, I'll show 'em a thing or two."

Gurney, damn him, had laughed. "You watch too much television, little boy. Talk about small-town cops, I can tell you one thing, you're pretty small-time yourself."

One of the cops had come out behind them, just then, and Marv knew he had heard Gurney from the grin on his face.

He could have hit both of them. And by the time he'd listened all the way home to Pa's jawing, he'd thought he'd never quit shaking; if he'd had to take much more he might have exploded in ten different directions, let 'em see then what happened when people pushed him around. But he'd have to get along with Pa, and talk him around so he'd know it was Verna and Jody who'd caused all the trouble. Pa'd stick with him, Marv was sure of that, if it ever came to a showdown.

He stared at the ceiling.

Little boy. Small-time. And the cop listening, grinning.

With a groan, he rolled over and buried his face in the pillow.

In the back yard Addie hung the last of the clothes on the line. Wiping her damp face with the corner of her apron, she picked up the empty basket and went back to the house.

She hesitated on the steps in the dull glare of sunlight, looking out toward the west and north where large thunderheads lay piled in rounded pyramids that glistened white and creamy where the sun struck them. She hoped the clothes would have time to dry; she was late getting them out, and it had been such a big load she dreaded the thought of having to rush out to pull them off the line still damp. But when she thought of the weather breaking, of having the heavy breathless air washed clean by a hard shower, she knew she would gladly do the clothes over again, even go out to gather them in the drenching rain if need be.

Rain. She savored the sound of it, the taste of it, in her mouth. The memory of it pouring in thick gray curtains across the Hill, blown by the wind, alive with brilliant streaks of lightning. Rain filling the ditches, running across the yards and graveled roads, pushing, hurrying, spurting down the eroded gutters along the side of the red clay Hill. Then, when the wind and noise were spent, the slow quiet drizzle that would go on through the night. Summer rain, dripping gently on the tin roofs, the sweet white magnolia blossoms, the green oak outside her bedroom window, the wet saturated earth.

She sighed. Leaving the empty basket on the porch, she went inside. The kitchen was stuffy and airless, and she went through it to the front part of the house, carefully averting her eyes from Marv's bedroom door. She had pulled the shades and closed the windows earlier, so that the living room was dim and shaded, but it was not cool and the shut-up air smelled of stale cigarette smoke. She grimaced and opened the door to the porch.

The baby was there in his playpen, talking contentedly to himself, wearing nothing but a diaper and the damp crumbs from a cracker he was eating. Mrs. Hackett rocked in her chair, brought over that morning by Gurney, and Bob McGee perched on the porch railing, ball cap on the back of his head, one foot propped on the playpen.

Addie regarded him with disapproval. "Please move your shoe," she said. "It's dirty and germy, and the baby teethes on that wood."

Bob took his foot away quickly. "Sorry," he said. Then, as if apology wasn't enough, he took a handkerchief out of his back pocket and wiped the top rail of the playpen where his shoe had rested. Glancing up to meet Addie's frown, he grinned and said, "It's clean, Addie, this is the first time I've touched it since I put it in my pocket."

Addie sniffed. "It's still a handkerchief."

"That's right," Bob said, holding on to his grin, "but believe me, not many germs could live through one of Ma's washings."

"For the Lord's sake," Mrs. Hackett said, "a few germs ain't gonna hurt that baby. Everybody's gotta eat his peck of dirt." She waited until Addie had sat down in the swing and added slyly, "That cracker he's gnawing on fell out on the floor a coupla times, and Billie Mae just blowed it off and gave it back to him."

Addie jumped up. "Mama, I thought you said you'd watch him for me." She snatched the soggy piece of cracker away from Neal and he stared at her with wide reproachful eyes. "You don't want that dirty old cracker," she said, but his mouth puckered up stubbornly and he let out a tentative cry of rage. Addie held out her arms and the cry dwindled away as she picked him up.

"Now you've done it," Mrs. Hackett said. "Try to put him back in that pen again and he'll scream the neighborhood down."

Addie sat back down in the swing with Neal in her lap. "It's almost time for his lunch. I'll just feed him and put him in for his nap."

"If you can get your mind off that baby for a minute, I've got a piece of news you might like to hear."

Addie looked up at her mother, noticing for the first time how bright her eyes were and the way she was smiling, pleased and amused and excited all at once.

"Something about Jody?" she asked, not daring to hope.

"I know where she is," Mrs. Hackett said with enormous satisfaction. "That man who called a few minutes ago told me just where to find her."

Addie let out the breath she was holding, but her chest still hurt with the pressure.

"I was just telling Bob. We're trying to decide what to do about it."

"Oh, Mama," Addie said unsteadily. "I can't believe it. Is she all right? Where's she been all this time, and where is she now? Did you call Verna yet?"

"Not yet. Might not call her at all, I haven't made up my mind."

Addie stared at her. "What do you mean, you might not call her at all? Mama, where is Jody? Tell me this minute, you don't have any right to keep it back from me."

"I'm not studying anybody's rights," Mrs. Hackett retorted. "Jody's a smart girl, she's done better for herself than I expected. It don't seem fair to spoil everything for her, let Gurney and Verna go hauling her home like one of them juvenile delinquents."

"Where is she?" Addie repeated flatly. "Tell me, Mama."

"Working in tobacco for some farmer south of town. That was him called, seems he read about her in the paper. Sounded like a right nice old man, and he didn't want to tattle-tale but he was a father himself and knew her family would be worrying."

"Working in tobacco?" Addie said faintly, and Bob laughed.

"Hot work," he said, "this kind of weather."

"At least she's getting paid for it," Mrs. Hackett said, "and that's more'n she ever got for slaving away at home." She shook her head, chuckling. "You got to hand it to her, Bob, a cat always lands on its feet. She's only been gone since Saturday night and she's already found a job and a husband and a boss who worries about her 'cause she reminds him of his daughter."

The silence on the porch was complete. Bob's grin faded and he stared soberly at Mrs. Hackett.

"What d'you mean, a husband?" he asked coolly.

Mrs. Hackett chuckled again, sounding a little as though she were crowing. "That's what he told me on the phone. She and some man come to work for him, told him they was married. When I asked him was he sure, he said that's all he knew about it. But I reckon they're living right there on his farm, in his house, as man and wife, or he wouldn't say a thing like that."

Bob said abruptly, "I don't believe it," and Addie made a choking sound in her throat. "Oh, Mama," she whispered, "it can't be that way, it can't."

"If you mean she can't be married, you're right. It takes longer than she's been gone to fix up getting married in this state."

"There's South Carolina," Bob said. His thin brown face was grave, thoughtful, a little tired. "It's an old trick, maybe we should have thought of it before." He started to shrug, gave it up, and looked down at his hands. "Only thing, I didn't figure she knew any guy that well, except maybe me."

"She didn't run off to South Carolina," Mrs. Hackett said. "This fellow didn't have a car, the one he was riding around in got wrecked somehow."

Slowly, narrowed, Bob's eyes came back to her face.

"You know him," Mrs. Hackett said. "Tay Brannon's the name."

He didn't say anything for a long moment. Then he gave a faint low whistle, letting it trail out to nothing.

"Well, what d' you know about that," he said softly.

"Not as much as I'd like to. I'd sure Lord like to know how they ran into each other."

"Maybe they had it all planned," Bob said, no expression in his voice. "Didn't Marv bring him up here to the house?"

"He didn't stay but a few minutes, there wasn't time to make any plans. Far as I know he came with Marv and went off with Gurney right away. Might have said hello and goodbye, but not much more."

Bob was silent. Slouching against the railing, he put his hands in his pockets and stretched his long legs out before him, looking down at them soberly.

From the swing Addie asked carefully, "Mama, who is Tay Brannon?"

Mrs. Hackett didn't answer her. Her bright eyes on Bob, she said, "You saw him, you know a little something about him. Think she's got hold of more'n she can handle?" She watched the flicker of anger touch his face. "You said he was tougher than Marv, you wouldn't want to tangle with him unless there was good reason. Maybe this is all his idea. Jody's no match for him, I expect, and she's probably got her hands full and don't know the first thing about getting loose of him."

"Maybe," Bob said flatly.

"On the other hand, this fellow on the phone seemed to think she was getting along fine. He come right out and said we could leave her there and not worry, he wouldn't let her come to any harm."

Addie pushed the swing back and forth, lifting her feet as she came forward, pushing back with her heels, concentrating on the steady motion with an effort, fighting the nausea in her throat. It was all wrong, terribly wrong, it was mixed-up and confused and frightening beyond anybody's ability to straighten it out. Jody, running off with some man, working in tobacco, living at that strange man's farm, saying she was married. Addie's mind stopped there, unable to go on thinking about it, and she stared at her mother and Bob Mc-

Gee, wanting to scream at them that they were wrong, too, they had no business talking it over as if Jody was somehow more theirs than Addie's or Verna's, as if they had every right in the world to decide what ought to be done.

"Maybe I better run out and take a look for myself," Bob said, still with that flat cool voice.

Mrs. Hackett nodded, satisfied. "You've got the address. I'm easier in my mind, now we know where she is, but I don't mind saying I'll sleep better once you've talked to her, face to face."

"Verna'd be easier in her mind, too," Addie pointed out, "if you'd tell her Jody's been found."

"I'll tell her," Mrs. Hackett said, "but not till I'm good and ready. I want to know how things are, give Jody half a chance to work things out for herself. Once Gurney finds out, the fat'll be in the fire for sure."

Behind the screen door someone moved, a thin shadow against the gloom of the darkened living room.

"Once Gurney finds out what?"

Marv stepped out on the porch. His face was pale, pasty-white, and his long dark hair fell across his forehead limply, damp with sweat. But his eyes glittered, alive and intent, as he looked from Bob to Mrs. Hackett.

"So you've found Jody," he said, and smiled.

It wasn't a pleasant smile, and Addie, her heart stopped for a long painful beat, thought he had never looked so much like Gurney. Only she had to admit that Gurney would never sneak up on anybody like that, eavesdropping, tiptoeing around in a dark house so he could hear without being heard. There was one thing you could say for Gurney, there wasn't an ounce of sneak in him; he came out in the open with everything, and if you didn't like it you could usually hear him coming and maybe get out of his way.

"Well, well, looks like you've all been pretty busy." Marv pushed the playpen out of his way with one foot and leaned indolently against the house siding. "Where'd you find her?"

Bob didn't speak. He studied Marv indifferently, coldly.

Mrs. Hackett sighed. "I forgot you was to home, Marv. You had any manners, you wouldn't creep up on people that way."

He laughed. "Can't think of a better way to find out what I wanta know." Looking at her with the laugh still twisting his mouth, he added, "You might as well tell me where she is, I'll find out sooner or later."

"I don't know as it's any of your business where she is," she said. "If it wasn't for you she never would've run off in the first place."

His face turned hard, impatient. "Don't give me that. I don't give a good damn why she left, I just wanta find out where she went to."

Mrs. Hackett rocked back and forth. "Why?" she asked. "Why're you so all-fired anxious to find her?"

"Hell, you know as well as I do why. Verna's all the time running over to your house to tell you every time she blows her nose, don't try to kid me you don't know all about her putting the cops on me."

"Seems to me I did hear something like that, but I don't see what Jody's got to do with it."

"Plenty, for Christ's sake. They saw that blood on my clothes and figured I did something to her. They won't believe anything I say, not with her still missing."

"Whose blood was it, then?"

"I had a fight with some guy," Marv said sullenly. "It's none of your damn business whose it was."

"Why don't you find him, let him tell the police what happened?"

"I don't know where he is, is why, and I ain't about to look for him."

"Can't say I blame you for that," Mrs. Hackett said promptly. "No need to push your luck, I expect you'd

200

be in a worse fix if you found him." She met his suspicious stare blandly and added, "If I was him I'd be looking for a chance to get even. But maybe this friend of yours is too much of a coward, you know more about him than I do."

He glared down at her. "Listen, old lady, I've heard enough. You tell me where I can find Jody or I'll call Gurney and let him get it outa you."

Bob McGee lighted a cigarette and flipped the match into the yard. Then he stood up, easy and quick, and pulled his ball cap down over his eyes.

"You talk too much, Marv," he said. "I'm kinda tired of hearing you run your dirty mouth."

Marv looked at him, surprised. "If you don't like it, bud, you know what you can do about it."

"Yeah," Bob retorted, "and if you don't watch it I just might."

Marv laughed. "Try it. Go ahead, you chicken," He put one hand in his pocket, slowly so that Bob wouldn't miss the gesture. "You talk right much yourself, not having anything to back it up with."

"I don't need a knife to take care of you," Bob said. "You're just a lousy kid, what I oughta do is wash your mouth out." He paused, with a contemptuous half-smile. "But I don't have to go to all that trouble. All I need's a phone and a chance to tell the cops about a black Chevie that was stolen last Saturday night, and they'll cut you down to size for me."

Marv stared at him. "You bastard," he said between his teeth.

"Both of you stop it," Mrs. Hackett said firmly. "I won't have a fight on Verna's front porch for everybody on the street to see." When neither of them paid any attention to her she raised her voice. "Bob, it won't do no harm to take Marv out there with you. He knows about it now, ain't nothing we can do but let him see she's okay. Then maybe he won't be blamed for something he didn't do."

Bob turned his head. "You crazy?"

"Maybe," she said calmly. "Jody might not like it, but there's other people involved. We got to be fair."

Even Marv seemed a little astonished. But he said morosely, "It's about time you thought about somebody besides Jody."

"I just wish I could go with you," Mrs. Hackett said to Bob. "Lord, I'd give a year of my life to see it, and I ain't got many to spare."

For a brief moment Bob's face showed a dawning comprehension, then he wiped it carefully blank.

"That's right," Mrs. Hackett said. "Don't know but what it's the best way, all things considered."

He grinned. "You're an ornery old woman," he said, his voice light and amused, even affectionate. "The Devil's gonna find you out one day and you'll go up in a puff of smoke."

"Then you can go to Mass and pray to one of them heathen idols to save my soul."

"I don't know what you're cooking up," Marv said, "but I'll tell you one thing, I'm bringing Jody back and nobody'd better try to stop me."

Mrs. Hackett smiled. "Bob ain't gonna try to stop you."

"He damn well better not," Marv said impatiently. "Jesus, we going or ain't we?"

"Don't rush me," Bob said. He waited until Marv had gone down the steps, then winked at Mrs. Hackett. "Keep your fingers crossed I'll come back in one piece."

He pushed his cap back, took the steps two at a time, and sauntered down the walk beside Marv, whistling a little snatch of song under his breath.

Addie watched them go silently. She smoothed Neal's hair, feeling it fine and silky under her hand, and pulled the end of her cotton belt from his mouth where he had been happily chewing it.

"My Lord, Addie, I'd give a mint of money to see

Marv's face when he finds out Jody's been with that Brannon boy all this time."

Addie said nothing. Her mother rocked briskly, cheerfully.

"Life's long and ugly and aggravating, it's enough to make you puke, but there's times when things go together so tidy and neat you want to yell from feeling so good about it."

Addie, who didn't feel good about anything, roused herself enough to say, "You never told me who Tay Brannon is."

Mrs. Hackett grinned. "He ain't no coward, afraid of a little knife, I can tell you that. He's gonna be mighty glad to get hold of Marv, and unless I miss my guess he'll have some say in whether Marv drags Jody off home the way he's planning."

A number of urgent questions crowded Addie's mind. There was so much she didn't understand, so much going on that still seemed strange and confused to her. They had kept things from her, she realized that now; from the very beginning it had been like a conspiracy, with her on the outside of a tight closed circle that never opened a crack to let her in.

She looked at her mother, still grinning so widely that her dentures showed white and gleaming below their bright pink gums. Her narrow wrinkled face had a little smear of dirt on one cheek and her hair was all rumpled, standing on end where she'd run her fingers through it. Even her dress, tasteless, ugly with brilliant purple and red morning glories blossoming all over it, looked rumpled; she had worn it the day before and it was soiled and wrinkled where Gurney had picked her up and put her on the bed.

Old and soiled and ornery, Addie thought, yet she was inside the circle, nobody tried to push her out, she was in the center of everything that went on.

Addie closed her eyes and leaned her head against the chains supporting the swing. Her mother. Gurney,

Verna, Marv. Bob McGee. Jody, whom she had loved.
It was easy to say that they lived in the same world
and breathed the same air, they walked up and down
the same streets and spoke the same language. But it
wasn't the same, she had known it for a long time.
They were different from her, all of them, even the
words they used had different meanings. They lived in
one world and left her alone in another.

She tasted the bile of nausea in her throat, so acrid
that it made her eyes burn. For a moment she sat
quietly, her eyes closed, distressed that she should feel
so ill and tired with half the day still before her to be
lived through somehow. She had to iron the big washing she'd done for Verna and cook dinner for the
children. For Gurney and Marv, too, they'd raise the
roof if a hot meal wasn't put on the table before them
the minute they wanted it, that was men for you. On
top of everything else her Circle was meeting at seven
o'clock, and she'd promised to go by the church early
and fix the refreshments. But she didn't have to go to
a lot of trouble for cake and lemonade, unless she decided to bake one of her angel food cakes with boiled
icing. Maybe she could find the time, the ladies in her
Circle always said such kind things about her baking.

She opened her eyes. Neal was almost asleep, his
head nestled comfortably against her, and she spoke
quietly so she wouldn't rouse him.

"What do you think Verna'll do about Jody when
she comes back?"

Mrs. Hackett shrugged. "If she comes back," she
corrected. "It's not Verna I'm worried about, it's what
Gurney'll do. Both of 'em ought to thank God, if they
get her back, but that ain't saying they'll have any
more sense than they ever did."

"She ought to be punished," Addie said. "I don't
know what Verna can think of, but she'll have to do
something."

Mrs. Hackett turned to stare at her. Her grin was gone now, with a sharp click of her teeth.

"What do'you mean, punished?"

"Verna's got Billie Mae to think about," Addie said, "and little Neal. It's not good for children to have somebody like Jody around, it's worse than indecent." She heard her voice rising and forced it down, remembering with a terrible grinding embarrassment the way she had screamed at Gurney, losing all control, making a fool of herself. "Running off the way she did, living with some man, lying about being married, I don't know but what it'd be better if she never came back."

Her mother couldn't seem to find any words. She looked at Addie silently.

"Verna could try locking her up, I guess," Addie went on, "but it won't do any good, she'll be in trouble again soon as she gets half a chance. Girls like that always do, look at Ruthie Maness."

"Jody ain't Ruthie," Mrs. Hackett said at last.

"Maybe not now, but there's no doubt Ruthie started the same way. If Verna can't see it somebody ought to tell her, it's a sin and a shame the way girls behave on the Hill."

Her mother gave a weary sigh. "You ain't gonna tell her any such thing, Addie. I'm warning you, don't meddle in something you don't know anything about."

Addie didn't want to know. She was so grateful for not knowing that she felt like going down to the church, that very minute, in the middle of a Tuesday, to get down on her knees and thank God for her blessed ignorance.

She was aware of her mother's frowning disapproval, but it didn't bother her. None of it really mattered any more, she had been crazy to get so upset about things. She had a queer notion that she'd never been on the outside of the circle, after all; she was in the center of it, it was hers alone, she could feel it closing around her, warm and tight and secure.

"I'm going to feed Neal his lunch," she said. "If you see Billie Mae, call her in." When Mrs. Hackett didn't speak Addie went on kindly, "It's time for you to eat, too. You come lie down on Verna's bed and I'll bring you a tray."

"I ain't helpless, I'll eat in the kitchen."

From a distance of great calm Addie said, "Oh, well, you look so tired I thought it'd be nice."

"I'll make out," Mrs. Hackett said shortly. "Bring a tray out here if you want to, I feel like eating by myself."

Addie lifted the warm heavy weight of the baby and went inside, glad that she wouldn't have to share the children with anyone. She'd cut their Jello into stars and moons with a cookie cutter, and maybe fix chocolate milk for them, and they'd have a party, just the three of them.

Despite the heat outside, Mr. Causey's kitchen was cool and pleasant. The trees had shaded the house from the sun all morning, and now that the big thunderheads had rolled in from the west, blotting out the light, the inside of the house still retained some of the quiet coolness of dawn.

Jody, frying ham in a black iron skillet, hoped it wouldn't rain before they filled the barns. Mr. Causey had gone off in his truck that morning, when the clouds first began to pile up above the trees, to see if he could find an extra crew to fill his two remaining barns before the weather broke. Somebody had promised him six men for the afternoon and two of his neighbors said they'd help out, but from the look of the sky and the feel of the heavy air Jody was afraid they'd be cutting it pretty close. She and Belle had come up to the house to fix dinner, but if the men decided not to leave the fields it'd be a matter of carrying food down

to the barns where one or two at a time could grab a
bite to eat without holding up the rest.

"Will a hard rain hurt the crop?" she asked Belle,
thinking not only of Mr. Causey but of Eddie and
Belle, trying to pay off their debts and the mortgage
on their farm.

Belle only shrugged and said, "Hail can make a
mess, and I've seen a storm with a lot of wind lay
tobacco right out flat. If it's just rain it'll be okay, only
the fields might be too wet to work for a couple of
days."

"I couldn't be that calm about it," Jody said ruefully, "not knowing which it'll be."

"You take what comes and make do with it," Belle
said. "I don't know there's much anybody can do to
change it."

"That doesn't keep people from worrying."

Belle added a heaping spoonful of sugar to a pitcher
of hot tea. "Oh, I worry. I worry so much I have to
set aside special times, so I won't forget anything."
She tasted the tea, grimaced, and added more sugar.
"I just don't believe in spinning my wheels, honey.
You want to know the truth, I've got too many worries I can do something about, like am I getting too fat
and is Eddie sneaking too many looks at that little gal
down the road who came home from up north with a
divorce and her hair conked."

"What does Eddie worry about?"

"Important things, I guess. Bills, the price of tobacco,
white folks, who's going to get elected president, atom
bombs, cops." She looked up, shrugged. "Isn't that
what a man's for?"

They smiled at each other.

Then Belle said briskly, "You run down and ask
Mr. Causey if he wants us to bring the food down
there. We can make sandwiches out of this ham, and
the tea'll go like it is without too much trouble."

When she stepped out on the porch Jody noticed

that it had grown darker, and the air was so still and motionless that the leaves on the tall oak by the back door drooped, melancholy and lifeless, dull dry green against a dull black sky. But they wouldn't have long to suffer. She could almost smell the rain, and a low rumble of thunder followed some distant lightning hidden by the trees.

She heard a car turning off the road and paused on the steps, hoping it was bringing the extra workers. They wouldn't have much time, but you could never tell about a storm; sometimes it threatened for hours, grumbling all the time, and ended with a few scattered sprinkles.

She was crossing the yard, heading for the barn, when a car door slammed behind her, and then another, and she turned to see Bob and Marv coming around the corner of the house.

She stopped short, staring at them.

They didn't stop. They walked toward her, unsmiling, taking their time, not hurrying because she was caught there in a trap between them and the house.

Even then, for a split second of panic, she considered running. But there was no place to run except toward the fields where Tay was, and she still had a chance to keep Marv from knowing about that.

"Well, what d'ya know," Marv said, "it's Jody." He halted at last, no more than a couple of feet away, and gave her a small unpleasant grin. "Don't you think it's about time you trotted along home, honey, you left things in sort of a mess."

She still didn't speak. There was a hard obstruction in her throat and she was afraid of the way her voice might sound, giving her away. Letting her eyes slide over Marv, she looked past him to Bob McGee.

"Hello," he said, "long time no see."

His face grew longer and narrow when he smiled, the way it always did, and somehow she was comforted, seeing him so much the same, still wearing his battered ball cap, letting her know from the way he talked and looked at her that he was still on her side.

"How'd you know where I was?" she asked him then, and because it was Bob her voice held steady.

"Some guy called," he said, "and Mrs. Hackett talked to him. He said you were working for him, told her where he lived."

"Mr. Causey?" Jody said blankly.

"A farmer," Bob said, "I didn't catch the name."

She sighed, letting her shoulders slump wearily.

"What difference does it make, who called?" Marv said. "Look, kid, I'm in a rush, I've got to see a cop or two. Come on, the fun's over, you're going home with us."

She kept her eyes on Bob. "Is that why you came, to take me home?"

"Not me," he said promptly. "You like working in tobacco, it's your funeral. No reason I can see why you oughta go home unless you're tired of smelling the damn stuff." He shook his head gravely. "You should've taken up smoking, honey, it's easier on that end of the cigarette."

She smiled faintly. "But it doesn't pay as well."

Marv said something under his breath. "I'm tired of all the yakking, Jody, let's go."

She looked at him directly for the first time.

"I don't have to go anywhere with you."

"The hell you don't. Get a move on, I'd hate to have to drag you to the car."

"You can't tell me what to do," Jody said carefully. "You're no kin to me. You're not anything to me, if it comes to that, so you'd better go on and leave me alone."

"I ain't going till you go with me," Marv said angrily, "you can get that through your thick head right now. Them damn cops blame me for you disappearing, they even act like they think I murdered you or something. You got to tell 'em you're okay, dammit, and get me off the hook."

Jody stared at him incredulously.

"Tell her about the blood," Bob said amiably. "That ought to make her eager as all hell to help you out."

"It was just from a nose bleed," Marv said, goaded, "I don't know why you keep talking so damn much about it."

"He says he had a little trouble with that Brannon guy," Bob explained in an expressionless voice, his eyelids drooping so that he looked a little like a long-faced, long-legged eagle. "He beat him up good, though, you know our Marv, and now them nasty cops think it's your blood all over his clothes."

Jody was speechless, taking it in. For another minute or two the tension inside her held, tight and precarious, and then, all at once, it let go. She couldn't help it, she began to laugh, and then she couldn't seem to stop.

"Yeah," Bob said, "terrible thing, ain't it?"

"Laugh, go on. I'm glad you think it's so goddam funny." Marv's face was pale, his eyes too bright. "But you can get one thing straight, sweetie, I'm gonna take you back with me whether you wanta go or not."

Jody saw the glitter of hatred in his eyes and knew she had been wrong to laugh at him. He'd never leave her alone now, she was sure of it, he'd stay there, stubborn and furious, until she knuckled under to him. He'd find out about Tay, and there was no way of telling what kind of lies he'd tell about him to Mr. Causey, with Eddie and Clay and Lacy, and, in a few minutes, the extra men coming to help, all there to hear the lies, and maybe one of them believing enough, suspicious enough, to call the police.

She couldn't see that she had much of a choice.

"Don't give me such a hard time," Marv said, "or I'll call Pa to come out and help me." He gave a short hard laugh and grabbed her arm. "He'll knock some sense into you."

She stood very still, hating the feel of his hand on her, knowing she must tell him she'd go with him and yet unable to force the words out.

Beside him Bob hunched his shoulders restlessly. "Leave her alone, Marv," he said. "She don't have to go home if she don't want to."

"You keep out of it." Marv tightened his grip on Jody's arm. A long low roll of thunder came with his words, and in the gloomy light his face glistened, pale and thin and sharp. "Let's go, you can send for your things later. I ain't about to let you outa my sight."

"She's not going anywhere," Tay said from behind them. "Take your hands off her."

Marv whirled around. For a long minute he didn't speak, and in the silence Jody could hear the queer gaspy sound of his breathing.

"My God," he said then, "where'd you come from?"

Tay came forward from the back corner of the house. He'd put on his shirt so hurriedly that he hadn't had time to button it, and his hands were black with tobacco gum.

"You look like a damn field nigger," Marv said, still in that quick breathy voice. "Jesus, you been working in tobacco, too?"

"Sure," Tay said. "You looking for a job, Marv?"

Marv laughed, but it didn't quite come off. "I was looking for Jody. If I'd known she was with you I wouldn't have been so worried."

"I'll bet."

Tay stopped, a foot or so in front of Marv. He hadn't looked at Jody, but now his eyes flickered from Marv to Bob, paused a moment, then came back to Marv. His face was still and cold, the way Jody had seen it that first night in the Dowd kitchen, with so little expression in it that there was no way of telling what he was thinking or feeling.

"I'm surprised you weren't worried about me," he said, "instead of Jody."

"I was," Marv said quickly. "I was real torn up about it, man."

"You scared I might want to come back and take a piece out of your hide," Tay asked, "or did you figure you were pretty safe, I'd either bleed to death or I'd be in jail, taking the rap for wrecking a hot car?"

"Listen, I ain't that kinda creep. Soon as I found a telephone I called 'em to send out an ambulance."

"Thanks."

"How was I to know you meant to take off like that? Somebody had to go get help. You were out cold, it had to be me."

"Yeah," Tay said. "You're some angel of mercy, aren't you?" He regarded Marv silently for a moment, then said flatly, "I suppose that was why you dragged me over under the wheel, so I'd be more comfortable while you went for help."

Marv shrugged. "Okay, so I chickened out. I was all shook up, man, I couldn't think straight."

"Maybe it's time you started."

"Come on, don't be like that. Let's forget the whole damn business, we both got away and they ain't got a thing on us. I maybe did the wrong thing, I'm sorry as hell, but no sense in making a big thing about it now, it's all over and done with."

"No," Tay said, "not quite."

"I don't know what you got to be sore about. Hell, you was out screwing Jody all this time and I was getting the blame for it."

Tay hit him, his fist coming up from his side so quickly that Marv had no time to see it and duck. The blow caught him on his chin, clean and hard, and he lurched back, stumbled, and then fell on the dirt driveway with a frantic scrabbling of hands and feet.

He was up again in an instant, cursing, his hand going to his pocket. Jody knew what was coming and closed her eyes, sickened, only to open them again immediately because it was worse to be in the dark.

The switchblade was ready in Marv's hand. Crouching slightly, arms extended, he moved slowly toward Tay.

"Okay, you asked for it," he said, his voice high and tight with rage, "now you're gonna get it."

With a small distinct click, the knife flipped open. Tay didn't move. He watched Marv's eyes, his own narrowed and wary.

"What's the matter," Marv mocked, "you chicken? Come on, I wanta see can I cut up that other arm a little."

"I don't think," Bob said pleasantly, just behind Marv. "Drop the knife, little boy."

"Keep outa my way," Marv said savagely.

There was another click, and Marv's face looked drawn and sick with fury.

"You heard what I said, drop it."

Bob held his switchblade carelessly, almost indifferently, prodding Marv gently with the tip of the knife.

Marv dropped his knife. Bob put out one foot and kicked it away; it slithered across the grass and stopped at the edge of the pink-and-white petunias circling the old well.

"Now let's see how tough you are," Bob said, "without the hardware. Go on, beat him up like you did before, Marv, give him another bloody nose."

"Goddam it," Marv said, his voice breaking a little, "you goddam lousy bastard!"

Bob moved back. He took Jody's arm and pulled her aside, still holding his knife open in one hand.

"He's all yours," he said to Tay. "Have fun."

"Thanks," Tay said.

He took a step forward and Marv retreated a step.

"I'll have the cops on you," he said desperately. "I'll tell 'em you stole the damn car, I'll swear out a warrant for assault!"

Tay smiled and hit him again, square in the face.

It wasn't a pretty fight. It wasn't meant to be. Jody saw that from the beginning Tay intended to beat Marv up and he went about it with a cold deliberate violence, never losing control of himself, letting nothing show in his face, no passion or hatred or anger, nothing but the single-minded determination to beat Marv senseless if he could, however he could.

Marv fought back, trying to defend himself, swinging wildly. But Tay didn't give him an inch; he hit him and stood over him until he dragged himself to his feet, and then knocked him down again. When Marv didn't get up quickly enough, Tay grabbed him by the shirt and hauled him up to hit him, and once, when Marv lay on his face, groaning, Tay kicked him until he struggled to his knees. Pulling him up by his collar, Tay spun him around and let him have it again. The blow sent Marv staggering back against the well, then he doubled over and slid to the ground, hair hanging down over his eyes, the blood dark and thick on his battered face.

Mr. Causey came across the yard.

"That's enough," he said. "Whatever he's done, you got no call to try to kill him."

Tay looked at him a little blankly. Then lifting his head, he saw Eddie and Belle standing by the back porch, and Clay and Lacy at the corner of the house. His eyes came back, rested briefly on Mr. Causey's face.

He glanced down at Marv's inert body indifferently. A couple of feet away the knife still lay among the flowers, and he bent to pick it up, jiggling it carelessly as if to test the feel and heft of it in his hand. He snapped it shut and put it in his pocket.

Without a word, he walked across the yard to the house and went inside.

Behind him in the yard no one spoke or moved. In the dark still air a rumble of thunder sounded loud and harsh.

Mr. Causey knelt beside Marv. Bob went over too, pushing his cap back, going down on one leg.

"He's okay," Bob said. "He only folded up because it was easier than taking any more."

Mr. Causey looked down at Marv thoughtfully. "Think anything's broken?"

"Plenty, I hope," Bob said, "but I don't aim to try finding out, the shape he's in. Reckon we ought to get him in to town, let a doctor clean him up."

Eddie came up then, his dark face smooth and blank, his voice without expression. "Want me to carry him inside, Mr. Causey? It's gonna let go pretty soon, be kinda damp lying out here."

Jody walked past them, keeping her eyes away from Marv. At the steps she met Belle's eyes, soft and black and worried, and heard Clay's low excited voice as he said to Lacy, "I never seen anything like that, he liked to splattered that guy all over the yard," and Lacy's answer, "I ain't surprised, you got to watch out for them quiet ones. He's just lost his job, though. Mr. Causey won't stand for anything like this going on."

Jody held the screen door carefully so it wouldn't slam behind her. Then she ran down the long porch, through the front hall, up the stairs with their smooth polished treads. As she reached the top of the steps he came out of the bedroom, carrying his small suitcase and his leather jacket, and they both stopped abruptly, staring at each other.

"I'm leaving," he said into the silence. "You coming with me?"

"Yes," she said.

He didn't make a sound, but he looked, for an instant, as if he'd let out his breath with a long sigh.

"Get your things," he said. "We don't have any time to waste."

She went past him into the bedroom. Putting her green dress and pajamas in the paper sack, she turned away quickly without looking at the dark furniture and the white counterpane and the lamp with pink roses. It was easier to pretend it was only a hotel room she was leaving, cold and impersonal, and she told herself it was a shame she had made the bed up so carefully when it would only have to be undone now, and the sheets taken off to be washed.

He was waiting for her at the bottom of the stairs.

Not speaking, he took her paper sack from her and put it under his arm. They walked together through the hall and down the porch to the back screen door.

Marv hadn't moved, he still lay flat on the grass, eyes closed in his bloody face. Mr. Causey, Eddie, and Bob stood around him, talking in low voices. They turned, seeing Jody and Tay, and Mr. Causey came toward them, frowning slightly.

"I'm sorry about the tobacco," Tay said.

After a pause Mr. Causey said, "Don't worry about that."

"I don't like walking out on a job."

"It's not the job that matters so much." Mr. Causey's frown deepened, touched his faded blue eyes. "You ought not to do it this way, son, it won't settle anything to run off. If that boy there was in the wrong and deserved the kind of beating you gave him, you ought not to have anything to worry about."

"You planning on turning me in to the cops?" Tay asked coolly.

"I wasn't thinking about that."

"He will," Tay said, with a brief gesture toward Marv. Then, his eyes meeting Mr. Causey's, he asked, "Could you see your way clear to lending me your truck? We got to get some place we can catch a bus out of here."

Mr. Causey hesitated. "I had an idea you'd been in trouble," he said slowly, "but I took a chance on you. I never held with them that think a boy's bad for life once he gets started the wrong way." He shook his head, sighing faintly. "You seemed to be a pretty good kid. I thought you'd probably worked it all out of your system and things would be different, once you knew somebody was willing to meet you halfway."

Tay said nothing. He held himself very still, tight, almost without breathing.

"I helped a lot of boys in my time," Mr. Causey went on, "and not one of them's ever made me sorry I did what I could for them. They tried to do the right thing, kept out of trouble, went on to be decent kind of men."

"If you're saying no about the truck," Tay said carefully, "it's taking you a long time."

Mr. Causey looked disappointed, even sad. "You ought to know I couldn't say anything else." After a pause he added, "You might stop thinking about yourself for a minute and give the girl a little consideration. Her folks are worried sick about her. I know it for a fact because I talked to somebody there at her house just this morning."

Tay's mouth hardened, but he only said, "So it was you who told on us," and left it at that.

"I'm a father myself," Mr. Causey said, "and I know how a father feels about his daughter. I wanted to tell him she wouldn't come to any harm, not if I could help it."

For a queer blank moment Tay seemed to have nothing to say. Then, his voice even, he asked, "Well, did you tell him?"

"He wasn't to home. But he'll be there the next time I call, and I hate thinking about telling him now that I let you take her off like this."

Tay shrugged. "Don't try to stop me."

"I won't," Mr. Causey said. "Maybe you're the

217

kind would beat up an old man as quick as anybody else, and I can't see that would do any good for Jody or make you change your mind."

"That's right," Tay said.

"I can't figure you out," Mr. Causey said. "I gave you a job and took you in my house. I was willing to give you a chance and any help I could, and this is the way you pay me back." His voice thinned out, sharp and nasal. "You're one of those that looks for trouble and always finds it waiting for you. You don't care about anybody but yourself, it won't bother you any that maybe you're ruining a girl's life the way you ruined your own."

Above them a wind began to move in the trees, rustling, whispering, teasing the dry leaves.

"Thanks for the sermon," Tay said.

Jody, watching him, saw his eye leave Mr. Causey, dismissing him, and rest briefly on Eddie's truck in the driveway. Then he looked at Eddie, standing a couple of feet behind Mr. Causey.

With a desolation that was deeper and heavier than despair, Jody knew she should reach out to him, pull at his hand, warn him not to ask Eddie, not in front of so many white people. But she held her breath, pushed back the words, put her hand in her pocket to keep from touching his. There was nothing she could do to save Eddie. Whether Tay asked him or not it would still be the same, there was no way to make it easier for any of them.

Tay didn't ask. His eyes met Eddie's for a long silent moment; then, abruptly, he turned away.

"Come on, Jody," he said. "Let's go."

Eddie's face didn't change, it was still smooth and blank and dark, wiped clean of any expression. But his eyes looked old and tired, almost sick, and he swung around suddenly and walked across the yard, back toward the fields, with his shoulders hunched and drawn in, his head lowered so that he stared at the ground.

Tay held out his hand and Jody took it. They started toward the corner of the house, walking together in the ruts of the graveled driveway, and behind them no one spoke or tried to stop them.

Then Bob said, "Hold on a minute."

Tay paused, turned slightly. He and Bob regarded each other silently, coldly.

"She don't have to go," Bob said finally, "not unless she wants to."

"I gave her a choice." Tay added, his voice remote and somber, "But it didn't make any difference, I'd take her whatever she said."

"Is that so?" Bob said softly, and took his hands out of his pockets.

"You're a bigger fool than I think if you figure this is any time for her to be going back home."

Bob didn't move his eyes from Tay's. After a moment he smiled faintly.

"You okay, honey? I can't let you go off without being sure. Mrs. Hackett'd skin me alive."

She nodded, all the words she might have said sticking painfully in her throat.

He reached in his pocket and pulled out his car keys.

"Catch," he said, tossing them to Tay. "When you get through with it, park it some place and mail me the keys."

It seemed a long time before Tay said, "Thanks."

Bob shrugged. "I don't want my girl walking."

Tay turned away and started toward the car. Jody followed him, feeling the cool wind on her face, hearing it work up to a roar in the tops of the trees.

"I owe you for a couple of days' work," Mr. Causey said. "If you wait I'll get the money."

"Don't bother," Tay said without turning around. "It's on the house."

Jody wanted to look back and smile at Belle. But she knew now that she couldn't trust Mr. Causey, and there was no way of telling how much trouble they'd already made for Eddie and Belle. Tay was holding the car door open for her and she got in, sitting stiff and straight while he put their things in the back seat, slammed the door, and went around to the other side to slide in under the wheel.

It took three tries before Bob's old car started. Jody, looking through the windshield, stared silently at all of them standing there in the yard watching—Belle, Clay and Lacy, Mr. Causey, Bob. Then the motor caught and Tay backed down the drive, and the house cut off from view the ones left behind.

Tay turned the car with a little spurt of dirt and pebbles under the tires, and as they drove down the driveway Jody could see the rain advancing in a long gray line over the fields across the road.

Once they were in the open the wind slammed at the side of the car and the rain engulfed them. Tay didn't say anything. He might have been a million distant miles away, a stranger who'd picked her up but didn't figure he had to furnish conversation along with the ride. It'd been the same way the night she met him, when they went through the woods and down the river, two separate people with the darkness between them and no easy words to reach each other.

There still weren't any words, at least none that were easy, and the gray half-light of the storm was as lonely as the dark. Worse, maybe, bleaker and emptier. You couldn't fool yourself about the distance between them; there it was, cold and hard with silence, wider than the width of the car seat with its worn upholstery and grease spots.

But she knew better now; she didn't mind that it wasn't easy.

Suddenly, without turning his head, he asked, "Is that true, what he said? Are you his girl?"

"No," she said. "He didn't mean it that way."

He didn't speak again. Jody was silent, too, watching the rain streaming down the windshield and the bright streaks of lightning and his hands on the wheel.

⟨12⟩

HE drove the way he did everything else, as if he knew what he was doing. He kept his attention on the road and the car, but he wasn't tense about it; whatever he was thinking, he didn't let it touch his driving.

Jody leaned her head back against the seat, waiting, watching him, worried only because there was so little she could do for him. Nothing, really, unless simply being there, not pushing him or asking anything of him, might help him to feel less alone.

Once he pulled off the road at a small Esso station and bought a few gallons of gas. He asked Jody if she wanted anything to drink, the first time he had spoken to her for thirty minutes or more, and when she shook her head he sprinted through the rain to the station and came back, dripping wet, with a pack of cigarettes.

"I'd forgotten you smoked," she said idly, not thinking.

"Too expensive when you're out of a job," he said briefly, and shrugged. "I can get along without it."

But she could tell, from the way he smoked the first cigarette, how much he'd missed it, and she wished she hadn't said anything. She wondered, then, how much money he had. Not much, if he'd gone without cigarettes all this time, and now he'd spent two dollars on gas. She wanted to give him her ten dollars, it was only fair, but she wasn't sure, remembering how he'd refused to take any money from Mr. Causey for a day-

and-a-half of hard work, that she knew how to offer it to him.

He drove on, not speaking again, and for another twenty minutes Jody waited it out patiently, quiet and small in her corner of the seat. She turned her head slightly to look at the drab outskirts of a small town, unkempt and sodden in the rain, and wondered, without caring very much, where they were. It was like a hundred other towns, with it's gas stations and used car lots and diners, and when they paused at a stop light the stores along the main street were as ugly and anonymous as those on every main street she had ever seen. It amused her slightly to search the window displays of hardware and cotton dresses and school supplies, trying to find the name of the town; but the game defeated itself, there was nothing she hadn't seen before, from the familiar sign over an A&P store to the Marine and Army and Navy recruiting posters outside the post office.

Unexpectedly, Tay pulled the car into a diagonal parking space and turned off the ignition.

For a minute neither of them spoke.

Then she asked, "Do you know where we are?"

"I didn't notice the name. It doesn't matter, we've come far enough to stop for a few minutes."

Before he got the words out he began to shake. Not much at first, so that she hardly noticed it and couldn't make herself believe that it was happening; and then before she could say anything or make a move toward him he was shaking violently, all over, his shoulders taut and jerking under his damp shirt, his teeth chattering together. His face was suddenly wet with sweat, and pale under its tan; she could see the muscle along his cheekbone pull and jump, uncontrolled.

He held on to the steering wheel until his knuckles were white, but it didn't seem to help. Nothing helped, but he didn't make a sound, or even look toward her. He just kept fighting it, alone, refusing to give in to it, finally putting his face down against his hands with a little gasp of breath between a groan and a sigh.

Jody slid across the seat. She put her arms around his waist, the only part of him she could reach, and pressed her face against his shoulder.

"Let go," she whispered. "It's no good to hold it in, it only gets worse."

He tried to speak; she could feel him stiffening, making a final desperate effort.

"It doesn't matter," she said gently. "Be quiet, don't say anything."

The cars on either side were empty, and the rain drizzled a wet curtain across the windshield. No one could see them, and no one looked; the few people passing by on the sidewalk were busy with umbrellas, hurrying, looking down at their feet to avoid wet puddles.

But she wouldn't have let go of him if the whole world had come to peer curiously through the windows.

Close to him like that, her arms tight around him and her cheek against the hard firm flesh of his shoulder, she could feel his tension draining away, easing. Finally the shaking stopped and he grew still and quiet under her hands, but she didn't move away or loosen her hold on him.

"I'm sorry," he said then, and after a long pause added, "For all of it."

"For all of what?"

He didn't say anything. Neither of them moved. The rain kept on, and the people scurrying by on the sidewalk, and the traffic behind them on the main street.

Then he lifted his head, which meant that she had to move her own from his shoulder. She took her arms back, too, but she didn't move very far away.

"You were right," he said, "there's never any end to it." He looked spent and worn, and somehow older, needing a shave, his eyes tired and frowning. "Once you start off wrong, it all seems to go the same way.

It's like getting out of step when you're marching, sometimes you never find the right timing again, you keep making the same damned mistakes over and over."

She wanted to touch him again, if only to put her hand over his on the wheel, but it was different now, it was up to him.

"I'm sorry I lost my head," he said. "Sorry I fixed it so we couldn't stay on at Mr. Causey's. Sorry I fouled things up for you, worse than they were before. Sorry about the whole damn mess."

He gave a short bitter laugh.

"Sorry, Jesus, being sorry doesn't help much."

"It wasn't your fault, what happened."

He shook his head, not accepting it.

"What'll we do now?" she asked, wondering if he'd already decided, if maybe he'd had it all figured out in his mind what they'd do and where they'd go if anything went wrong at Mr. Causey's.

"Keep going," he said. "Any place, just so it's a long way from here. They'll know we're together now, and that we've got a car."

After a moment she said slowly, "Maybe we ought not to stay together." He didn't answer that at once, and she went on, "It's worse for you than me."

They'd never stop looking for him now, she knew that. It was bad enough with only Marv to tell his lies, once he could talk again, but now there'd be Gurney, too. He'd never rest until he could settle things for Marv and even the score.

"Don't look like that," Tay said abruptly.

She raised her eyes and met his. "It'd be safer for you if we weren't together. It would have been all along, I was just too stupid to see it. Marv was looking for me, he didn't even know you were there."

"Forget about Marv, will you?"

"You've got enough trouble, without me."

"If I'd never seen you, I'd still have trouble."

She looked away from him because it was easier that

way. "You've been telling me all along that I ought to go home."

He was silent for a moment. Then, his voice flat and tired, he asked, "Do you want to?"

She shook her head, staring blindly out of the window.

"If you figured it'd be hard before, you ought to know what it'll be like now."

"I don't have to go back there," she said with despair. "There're other places in the world."

But it was a losing battle and she knew it; she'd lost the same one before.

"Like Charlotte," he said. "I knew we'd come back to that."

A woman came between the cars, her arms full of packages. She closed her umbrella and climbed in the next car, not even looking their way. Jody watched absently while she put her packages in the back seat, unbuttoned her raincoat, and finally started the car and backed away.

"Is it me?" he asked slowly. "Is that the reason for all this, you just don't want to stay with me?"

She had never imagined he would think that. She turned her head quickly and caught him unawares, his guard down, something in his eyes she hadn't seen there before. For a minute they stared at each other, intent, wordless, and she knew, from the way his face changed, what he had seen in hers.

But she had to say it. "You know it isn't that."

He smiled, the warm easy smile that came so rarely. "I hoped not," he said, "but I wasn't sure."

He put his hand on her face. Holding himself very still, only his hand touching her, he looked down at her with the smile still on his mouth.

He didn't kiss her; he didn't have to.

"I think we'll stick together," he said gently, "from now on."

Another car pulled in beside them and a man got out, looking in at them curiously.

Tay took his hand away. But they were still very close to each other, so close she could see the pulse beating in his throat.

"You can stop worrying," he said, "I've got everything worked out. How would you like to go to the beach?"

"What would we do at the beach," she said, and had to stop to take a breath, "at this time of year?"

"Swim. Lie in the sun. Rest up from pulling and handing tobacco."

"Only if we can stay in the best motel, with room service and meals sent in."

"Sure, the best, you think I'd take you any place third class?"

"On second thought," she said, "it might be fun to be beachcombers. You know, go barefoot all day, and sleep all night on the beach."

"It might come to that, but I've got a buddy at Myrtle Beach who'd give us a meal and a place to sleep till I find a job." His voice sobered. "We were together for two years in the Army, he told me to look him up if I was ever in that part of the country."

"Jobs aren't easy to find at the beach, not in August."

"If we can't pick up something there we'll move on. South, maybe, I wouldn't mind seeing Florida again."

She hated to keep objecting, finding fault. He had the familiar look of knowing what he was doing and how to do it, and she had never wanted anything in her life as much as she wanted to leave it up to him, to do what he said without question, to shift all her troubles to his shoulders the way she'd done since the moment they met in the woods that first night.

But she couldn't now, it wasn't fair, everything had changed.

"Would we take Bob's car all the way to Myrtle Beach?"

"I figured on leaving it here. If I mail him the keys now he can pick it up tomorrow, it's not more than an hour's drive."

"We don't have enough money to take the bus."

"You have," he said. "I'll thumb."

She stared at him.

"You know, hitchhike."

"You mean we wouldn't go together?"

"It won't be for long," he said, amused by the panic in her voice. "I bet I'll get there before you do."

"If they don't pick you up."

"Stop worrying. I'll be careful not to thumb a ride with a cop."

"The beach isn't very far away," she said doubtfully. "What if somebody from home sees us?"

He shrugged, but some of the weariness was back in his face. "We'll just have to keep moving."

"But you came back this time to stay," she said, watching him. "You said you were homesick, and tired of being on the move."

"There're other places in the world," he said mocking her own words. Then he added quietly, looking down at her, "Sometimes you don't have a choice, it's made for you. I'm not kicking, not this time."

He took the keys out of the ignition and put them in his pocket.

"I saw a hardware store down the street," he said. "I'm going to see if I can get a box and some paper, and we'll get these keys in the mail. This is as good a place as any to leave the car, it's across the street from the bus station and nobody'll think much about it being parked here overnight."

She could see, in the rear view mirror, a big Greyhound bus parked in front of a drug store. It wasn't much of a bus station, even for a small town, but it was on the main north-south route and plenty of buses would be passing through.

"When I get back you can give me Bob's address. Then I'll go over and ask when the next bus leaves for South Carolina." He gave her a brief warm smile, and she felt as if he'd touched her. "Sit tight, and don't talk to any strangers."

He opened the door, slammed it, and jumped a pool of water to the curb.

Jody watched as he walked down the sidewalk, careless of the rain, one hand in his pocket and the other swinging free. He looked very brown in the gray rainy light, brown and hard and tough, and in his damp shirt and jeans he seemed all shoulders and no hips. She liked seeing him like that, walking alone, not knowing she was watching, and she leaned forward, keeping her eyes on him until he disappeared inside the hardware store.

She sat quietly for a while, waiting to see if he'd find what he wanted or come back out immediately. When he didn't appear again she sighed, opened her purse, and took a five dollar bill from the worn wallet inside. Then she rummaged in the bottom of the purse until she found a safety pin. Careful to put the bill where it couldn't be seen unless someone opened the door, she pinned it to the seat.

Turning to look back across the street, she read the destination sign on the front of the bus. It wasn't any surprise to her; she had known, as soon as she saw that the bus was headed the way they had come, what the name would be.

She drew a deep breath and held it. Then she let it go, unsteadily, past the tight knot in her throat.

Grabbing her paper sack and purse, she got out of the car and closed the door. She had to pause at the back of the car, waiting for a break in the traffic, and she held the paper sack over her head, narrowing her eyes against the rain.

Across the street the bus driver came out of the drug store and swung up into the bus. She took a chance, darting between two slow-moving cars, and reached the door of the bus just as the driver reached over to pull it shut.

"Do I have time to get a ticket?" she asked hurriedly, knowing that she didn't, and he grinned down at her amiably.

"Hop in, it's wet out there. I'll take your money, I'm behind schedule already."

She paid him gratefully and put the change in her purse, grabbing the arm of a seat to balance against the jolt as the big bus pulled away from the curb. Sitting down in the nearest empty seat, next to a plump middle-aged woman who roused herself to smile and nod, she stared straight ahead through the enormous expanse of windshield with its wipers that swept the rain aside in two great arcs.

The bus lumbered past the post office, the A&P store, the traffic light. Past the store fronts, past the gas stations and used car lots and diners on the edge of town. Then, with a steady roar, it seemed to settle itself on the highway, heading north.

Jody closed her eyes at last. She leaned her head back against the high seat, keeping her mind carefully blank.

But it was a mistake. Putting the back of her hand tight against her mouth, she opened her eyes and stared ahead again. Her throat was dry and sore, as though she was beginning a cold, and her head ached, but worse than anything else was the sick panic, rising inside her like rain water overflowing a shallow gutter, whenever she thought of him coming back to the empty car and finding her gone.

"Are you feeling all right, honey?" the woman beside her said softly in her ear. "Can I do anything for you?"

The panic rose another notch.

"I'm okay," Jody said hastily, and added, "Thank you."

"You look sick as a dog," the woman said, her voice solicitous, slightly curious. "You musta run too hard, trying to catch the bus. Why don't you put your head down on your knees, sometimes that helps."

Jody shook her head, gone beyond words, praying silently that the woman would leave her alone.

"My land, your eyes are bigger'n your face," the woman said. "You're white as a sheet, too, you ain't got a bit of color. Better put your head down, honey, you don't wanta faint right here on the bus."

As a last resort Jody closed her eyes again, shutting out the woman and her kind friendly face.

"That's right, you rest and maybe it'll pass off. I'll just open the window, fresh air's always good for car sickness."

The cool damp air struck Jody's face, blew her hair back. She took deep breaths of it, smelling the rain and the steamy cement of the highway and an occasional tang of exhaust fumes.

She sat like that for the rest of the trip, not daring to move or open her eyes. The miles seemed endless, going back, but just as she was beginning to think despairingly that she couldn't stand it much longer, the bus began to slow down, lurching a little as it turned corners and stopped and started at traffic lights, the roar of its motor gradually diminishing as it neared the center of town. Then it made a sharp left turn, pulled up the slight incline to the landing platforms at the rear of the bus station, and stopped with a final belching of exhaust and noise.

For a minute the sudden silence was strange and unfamiliar. Then the usual bustle of arrival and departure began, and Jody opened her eyes to see the aisle filled with passengers, reaching for their bags on the racks overhead, straightening their clothes, moving toward the door.

Beside her the plump woman gathered up her purse and gloves and said, "I hope you feel better, honey. Is anybody to meet you?"

Jody smiled faintly. "Thanks, I'm fine."

She waited for her chance to step down into the aisle and moved with the crowd down the steps and out of the bus. The platform behind the station was hot and stifling, crowded with people; the rain had stopped and the late afternoon sun had broken through the clouds again, weak and pale, glittering on the wet steamy asphalt and the pools of water in the parking lot.

Jody went into the stale air-conditioned cold of the station. Finding a telephone booth, she closed the folding door and looked in her wallet for a dime. Dropping it in the slot, she lifted the receiver and dialed a number.

She leaned against the wall, shoulders slumped, and listened to the ring on the other end.

Addie answered. "Hello, this is the Dowd residence."

Jody stared at the telephone numbers scribbled in pencil on the wall, the names, the obscene words.

"Hello," Addie said again, "hello?"

"Addie, this is Jody. Is anybody there but you?"

Now the silence was at Addie's end, humming through the wires.

"Jody?" she said at last, her voice thin and queer. "Is this Jody?" Not waiting for an answer she went on, "Where are you, where are you calling from?"

Jody could hear Mrs. Hackett, close to the phone, saying, "Give it to me, Addie, you don't deserve to speak to her," and then her voice was loud and firm in Jody's ear. "It's me, Jody. My Lord, I didn't expect you to be calling."

Jody sighed and rested her forehead against the telephone on the wall, letting the dial circle press painfully into her skin.

"I just got here," she said. "I'm at the bus station."

"I thought you had Bob McGee's car, what were you doing on a bus?"

"I came home," Jody said.

"By yourself?"

"Yes."

There was a short pause.

"I'm sorry to hear that. Bob called, when he got a chance, and told me all about it. It took a load off my mind, knowing you had somebody to look after you for a change."

"Don't," Jody said, "please."

She couldn't say any more, but she knew it'd be enough.

"Well, I won't ask a lotta questions now," Mrs. Hackett said. "I hate a pesky telephone, anyway. You come on home, Jody, there's only Addie and me here, looking after the kids."

"Where's Marv?"

"In the hospital, where'd you think? Verna and Gurney went over, soon as Bob let 'em know what had happened, but Verna had to go back to work after she found out how he was. Gurney's still there, I don't doubt, turning the whole place upside down."

Jody kept her voice even. "Then he's okay? Marv, I mean."

"There's nothing broken or ruptured, if that's what you wanta know." Mrs. Hackett laughed. "But Bob said he was really putting on a show, moaning and groaning, carrying on like he was about to die any minute. He's a fool, I always said so. If I was a man I wouldn't want the whole world to know I'd been beat up like an old mashed potato."

"I guess I'd better go by the hospital," Jody said wearily, "before I come home."

"Tell me something," Mrs. Hackett said. "Is that what you come back for, to weep over Marv Dowd and wring your hands and say you're sorry? If that's

233

the case you've lost what sense you had, he deserved every lick of it and don't you forget it."

"Gurney won't think so."

"Well, you know Gurney," Mrs. Hackett said soberly. "He's been listening to Marv, and Marv's been raving. He's accused that Brannon boy of everything in the book. Bob says to hear him talk he tangled with a criminal right out of Alcatraz."

"That's why I came back," Jody said.

After a moment Mrs. Hackett said, "I wish I was with you. You ought not to go over to that hospital by yourself."

"Don't worry," Jody said. "I'll be okay."

"You must've found a lotta starch some place," Mrs. Hackett said thoughtfully, "to go putting your head in the lion's den like that."

Jody smiled slightly. "You'd be surprised at the things I found."

"I'm never surprised," Mrs. Hackett retorted. Then she said, "Go to it," and hung up.

Jody went in the rest room and changed her clothes. The green dress was wrinkled from being folded in the sack, but it looked better than her slacks and shirt which were rumpled and soiled and still smelling faintly of tobacco. She washed her face and put on fresh lipstick, wondering how long she had looked so pale and queer, not surprised that the woman on the bus had been alarmed.

When she finished she walked through the bus sttaion, glancing with longing at the people eating in the small restaurant; she hadn't eaten since breakfast and her stomach felt as if it was stuck to her backbone. But she didn't stop, or look a second time; she went on out into the hot damp afternoon.

It wasn't a long walk to the hospital, no more than six or seven blocks, but her feet were dragging by the time she reached it.

She paused on the sidewalk, looking up at the old

brick building with its lowered shades and square black air-conditioners in each window. Then, lifting her shoulders, she ran up the steps quickly and pushed through the swinging glass doors into the waiting room.

It was dim and quiet inside, and permeated with the smells and sounds peculiar to hospitals. Looking around, trying to get her bearings after the brightness outside, she saw Gurney and Bob McGee standing by the window across the room. They didn't see her at once, and she had a minute or two to cope with the surprise of seeing them there together. She couldn't hear what they were saying, they were keeping their voices low, but it was obvious, from the look on Gurney's face, that they were arguing about something.

Then Gurney looked up and saw her.

At first his face was merely blank. Then his heavy brows snapped together and he scowled, one corner of his mouth turning down.

"For Christ's sake," he said, "look who's here."

"Hello, Gurney," she said.

Bob swung around, a startled frown on his face. But she didn't look at him. She kept her eyes on Gurney; it was Gurney she had to deal with.

"So you decided to come back," he said flatly. "What's the matter, that fellow have enough of you, send you home already?"

He stood looking at her another minute, his hands clenched, and then, abruptly, he lunged across the room toward her.

Her breath caught, but she stood her ground. From the corner of her eyes she saw Bob move at the same time, coming after him.

"My God, you must not've been any damn good at all," Gurney said, "can't even shack up with a bum and not get kicked out."

He loomed over her, big and dangerous.

"Is Marv better?" she asked steadily.

235

"Jesus, I oughta beat you black and blue, let you see how it feels."

"Don't take it out on her," Bob said, "she didn't do it."

Gurney ignored him. He stared down at Jody, his eyes hot and angry.

"I don't know why you come back, Christ, we got no use for any dirty little tramp. You coulda just kept going and never come back, it'd suit us fine. You made your bed, dammit, now you can lie in it!"

She listened because she had to. There was no running away this time. She'd known how it would be, but somehow it didn't seem to matter so much any more. She didn't feel like the same person, that was all; she'd been a long way and she'd brought something back with her she didn't have before.

"I got a warrant for that boy friend of yours," Gurney went on, "but, hell, I oughta have the cops pick you up, too. You're in it as deep as he is. Marv told me how the two of you tried to pin a rap on him for something he never did. I ain't gonna stand for it, I'll tell you that right now!"

He looked mad and goaded enough to hit her, and she wasn't surprised when he reached out and grabbed her shoulders.

Bob took a step forward and said, "I'm warning you, Gurney, leave her alone."

Gurney's grip tightened painfully on Jody's shoulders.

"Why'd you have to do it?" he asked, low, his voice quick and hoarse. "Why'd you run off like that, and not tell anybody where you'd gone?"

She shook her head helplessly.

"I hope to God I never have to go through anything like that again, Christ, I almost went crazy, worrying about you."

He took his hands away from her, moved them back almost at once as if he had no control over them, and finally, with something like desperation, jammed them in his pockets.

"Just tell me why you did it," he said again, roughly. "I never did anything to hurt you, you know I didn't. At least I never meant to, I swear it. Whatever was wrong you coulda told me instead of running off with some guy you never saw before."

Jody took a breath and held it. Then she let it go, gently, carefully.

"It's why I've come back that matters," she said. "You'd better tell Marv that I'm here so he won't get caught in a lot of lies. I wanted to make sure somebody would be around to tell the truth."

Gurney's face was oddly, unnaturally quiet; he seemed to be listening to something beyond the sound of her words.

"Don't take that bum's side against Marv," he said slowly. "Don't do it, Jody."

"I told you," she said. "That's why I came back." She saw the way his body tensed, the flicker of anger in his face. But she went on, softly, "If it wasn't for wanting him to have a break, this once, I'd still be with him. I'd never have come back at all."

"You belong here to home," Gurney said, "and from now on it's where you'll stay."

"Maybe," Jody said, "and maybe not."

He stared down at her. "You don't mean that. You're just a kid, you don't know what you're talking about."

"It's not the same any more," Jody said. "Don't push me too hard, Gurney, or I'll leave again."

His eyes narrowed, glittered behind the dark lashes. He started to speak, then rubbed his mouth with the back of his hand. Swinging away from her, he went over to the window and stood there, his back to the room, one hand on either side of the window.

"You got a nerve," he said finally, "running away from home with some no-good tramp, letting him beat up Marv till he almost killed him, then, dammit, coming back here like you was queen bee, telling me where to get off."

His words sounded uneven and twisted, as if he found it difficult to shape the words separately and get them past his rigid mouth. He didn't turn around, and his big shoulders under the white coveralls were stiff and taut.

Jody walked across the waiting room and sat down on the arm of the sofa, hugging her arms against her, her head bent.

She could feel his hurt and pain and confusion inside her, not like her own but an extension of his that reached down into some deep vulnerable place, secret and dark, that was impossible to guard or defend. But she sat still, fighting it, knowing there was nothing she could say or do. It wasn't her place to comfort him. Verna was his wife, it was Verna who'd have to heal his hurt.

Bob came to her rescue. He was slouched against the wall, casual, apparently disinterested, but his eyes, going from Jody to Gurney, were thoughtful.

"She didn't have anything to do with Marv getting beat up," he said. "I been trying to tell you that. I was there and I saw the whole thing. Marv asked for everything he got, and if he says different he's lying."

Gurney turned. "I ain't saying he wasn't due a hiding, he's a regular little bastard when he wants to be. But you seen him, Bob, my God, the guy didn't have to beat him to a bloody pulp."

Bob shrugged. "Marv pulled a knife on him."

"Marv said he had to," Gurney said angrily. "The guy was dangerous and he was scared. Jesus, anybody has a right to defend himself."

"Yeah, he was scared, all right. Scared yellow, the way he was the night he wrecked that car."

Gurney's face darkened. "That's another thing, nobody's gonna accuse my boy of stealing and wrecking a car, and get away with it. I've signed a warrant for assault, and when they pick Brannon up for that they'll want to ask him a few questions about that damn car."

"If they pick him up."

"Listen, I'll see him in jail if I have to scour the country for him myself."

"You may as well give it up," Bob said. "It don't work that way, Gurney, no matter how you try to pretty it up it'll still come out the same."

Gurney hit the window sill with his fist. "Not for Marv," he said bitterly.

"Marv stole the car," Bob said, unmoved, "and it was Marv who wrecked it. I know people who'll go on the stand and swear they saw him driving it, and I'll be right there to testify I heard him admit the whole thing before witnesses, wreck and all."

Gurney stared at him, the flush dying out of his face and leaving it white and drawn.

"What's the matter with everybody? None of you ever saw that Brannon guy before Saturday. He blew into town and got into trouble and then he blew out. It's the way guys like that operate. He's not worth a red nickel to anybody. For all you know he's just a two-bit punk with a record as long as your arm. I can't figure it, Christ, how come everybody's so quick to take his side against Marv's?"

Bob's smile wasn't amused. "And how come you're always so sure everybody's wrong but your boy Marv? Knock it off, Gurney, this time he stretched his luck a little too far."

Gurney couldn't seem to find anything to say. Jody looked away from his face and fixed her eyes on her hands, noticing that they weren't entirely clean of tobacco gum. She could see a tiny dark smudge in each palm. Maybe it had to wear off, she'd scrubbed them till they ached.

"Dammit, Bob," Gurney said finally, "it's my son you're trying to railroad off to jail!"

"I'm crying," Bob said. "So will the cops when they hear the other side of the story." He shrugged, turned and gave Jody a reassuring smile. "I've got to get back to work. You want me to give you a lift home, honey, or have you already got a ride?"

She knew why he had put the question that way, but there was no way to tell him, with Gurney listening, that his car was in a little town fifty miles down the highway and that Tay was on his way south, hitchhiking, out of their reach. Alone, the way he'd always been, with five dollars in his pocket and no place to go. Thinking he had to keep moving to stay ahead of the police, thinking he had no friends but an old Army buddy who might take him in for a night and a meal. Knowing she'd left him but not knowing why.

"Thanks," she said evenly, "I'd like a ride."

"Jody, you're back!"

Jody's throat tightened, hearing Verna's low slurred voice, seeing her there in the door with her cheeks wet and her mouth trembling.

"Mrs. Hackett called me and I couldn't believe it, I was afraid to, not till I saw you with my own eyes."

She came across the waiting room at a run and dropped down on the sofa beside Jody, letting her purse fall unheeded to the floor.

She put her arms around Jody and held her tightly. For a long while, wordless and shaking, she cried into Jody's hair, and the sound was forlorn and childlike in the silent waiting room.

Then Gurney said abruptly, "Take it easy, Verna. She's back, for Christ's sake, you can bawl over her when you get her home."

Verna straightened her shoulders. She raised her head and wiped her face with the backs of both hands, and smiled unsteadily.

"I never saw anybody look so good to me. You okay, honey, is everything all right?"

Jody just looked at her, close to tears herself.

"You look like you've been sick," Verna said, her eyes searching Jody's face. "You've got big circles under your eyes, the way you always did when you were a kid and didn't feel good."

"I'm not sick," Jody said, and she had to stop before she went on. "Don't worry, Mom."

"Well, no sense in taking a chance, we'll go home and I'll put you to bed. I asked could I have the rest of the day off, in case it was really true you'd come back."

"That figures," Gurney said. "She comes straggling home after chasing around the country with some man, so you gotta take the day off and nurse her."

Verna sighed and pushed Jody's hair back from her face. "I don't care who she was with, she's home now."

"Yeah, with circles under her eyes yet. Ain't it a shame, all of it's our fault and none of it hers."

Verna stood up. "That's enough, Gurney. I don't wanta hear any more about it, here or at home."

Bob stood away from the wall. "I'll be waiting outside if anybody wants a ride," he said easily, to nobody in particular, and sauntered across the room and through the door.

Gurney watched him go, then shrugged. "Don't worry, I've said all I'm gonna say, I'm fed up with the whole thing. She can leave again tomorrow for all I care."

Verna regarded him silently for a moment. Then she asked, "How's Marv feeling?"

He laughed shortly. "What do you care?"

"Because I do," she said, a little puzzled. "Have you talked to him since I left, is he feeling better?"

"Go on home, tuck Jody up in bed, don't you worry about Marv."

"You're talking foolish, Gurney. What's the matter with you?"

"I'm fed up, is all. They bring my boy to the hospital, half-dead, and you can't get but five minutes off.

You gotta rush right back to work, you couldn't care less whether he lives or dies. Marv told me you'd always had it in for him and I'm beginning to believe it. Everybody gangs up on him, you're as bad as the rest."

It seemed to Jody that he was feeding his anger, deliberately trying to fan it into life. He didn't look like himself, his shoulders were slumped and his head down, his face tired and haggard.

"That isn't so and you know it," Verna said. "It's not easy to get close to Marv and maybe I haven't tried hard enough, but it's not because I don't care. How could I help caring, he's yours, isn't he? You care about Jody and she's mine, it's the same thing."

Gurney stared at her, his face stricken, bleak. He started to speak, and hesitated.

Then, with despair, he said, "He stole a car, Verna. It was him did it, not that Brannon guy."

"Oh, Gurney," Verna said softly. She walked across to him, put her hand on his arm. "Can't you do something, you won't let him go to jail, will you?"

"I doubt if I'll have anything to say about it," he said bitterly. "Looks like half the world's set to testify against him, he ain't got a chance." He looked down at Verna and said, his voice heavy, "If he's done something wrong, he'll have to pay for it."

"Maybe they'll give him another chance, Gurney, it's the first time he's broke the law."

"He don't deserve another chance," Gurney said morosely, "not unless he's changed his way of thinking. He really gave me the business, and he did it on purpose, lying to me, telling me a lotta stuff that wasn't so, making me look like a fool when I tried to stand up for him."

"Well, you'll always have to stand up for him," Verna said, "no matter what he's done." Then she met his eyes directly and went on, in the same quiet voice, "You knowing what he's done might make a difference to him. After all the times you wouldn't believe what anybody said against him, he probably figured he could just go on getting away with things."

"Okay, it's my fault," he said tightly, "have a hell of a good time thinking you was right all the time and I was wrong."

Verna's face softened. "Maybe you was wrong, Gurney, but only because you love him. It's the same way with me and Jody, I got a few mistakes to live with myself."

He lifted his shoulders, moved them a little as if they'd been cramped.

"Well, no need to chew it over all day. I better go up and see how he's doing, then get over to the garage." He put his arm around Verna, giving her a quick little hug. "You've had a hard day, honey, chasing around all over town. Come on up with me, then I'll run you home."

Close together, they walked across the waiting room. They didn't look at Jody, or even seem to remember that she was still there, sitting on the edge of the sofa.

She closed her eyes, wishing she could let go everything at once, thinking with unbearable longing of all the clean straight hospital beds upstairs with their empty pillows and the sheets turned back neatly, just waiting for somebody who was sick and worn out and tired to death.

Then she heard Gurney's amazed voice saying, "Well, for God's sake, look who's turned up."

She opened her eyes wearily.

Tay was standing just inside the glass doors, looking at Gurney. He took a couple of steps forward and stopped, waiting, holding himself straight and easy, head up, his hands hooked on his belt.

The room was still and empty, the silence broken only by the muted clatter of a hospital cart somewhere down the hall. Jody sighed once, and the sound seemed to go on and on, like a tiny rush of wind; she knew from his face that he had heard it and wished tiredly that she could have kept it inside her, but it came from too deep.

He didn't look at her. He kept his eyes on Gurney, and he didn't lower his head.

"How's Marv?" he asked at last.

"Living, no thanks to you."

Tay's face didn't change. "He had it coming. Once for Jody, and once for me."

"You're the one that's got something coming, buddy."

"Not from Marv."

"From me, then," Gurney said impatiently. "Dammit, you got no right to take the law in your own hands, beat my boy half to death. I took out a warrant for assault, Brannon, and them cops are gonna be plenty glad to see you."

Jody, seeing him standing there in front of Gurney, thought she had never known anybody to look so alone. She remembered how she had first seen him last Saturday night, leaning his shoulders against the refrigerator in the Dowd kitchen, a stranger to her, remote and wary, deliberately solitary and glad of his choice. It was the way he must look to Verna and Gurney now; but this time she could see past his locked face; she knew the strain and loneliness and trouble pushed down like a heavy lump behind, she had touched it and recognized it for her own.

Then he said, without heat, "I figured it'd be that way."

Gurney scowled at him. "Then why'd you come back? Jesus, anybody with good sense woulda kept on going and never looked back."

"I had a reason," Tay said.

His eyes moved past Gurney, found her. Dismissing Gurney without another word, he came toward her across the waiting room, and in the brief moment before he reached her she saw that he had lost the look of being alone. He didn't know there was a good chance he wouldn't be blamed for the stolen car, he didn't know that Bob McGee was on his side and that Gurney was bluffing; he didn't know any of the good things, only the bad, but he was looking at her as if none of it mattered to him at all.

He stood there for a minute, not touching her, looking down at her with his eyes sober and thoughtful, a little tired.

"You ought to have known it wouldn't work," he said at last.

"I tried," she whispered. "I thought it'd be better this way."

"I know what you were thinking," he said ruefully. "How to make things easier for me. Safer. Not so much trouble."

She was beginning to feel it, it was sinking in that he was there, that he hadn't gone on without her.

"But I never thought you'd come back, too."

He smiled faintly. "Didn't you?" Then, his voice muted, careful, he went on, "It wasn't getting away that really mattered, it was us being together. I've known it for a long time, I can't even remember when I wasn't sure about it, but it seemed to me a lot of other things had to be thought about first."

She sat very still and watched him, seeing how his face changed for her, opened up, quickened, came alive. The strain and the trouble showed now, but not the loneliness; he looked weary and spent and worn, and yet, oddly, content.

"The worse thing was thinking about how it'd be for you, coming home again after everything that had happened," he said. "I knew I couldn't let you come back without me, but if we tried it together there wasn't a chance they'd let me stick around long enough to be any help to you. I couldn't find any answer, no matter how I figured it."

She was too close to weeping to say anything. But he didn't seem to need any words, or any help; it was as if he had worked it out in his mind until he was sure of himself, and now that he had found her again everything had fallen into place for him and the only important thing left was to work things out for her as well as he could.

"But there was an answer, all right," he said. "I wasn't thinking straight about it. I guess it took you to show me where I was wrong." After a long silence he came back to what he was saying. "We talked about there never being any end to it, but I was wrong about that, too. You can stop running any time, just by going back to where you started."

She found her voice somewhere down in her throat. "Is this where you started?"

He smiled again. "Not quite, but near enough." Then he said gently, "Don't worry, we'll work it out. We have to, there's not any other way for us." He put his hands on her shoulders and pulled her up. "Just promise me you won't go chasing off again by yourself, whatever happens. The rest won't matter, if only I don't have that on my mind."

She nodded, and her own smile finally came, easy and slow, warming her from the inside out. "Sure," she said, "I promise."

For a moment he didn't move. Then, with a sigh that broke in the middle, his arms slid down around her and he put his face against her hair.

"Judas Christ," Gurney said, "the guy's got a nerve. Right here in the hospital, in front of God and everybody."

Verna's voice was low. "Leave them alone, Gurney, they don't care who sees."

"Well, hell, I do."

"Make like you don't even know them, then," Verna said. "Come on, let's go and see how Marv's doing."

"Listen, I'm not gonna have that kinda thing going on around my house. If she's coming home, she's gotta start acting decent."

"All right," Verna said, "you can sit at the front

door with a shotgun. But if you think you can keep him out, you'd better come on upstairs and ask Marv how to do it."

Jody heard them, but she didn't listen. She kept her eyes closed and held on to him as tightly as he was holding her, thinking, In a little while I'll tell him, when he lets me go so I can see his face, I'll tell him this time we've both come home to stay.

❧{ 13 }❧

THE sun had dropped behind the houses on the Hill, taking with it the steamy heat and hard glare of late afternoon. In the front yard of the Dowd house a faint hint of coolness rising from the damp ground beneath the forsythia bushes was all that was left of the storm; the muddy yard had dried hard again and the zinnias by the porch steps had revived in the sun and smelled as dry and musty as if they had never been flattened by a driving rain.

Nothing uglier than an old worn-out zinnia, Mrs. Hackett thought, but you had to give them credit, zinnias never gave up until you hoed them under.

Looks weren't everything, if it came to that, nor smell, either. Take them tulips Jody had tried to grow —there was a pretty flower, all right. But they came and went before you got a good look; there was nothing lasting about them. Or take a magnolia, as handsome as a white wax funeral flower; she guessed the Lord hadn't made anything in the world to smell as sweet and look as pleasing as a magnolia blossom opened out in the sun or wet with morning dew. But even from here she could see the big bruised flowers littering the ground under the tree in her yard, and knew they were already beginning to turn yellow where the wind and rain had torn them. You'd never think they'd be so delicate and puny, but there it was. She doubted if the Lord was trying to prove anything, though, it was too much to take on faith that He preferred a smelly old zinnia just because it was pig-headed and tough and kept blooming till you got to hoping you'd never see another one.

She rocked back and forth rapidly, setting her heels down with neat little clicks. Now and again she turned her head to look down the street. It was time for the men to straggle home from work and a number of cars had passed, some turning in driveways up and down the block, but, although she looked each time she heard a motor in low gear pulling up the Hill, none of the cars had stopped at the Dowd's. Bob McGee had his boss's car but she would recognize it, she knew, if she saw it again, and Gurney's car was as familiar to her as anything could be that she saw every morning out of her bedroom window; still neither of them came and it was beginning to look like they never would.

She'd hoped somebody would think to call her, let her know what had happened. She wasn't sure her patience could be stretched out much longer; there was nothing could sour your stomach like being so old you couldn't do anything but sit and rock, having to wait till everything was over and done with and people could slow down long enough to remember to tell you about it.

"It's almost time to eat," Addie said from the screen door. "I bought enough hamburger for everyone for supper, but I don't know how much to cook."

"Cook it all," Mrs. Hackett said.

"It'd only be wasted, if Gurney doesn't plan to come home to eat. Maybe I'd better just fix enough for you and me and the children."

"You know what'll happen if Gurney comes and there ain't enough on the table to suit him. He's likely to be out of sorts, anyway, so I wouldn't take any chances."

Addie sighed audibly. "Do you suppose Jody'll be here?"

"I expect, she's got to eat some place."

After a pause Addie said, "You shouldn't have told that boy where she was. He's caused her enough trouble already."

"Not as much as he's going to, I reckon, before he's through." Mrs. Hackett chuckled. "Thank the good Lord, that's the kind of trouble a woman can't get enough of."

"No, you shouldn't have told him," Addie said reproachfully, as if her mother hadn't spoken. "I didn't like him."

"I did," Mrs. Hackett retorted.

"That was plain enough," Addie said shortly. "Anybody would think you'd been sitting here on the porch all day, just waiting for him to show up."

Mrs. Hackett rocked briskly. "That's right, I knew he'd be coming along and I didn't intend to miss him."

For a moment Addie was silent with surprise. Then she asked slowly, "How could you know anything like that, Mama?"

"I got more sense than you give me credit for, is how. Besides that, I figured no man with the kinda guts he's got would let Jody get away from him once he'd had her."

Mrs. Hackett wasn't looking toward the door, but she could feel Addie's stiff disapproval all the way across the porch.

"I'd better put the meat on," she said distantly. "Please call Billie Mae in to clean up, Mama. I put a fresh dress on her, one I washed and ironed today, but she's probably covered with red mud by now."

Not entirely covered, Mrs. Hackett discovered, but she had to admit there wasn't a square inch of Billie Mae showing that looked anywhere near clean.

"You'd best go scrub before Addie catches up with you," Mrs. Hackett suggested. "Supper'll be on the table before long, and if you ain't took some of that dirt off there'll be the devil to pay."

Billie Mae looked unimpressed. "Can Linda stay and eat with me?"

They waited for her answer, their faces secretive and sly, balanced carefully on the edge of giggling, their little thin dirty legs held unnaturally still.

"I don't see why not," Mrs. Hackett said. "Is your mother to home, Linda? You go ask her first, so's she'll know where you're at."

"She's home," Linda said, "but she'd be real glad if I was to eat supper some place else. Maybe I'll even spend the night, if you'll let me."

Mrs. Hackett stopped rocking. "What kinda trouble's she in now?"

"My pa's in town," Linda said.

"Well, no wonder." Mrs. Hackett shook her head, looked down at Linda thoughtfully. "He making as much noise as ever?"

"He says he's gonna take me with him for sure this time, ain't no use her trying to keep me."

"I don't know why he talks like that," Mrs. Hackett said. "He's got no place for you, my lord, the last time Ruthie told me where he was he'd been living in a trailer somewhere down around the Marine base."

Linda hopped up and down the steps on one foot. "He's got folks some place, I heard him tell Ma. He's gonna bring the lady from the Welfare out to see don't she think I oughta go live with his sister."

Mrs. Hackett waited until Linda reached the top step again and said, "Stop that jiggling, it makes me nervous. Do you want to go with him?"

Linda shrugged. "Me and Ma get along. I ain't so sure his sister wants me living with her, it's just they all hate Ma."

Linda giggled and Billie Mae joined her. The telephone rang in the dining room and Mrs. Hackett listened until she was sure Addie had answered it.

"Well, you go get your pajamas and tell Ruthie you're going to be up here with Billie Mae for to-

night. And ask her to come by and see me after supper, I want to talk to her. I'll be home by then, you
tell her I'll be looking for her over to my house."

She watched them race down the sidewalk. Behind
her, Addie opened the screen door.

"That was Verna," she said. She walked across the
porch to the swing, sitting on the edge of it gingerly,
as if she had no time to be comfortable.

Mrs. Hackett said, "Well?" She had a notion that her
nerves were ready to jump right out of her skin, wanting Addie to hurry and tell what she knew, but she'd
waited this long, it'd be foolish to go to pieces now.
Besides, she was pretty sure she already knew how it'd
gone.

"They'll be home to supper in a few minutes."

Mrs. Hackett knew, from the tone of Addie's voice,
exactly what she'd say next.

"Her and Gurney and Jody," Addie went on dully,
"and that Brannon boy."

Mrs. Hackett didn't speak.

"I never thought Gurney would let him come here
to the house," Addie said, "and Marv still in the hospital." She stared across the yard, frowning. "It doesn't
seem right, any of it. Do you reckon Gurney and Verna
don't know about Jody living with that boy?"

"Marv's still got the use of his tongue, ain't he?"
Mrs. Hackett smoothed a wrinkle out of her dress.
"I'm sure glad I didn't let you talk me out of putting
on my good frock. Now we're gonna have company
for supper and I'm all ready for it, don't even have to
change my stockings."

"I won't be able to eat," Addie said despairingly.
"I can't sit at the same table with somebody like that,
I wouldn't know how to talk to him."

"No need to worry about talking to him," Mrs.
Hackett said. "He's not like Gurney, he's one of them
quiet ones without too much to say."

After a moment Addie said, her voice edged with

bitterness, "Well, I hope you're satisfied. She's back, and they're taking her in again just like nothing ever happened."

Mrs. Hackett snorted. "Don't you believe it. Plenty's happened, and every last one of 'em know it."

"Nobody would think it, the way they act. Verna could hardly talk on the phone she was so happy, like it was something wonderful to have Jody back again."

"It is, sure enough."

"Jody ought to be hanging her head in shame," Addie said, choking out the words. "She ought to repent of her sins, instead of throwing them in people's faces."

"Not Jody," Mrs. Hackett said with satisfaction. "She ain't got as much magnolia in her as I thought, not that one."

Addie looked at her curiously. "What do you mean, magnolia?"

"If you let that hamburger burn, Addie," Mrs. Hackett said, "you'll have Gurney to deal with."

"It's in the oven, I'm making meat loaf. Did you call Billie Mae?"

"She'll be back in a minute. Linda Maness is gonna eat with us, too."

"Mama, why did you have to ask that child to supper? I don't like Billie Mae playing with her so much."

"Ruthie's got her hands full, her husband's in town."

"Not much of a husband, if you ask me."

"Nobody's asking you, but you're right, he ain't much of anything. He's trying to get the Welfare to take Linda away from Ruthie for no good reason but pure spite, and I aim to do something about it."

"You'd better stay out of that business, Mama. Ruthie deserves any trouble she's got, it's not up to you to straighten out any mess she's made of her life."

"Might as well be dead," Mrs. Hackett said, "if you can't help people when they need it."

JAN COX SPEAS

Addie pushed back an untidy strand of hair that kept falling in her eyes. She moved the swing back and forth gently, leaning her head against the chain.

"I cooked some fresh squash," she said, "and a mess of green beans. Do you think anybody will want dessert? I baked that cake for my Circle meeting tonight, but we could use it for supper and maybe I'll have time to beat up some cookies to take to the church."

"Men always like something sweet," Mrs. Hackett said slyly, thinking how good the icing had tasted when she ran her finger along the bottom edge where Addie couldn't see. "Just cut a slice around, and maybe there'll still be enough for your Circle."

Addie nodded. She closed her eyes wearily, resting, letting the swing hang motionless.

Then she said, "I thought I might run downtown in the morning. They're having a sale at Bright's on winter clothes."

"Nobody but you could stand thinking about woolens, hot as it's been this week."

"You need a new wool bathrobe, Mama, your old one's coming apart at the seams. And I was thinking I might get a couple of sweaters for you, if they have any of those heavy ones that button down the front and have pockets."

"I expect I'll be glad to have 'em, come the first cold spell, but I can't work up any pleasure in the thought right now. That rain sure didn't cool things off much, the way I'd hoped."

Mrs. Hackett looked down the street and watched Billie Mae and Linda racing back up the sidewalk.

"It's a good thing Linda's gonna get some of your cooking," she said. "She's too thin, needs some meat on her bones." After a pause she added casually, "Ruthie tries her best, but it ain't always enough, broke as she is. If you could find a pretty remnant of piece goods tomorrow, maybe we could run up a new dress for Linda."

254

"Ruthie knows how to sew."

"She don't do as nice work as you, Addie. With school starting next month and all, I thought it'd do that child a world of good to look decent for a change."

"It won't keep the Welfare from taking her away from Ruthie, if that's what they've got in mind."

"I've got a few things to say to the Welfare," Mrs. Hackett said. "Wouldn't mind saying 'em to Ruthie's husband, either, if it comes to that."

Addie stood up. She walked slowly to the door, straightening her apron.

"I'd better put on some potatoes," she said, "or that meat loaf won't stretch to so many people. You want to come in and clean up now?"

"I'm clean enough," Mrs. Hackett said. "I'll just sit here and watch for the car."

Turning her head so that she could see the length of the Hill, she began to rock again.